REVENGE OF THE DESERT WOLF

BETA

RED ROCK PACK
BOOK 2

JD WOLFE

Note from Author

This is a work of fiction. Unless otherwise indicated, all the names,
characters, businesses, places, events, and incidents in this book are
either the product of the author's imagination or used in a fictitious
manner. Any resemblance to actual persons, living or dead, or actual
events is purely coincidental.
Edited by a really smart friend

Cover Design by JD Wolfe
jdwolfebooks@gmail.com

Another Note From the Author Because She Likes Words:

This book contains; violence, abuse, blood, gore, murder, and a mention
of the devil. It also describes in detail sexual acts and nudity. As well as
every known cuss word with some new made-up ones.

To the shifters hidden among humans, to the restless souls who refuse to fit into neat little boxes—may you never shrink yourself to make others comfortable.

To Hubs, proof that love isn't just about fate, but about the choices we make every day.

CONTENTS

Red Rock Pack

CONFIDENTIAL

Council of the Animal Society

Threat Level

1   2   3   ④   5

File Number	#69512735-24
Shifter ID Code	#W71981-F

Intended for Official Use Only.

CONFIDENTIAL

Name: Sheridan, Harper

Pack: Red Rock Pack

Pack Position: Beta

DOB: 07 | 19 | 82   **Age:** 41

Registered Animal: Wolf

US Citizen: Yes   **Language:** English

Height	5'5"
Weight	170
Hair Color	Blonde
Eye Color	R - Brown / L - Green
Skin Tone	Fair

Pack Information

Registered Address:
117 Stanley Dr
Lake Las Vegas, NV

Mate: Williams, Lucas
Humboldt Pack Beta

Alpha: Randolph, Charlotte

Enforcer: Devereaux, Jade

Pack: Unknown

Psychological Profile:

- Strategic and independent, with a preference for planning and foresight
- Seeks control over her environment and the safety of her pack
- Confident in her abilities, though struggles with how other perceive her
- May come across as aloof or overly critical; struggles with spontaneity

Humboldt Pack

CONFIDENTIAL

Threat Level
1 2 3 ④ 5

| File Number | #38593627-12 |
| Shifter ID Code | #W122581-M |

Intended for Official Use Only.

CONFIDENTIAL

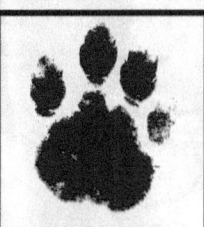

Name: Williams, Lucas

Pack: Humboldt Pack

Pack Position: Beta Male

DOB: M 03 | D 23 | Y 84   **DOB:** 41

Registered Animal: Wolf

US Citizen: Yes **Language:** English

Height	6'4"
Weight	185
Hair Color	Brown
Eye Color	Brown
Skin Tone	Medium

Pack Information

Mate: Sheridan, Harper

Alpha: Adler, Spencer

Enforcer: Sutton, Kai

Enforcer: Rowe, Jaxson

Registered Address:
41792 Goldrush Dr
Twodot, CA 95563

Psychological Profile:

- Highly perceptive and intuitive, able to read people and situations with precision, often seeing angles others miss
- Seeks purpose rather than power, though he may appear reluctant to lead, he carries the weight of responsibility heavily when it's placed on him
- Loyalty must be earned, but once given, it's unwavering—though betrayal is never forgiven

C.O.P.S

F ind All Files at:

TOO SOON TO CELEBRATE?

While reaching across the table for another slice, the fragrant smell of pizza toppings, fried foods, and human sweat fills Jade's senses. Her superhuman sniffer ensures she is hyperaware of her surroundings, but this level of "aware" is more than she's comfortable with.

Biting into the overloaded pepperoni pizza, her attention flickers to Harper, her friend and sister in everything but blood. Harper's newfound mate, Lucas Williams, is practically glued to her side. One hand grips Harper's shoulder in a possessive hold while he struggles to eat with the other. It's almost comical—Lucas clearly isn't letting go anytime soon. Not for food. Not for air.

Jade's lips twitch, a half-formed smirk threatening to break through her neutral expression. *I can't believe a plan of mine didn't end in murder,* she thinks, shaking her head slightly.

Somehow, they'd managed to take down Miles Barlow without spilling a single drop of blood—a first for her. That fact nags at her, a tiny spark of unease buried beneath the exhaustion of pulling it off.

But as she watches Harper laugh softly at something Lucas says, Jade lets herself enjoy the rare peace that hangs over the table, knowing it won't last. It never does.

Her shifts her gaze, scanning the room as the Red Rocks and their allies, the Humboldt pack, celebrate together. The echoes of their shared victory over a common enemy bounce off the pizza shop's walls, but Jade knows all too well that victory often comes at a cost. Both packs paid dearly—some scars visible, others buried beneath the surface.

Her focus returns to Harper, who fidgets slightly under Lucas's arm. Most wouldn't notice the subtle shifts, but Jade does. She knows Harper's body language better than anyone. The slight downturn of her mouth, the way her fingers drum absently against the table—it's clear something has her worry wheels spinning.

Jade feels the familiar tug of her own protective instincts, sharp and unrelenting. It's a feeling rooted in the past, in a time when she was too weak to protect herself, let alone anyone else.

When they were kids, Jade's father was a staunch enforcer of the patriarchal traditions that ruled pack politics. Men led, women obeyed, and there was no room for dissent. His rule was absolute, enforced with an iron fist. At first, those fists landed hard—teaching obedience, as he'd call it—but as Jade grew, her resilience outpaced the bruises.

That's when the real torment began.

Words became his weapons, sharper than claws and impossible to heal. He wielded them with precision, digging into her insecurities, planting seeds of doubt that took root in the shadows of her mind. His cruelty evolved into an art, calculated and deliberate, designed to break her spirit rather than her body.

Jade learned quickly to mask her emotions, to shield herself from his barbed attacks. Tears were a sign of weakness; silence became her armor. But even armor cracks under relentless pressure. His voice still echoes in her memories, a ghost she can't quite shake, whispering doubts that resurface at the worst moments.

She survived, though. That's the part she clings to when the nightmares come—the part that fuels the fire in her now. She didn't just survive; she grew stronger, harder, more determined. But sometimes, in the quiet moments, she wonders if those cracks in her armor will ever fully mend.

Harper's dad was the exception. Mr. Sheridan believed in fairness and kindness, a stark contrast to the patriarchal cruelty of other packs. He taught Harper, Jade, and Charlotte—now their Alpha—that not all men led with fists. The Sheridan house became a sanctuary for Jade, a place where love wasn't a weapon but a balm.

Watching Harper squirm under Lucas's arm, Jade feels a pang of protectiveness so sharp it almost makes her flinch. Harper saved her once, just by showing her what a real family could look like. Jade vowed the night Mr. and Mrs. Sheridan helped the girls escape, that she would protect Harper and the rest of the Sheridan's, even if it meant her own death.

Well, except Ryder. Harper's oldest brother is the one Sheridan she'd gladly see flattened by a grand piano falling from a fourth-floor window.

But Harper's safety comes first. Always. As Lucas leans in to whisper something in Harper's ear, Jade's gaze narrows. She'll fix whatever's weighing on Harper's mind—she has to.

"Why is it that in a room full of love, the weight of worry presses the heaviest?"

Being the pragmatic one in the pack, Harper struggles to live in the moment.

Her pack, the Red Rocks of Las Vegas—an almost all-female shifter pack that made the desert their home—just defeated their enemies with the help of their new allies. Finding a common enemy, the Humboldts pledged their alliance, offering extra protection.

The asswipe, Miles Barlowe, alpha of the Cascade Pack, had come for their territory. His shitty pack tried to take Vegas from the Red Rocks four times. Each attack left devastation on both sides.

Now, the Red Rocks are down to just four; Charlotte, their Alpha. Jade, the pack's enforcer. Luna, the crazy genius. And herself—the worrywart. Technically, she's the Beta, second in power only to Charlotte. But she doesn't feel that badass right now.

Wolf shifters aren't supposed to have this much anxiety, right?

The scum, Miles Barlowe, is finally gone. Vegas is safe. Even better, he'll never walk anywhere but the concrete cell he's being locked into right now.

So what the fuck is her problem?

Looking around the diningroom of the small mom and pop pizza parlor, watching five giant males, six beautiful females, and one teeny human taking up the entire seven table dining room, celebrate the fact that the evil that has taken eleven of their sisterhood will never see the light of day.

Sitting on the red bench seat, Harper watches her Alpha with her newly found mate, Liam Dunne. A pairing none of them ever thought they would see. Harper was so happy for her alpha when she learned about Liam, but also has to admit it made it easier for her to tell the pack that she found Lucas. Harper snuggles into his side, feeling his inner beast vibrate with her closeness.

The Red Rock Pack has been through a lot over the years.

Charlotte, Jade, and Harper had fled a pack controlled by a tyrannical alpha male when they were barely of age. They chose Las Vegas as their new home—not because it was ideal for wolf shifters, but because no one else wanted it. The desert was harsh, but that meant no competitions.

After escaping, they learned survival skills from their sanctuary pack. They took those skills, built a home, and grew their numbers. Unfortunately, the war with the Cascade Pack cost them nearly everything. Now, only four remain.

This celebration isn't just about victory—it's about remembering the sisters they've lost.

Harper feels relieved. Accomplished, even. After all, they didn't even have to shed blood to take down their enemy. But still, that nagging feeling won't go away.

Her wolf feels it too.

Harper's human side is always overanalyzing, but her

wolf? Complete opposite—her only concern is which Joshua Tree to nap under.

Before Harper can dwell on it any longer, Kai's lighthearted voice pulls her from her thoughts.

"Isabell, you were amazing! Did you see his face when he realized he had been tranq'd?" Kai shoves another piece of pretzel bite into his mouth, smiling around the brown salt covered dough.

"I do nothing. No hero for standing." The little senorita's salt and pepper hair moves back and forth as she shakes her head.

"I can't believe we went into a battle, but have no new scars to show for it. Hey Spencer, why can't you be that smart?" Lucas asks with a smile.

"Its tough when you're surrounded by a bunch of idiots."

The crumpled up napkin that Spencer throws at Lucas from the next table hits its intended target.

The twenty something blonde server sets down the fiftieth pizza they've ordered.

"I am so sorry we've taken over the place." Harper apologies.

Looking up to Kai, the petite valley girl responds, "Are you kidding? You guys have been fun and not bad to look at." Giving a wink.

Harper side-eyes Luna, then hears the hiss.

"Luna! What have I told you about hissing at people? It's not nice."

The giggle that is in Charlotte's tone tells Harper she's not really mad. Love has done something baffling to her Alpha. Liam exercised the bitchy right out of her.

"Sorry, Char, but she deserves it."

Harper smiles at Luna, even though the tension is making her head feel like it's splitting in two. She has always been the worrier of the pack, and it's saved them on more than one occasion.

Wanting the packs to relax and continue to build their ally bond through this victory, she is tries to shake the nauseous feeling deep in her gut. The fact that her wolf hasn't stopped biting at her insides since she watched Jase— their local COPS agent—take the unconscious Miles away, doesn't help calm her doubts that this is over.

The Council Of the Paranormal Society, or COPS for short, is an agency that was established after Luna and Jon, her twin brother, were in such a terrible position they exposed the paranormal society. The Red Rocks found her and Charlotte knew Luna was special and needed a certain type of family.

Lucas must be feeling her anxiety through their fast-growing bond. Feeling his warm breath over her ear, "What's going in that beautiful brain baby?" shivers run down her neck with his words.

"So, should we be worried about Ethan?" Harper blurts. "I'm all for celebrating Miles going to shifter jail, but his pack is still out there." Harper looks around the group, then up to meet Lucas's eyes. "Sorry, it was bubbling."

The kiss he gently places on her forehead calms her only slightly.

"Way to kill the buzz, Harper." Jade rolls her eyes.

"Hey. She's right. I spent time with that pack, and Ethan has some weird connection to Miles. I guarantee he won't leave this alone." Nodding his head with his words. "I think we need to stay on guard."

"I agree." Charlotte pushes the grease covered plate towards the middle of the table. "It won't take long before the pack is in full blow havoc and what then? Will they have enough organization to come after us, or will the broken bond make them so sick they just go after each other?" Charlotte questions.

Blondie returns, leaning over the table right in front of Kai, exposing her cleavage as she sets down two pitchers of beer.

Smirking, Kai warns the bold little thing. "You may want to be careful, darlin. This one here." He points his thumb at the tiny albino beauty next to him. "She bites."

Harper hears the chomp of Luna's teeth, then watches the blonde slowly stand and stomp back to the counter like a toddler that just lost their favorite toy.

After filling pints around the table, Spencer sets down the empty pitcher of beer. "I could send a couple of enforcers to watch the Cascades. I agree. We need to keep an eye on their descent into madness."

"I'll do it." Jaxson nonchalantly volunteers.

Leaning forward, taking the warmth of his body away from Harper, Lucas answers Jaxson. "No. They've seen you now. Let's send Ryan and Ollie."

"Yeah, that's a good idea." Spencer lifts his tiny mate, Avery, off his lap and stands in one smooth movement. Harper watches as he pushes open the glass door, with his phone up to his ear. His voice trails off as the door closes behind him.

"Now, can we just relax and enjoy the peace for a minute?" Jade is picking up the plates and stacking them one on top of the other.

"You? Enjoy? You don't *enjoy* things, Jade." Luna laughs.

"Shut the fuck up Luna. I enjoy many things."

Luna places her elbows on the table, causing the forks to clink slightly. Batting her eyelashes with chin in her palms, looking up at Jade. "Like what?"

Stretching her eyes to the ceiling, clearly looking for

answers. Harper watches the *ah-ha* moment in Jade's black eyes that are now back on Luna.

"My knives."

"Ok. Fair."

Jade snaps her fingers. "My vibrator. *AND* the peace and fucking quiet of my room."

"Well, my room shares a wall with yours and from what I can tell, the vibrator doesn't allow for much peace and quiet." Jaxson states.

"And my room shares your other wall. I disagree. From what I can tell, even your hand doesn't want to fuck you." Maddy comes out of nowhere.

The whole group, oooooo's and yells buuurn at the same time.

Jaxson lifts his hand towards Maddy for a high-five. "Ok, little wolf, that was pretty good."

Harper sees the pride in Jade's eyes, but says nothing.

After paying the bill, Charlotte suggests, "Let's head back to the house and have a pool party."

"Dibs on the Flamingo floaty." Luna throws her hand in the air.

READY! SET! CHICKEN!!

A couple of hours later, they are all back at the ten-bedroom mansion the ladies bought for themselves. They worked their asses off to make it happen, determined to create a home big enough for the pack to expand... someday. Buying a sprawling mansion on Lake Las Vegas hadn't exactly been in the original plans, but when they found it, it just felt right.

The pool and three hot tubs sealed the deal for most of the pack, but for Harper, it was the massive, gothic-style kitchen that stole her heart.

This house wasn't just a home; it was a testament to everything they'd built for themselves. Each of them had carved out their own path in Vegas, using their skills and determination to thrive.

Charlotte, playing to her physical strength, built a top-level gym from the ground up.

Jade launched a badass security business catering to the high-profile playboys Vegas seems to collect like trading cards.

Harper is the hottest chef in town, with her restaurant, X'tase, earning three Michelin Stars since her arrival.

And then there's Luna.

Well, none of them really know what Luna does—she's some kind of genius computer chick. If the pack needs to know anything, Luna always gets it done.

All four of their jobs have intertwined a time or two. All four of their jobs cater to the world's rich, famous, and at times, *infamous,* people. Sin City proved to be the perfect place for these females to work their strengths.

Laying on the bed in her favorite part of the house, her den, Harper watches the beautiful male in front of her, feeling a tingle in all the right places. Admiring his broad shoulders and six-pack abs moving under his perfect light tanned skin. With all the grace of a fly fighting to get out of a web, Lucas digs through a bright blue duffle bag that is struggling to hold its seams.

"Where the fuck are my swim trunks? I know I packed them."

Harper startles when black fabric pops out of the web, waving proudly above his head. "Ha! For a second there, I thought I was gonna have to make an entrance with my dick hanging out," he says, clearly amused.

She blinks, realizing he's been thinking out loud. Before she can respond, he tilts his head, his tone shifting from playful to curious. "What's got you all worked up, baby? Our bond's tighter than a fine-tuned guitar string."

Leaning up on her elbows. "And here I was thinking I was doing a great job of covering it up."

"Not with me."

Her brain short circuits as Lucas slides the pure black swim trunks up to his belly button showing the definition in his powerhouse thighs. "Someone else maybe, but not with me." Making his way to the bed, he sits down next to her.

"Do you think we're celebrating a little too early?" Harper hears the edge in her own voice, the weight of her anxiety slipping through.

"Yeah. Maybe?" Lucas's voice is steady, but there's something unreadable in his dark eyes. "I think Ethan is crazy and reckless enough to try something stupid. But he won't have control of the pack."

He reaches out, fingers brushing her temple as he tucks a strand of blonde hair behind her ear. A simple gesture— too soft, too careful for the tension humming between them. His touch lingers, just for a second, before he pulls away. His jaw tightens, the muscle ticking beneath his skin.

"With Miles in prison, none of the Cascades can formally challenge for his Alpha position." The words come measured, controlled, but the unease beneath them flickers like a warning. "The bond is still intact, which means Ethan would have to break it somehow. I've heard it can be done, but it takes a hell of a lot of strength."

He exhales hard, rolling his shoulders like he's shaking off something heavy. His hands flex, fingers clenching and unclenching at his sides. Restless energy, like a tiger pacing behind steel bars.

"Without that bond, rallying the pack—hell, even organizing a hunt—would be nearly impossible."

Harper frowns, the unease settling deeper in her chest. "But you're not saying it's impossible."

Lucas hesitates, his jaw tightening for just a moment before he shakes his head. "I don't think he's strong enough. Breaking an Alpha bond... that's not something just anyone can do. It would take more power than what I think Ethan has, and even then, it would tear him apart in the process."

His confidence reassures her for a moment, but the nagging thought remains. Ethan might not have the strength, but desperation has a way of making people dangerous.

Harper knows she is being neurotic, but she can't seem to shake this uneasiness. "Unless he has more of that COPS powder."

Somehow Miles has gotten his hands on, not once, but twice, the highly illegal powder that the Council of the Paranormal Society uses to help control unruly shifters. It paralyses the shifter, making them incapable of changing into their animal or if shifted, forcing them back into human form all while creating a state of delirium.

"That shit is nasty stuff and shouldn't even be a thing," Harper chirps.

"Jase said the Council approved a search of the entire Cascade pack lands for any more vials. I think he'll do it. He seems like a good one."

Lucas's hand moves over her exposed belly, his touch gentle and unhurried. Her wolf is eating it up, practically purring with contentment.

Before Lucas, she never would've dreamed of wearing a bikini. There's a little more of Harper than the average female shifter—no cut abs like Charlotte and Jade seem to have effortlessly, or Luna's sleek, runway-model frame.

Harper loves her own cooking too much for even her shifter metabolism to keep the extra weight off. For years, she used to hide it, covering up in loose clothes and keeping herself in the background. But now... Lucas won't let her.

As she closes her eyes and leans into the soothing rhythm of his touch, her mind drifts back to the first time he made her feel like she didn't need to hide. The first time he made her feel safe in her own skin.

"Hey baby. I'm going to ask you a question that I hope you can answer honestly." Lucas takes her hand. "Are you truly comfortable in that shirt, or are you hiding those beautiful curves from the world?"

Turning her one brown eye and one green eye down to her shoes, "I don't know. I've just always worn flowy clothes." Harper tugs at the t-shirt. "but, maybe it is to hide, because it makes me more comfortable."

"Ok baby. Thank you for your honesty...now...go change. Put on something tight for me. I want to see those curves." Lucas put the crook of his finger under her chin and forces her to lift her eyes back to his. He then rubs his thumb slowly down her bottom lip. "Make no mistake, woman, those are my curves and I dislike when they are hidden."

"Hey baby. Where did I lose you?" He has stopped rubbing her and has a puzzled look on her face.

"Oh, sorry. I do think Jase is one of the good ones. Charlotte gives him a hard time, but he's always been respectful to us. He watches the Cascades closely, just waiting for them to step out of line. But until today, they never slipped up—so we had to make it happen ourselves. I still can't believe Jade came up with that plan. It's not her style at all."

"What time is everyone meeting down at the pool?" Lucas asks, leaning back against the plush white headboard, his dark eyes locked on her with a familiar, mischievous glint.

Harper raises a brow, her legs tucked beneath her on the bed. "Why?" she asks, though she can already see where this is going.

"I think you need me to fuck the anxiety out of you," he says with a cocky grin, his voice low and teasing.

Her breath hitches, but she doesn't let him see it.

Instead, she smirks, tilting her head. "Do you have any idea how sexy you are, Williams?"

"I might've heard it once or twice," he replies, closing the small space between them with a casual ease. His hand slides to her waist, fingers tracing the curve of her hip like he's memorizing her all over again.

"You're ridiculous," she whispers, though her pulse quickens as his lips brush the corner of her mouth.

"And yet, here you are." His voice is softer now, almost reverent. His hand shifts to her cheek, tilting her face toward him. "You don't have to carry everything, Harper. Not with me."

His words hit harder than she expects, and for a second, she feels the weight she didn't even know she was holding. Before she can respond, his lips capture hers in a kiss that's playful yet insistent. His hands slide down to her hips, and in one smooth motion, he shifts her onto his lap.

"Lucas—" she begins, but he cuts her off with a look, his hands holding her steady.

"Trust me, baby," he purrs. "You're perfect, and I want to show you just how much."

Her heart skips a beat as he leans them back further against the headboard, the soft fabric cradling them both. His hands guide her movements, lifting her slightly before settling her back down against him, his strength making it effortless.

"You're incredible," he whispers, his voice a mix of awe and heat as he watches her. His hands remain firm on her hips, helping her find a rhythm.

Despite the familiar stirrings of insecurity—her curves, her weight—his words, his touch, and the way he looks at her drown them all out.

"You're mine," he says, his lips brushing her neck as his

voice grows huskier. "Every part of you, Harper. Perfectly mine."

Her body moves with his, her breath mingling with his as she lets go, trusting him completely. The way he holds her, the way he moves with her, makes her feel more alive than she's ever felt.

Lucas's hands are everywhere—strong, sure, and reverent. They steady her hips, guiding her rhythm with ease, but his touch is more than just control. It's worship. His fingers trace the curve of her waist, his palms pressing firmly against her thighs as if anchoring her to him."

Look at me," his voice a rough whisper that sends a shiver down her spine. His dark eyes hold hers, filled with heat and something deeper, something that makes her chest tighten. "You're stunning, Harper. Do you feel what you do to me?"

Her cheeks flush, and she tries to look away, self-conscious as her curves press against him. But Lucas won't let her. His grip on her tightens—not rough, but firm, grounding.

"Don't hide from me," he says, his tone dropping even lower, almost a growl. "Not now. Not ever."

She bites her lip, her insecurities bubbling to the surface. "I'm not—"

"Yes, you are," he interrupts, his lips brushing hers, soft but insistent. "And I'll spend every day proving to you that you're perfect, Harper. This body, this heart, this fire in you —it's all mine. And I'll never stop wanting you."

His words unravel her, and when his hands slide up her back, pulling her closer, she lets herself believe him. For once, she doesn't try to argue.

He shifts beneath her, his strength effortless as he lifts her slightly, his movements deliberate, teasing. One hand steadies her hips, while the other slides up her back, his touch trailing heat in its wake. Then he leans forward, capturing a small pink nipple between his lips.

A sharp gasp escapes her as his tongue flicks over the sensitive peak, each stroke sending a jolt of pleasure through her. He alternates between gentle flicks and firm suction, his mouth skillful and intent. She throws her head back, as the tension in her core coils tighter with every sensation.

"Lucas..." she breathes, her voice shaky, barely more than a whisper. Her fingers dig into his shoulders, nails biting into his skin as if anchoring herself. The faint crescents they leave behind don't bother him—in fact, they seem to ignite something deeper. He groans against her skin, the vibration sending a fresh wave of heat spiraling through her.

"You feel so damn good," he groans, his head falling back against the headboard for just a moment before his lips are back on hers.

His movements become more hurried, the teasing edge replaced by raw, unrestrained need. She watches, heat pooling in her core, as he braces one hand behind him, digging into the mattress for leverage. His other hand grips her hip firmly, grounding her as his hips roll upward, driving into her with increasing intensity.

The heat between them is everything she's never experienced—everything she never thought she could have. Her breaths come in ragged gasps, her body trembling as she meets him thrust for thrust.

The sound of their bodies colliding fills the room, mingling with the low groans that spill from his lips and the unrestrained moans escaping her own.

Her wolf, so often quiet and indifferent when it came to

the men in her past, is alive now, howling in the back of her mind. Every nerve is on fire, her instincts screaming that this—this man, this moment—is what she's been waiting for.

"Harper..." he growls, her name rough and desperate on his tongue, like a prayer he can't stop repeating. His hand tightens on her hip, guiding her movements as they find a rhythm that's both chaotic and perfectly in sync.

Every thrust sends shockwaves through her, the pressure building with each stroke, until she's lost in the overwhelming sensations coursing through her body. Her wolf feels it too, a primal satisfaction thrumming through her as Lucas moves with her, his strength and devotion anchoring her in the moment. The wolf doesn't question, doesn't doubt —she *knows*. He's hers.

Her eyes lock on his face, and the sight nearly undoes her. His jaw is clenched, his brows furrowed, but his dark eyes stay fixed on her, blazing with a fire that sends her heart racing. His lips part as a groan escapes him, deeper now, more guttural.

The tension in her body coils tighter, ready to snap. She watches as his face shifts, the telltale signs of his climax drawing near. His breathing grows erratic, his grip on her hips unrelenting as his control begins to slip. That's all it takes. The sight of him—completely undone, lost in her— pushes her over the edge. Her climax crashes into her, wave after wave of heat and pleasure rolling through her, leaving her gasping and trembling in his arms.

Her wolf howls in triumph, her presence a powerful hum in the back of Harper's mind. It's more than physical— it's instinct, primal and unshakable. She belongs to him, and he belongs to her.

Her moans become louder, more insistent, as her body

clenches around him. The sound spurs him on, his rhythm faltering as he reaches his peak. He pulls her flush against him, his head falling back, a deep, groan tearing from his throat as he follows her into release.

For a moment, the world stills, and the only sound is the mingled sound of their ragged breathing. His arms wrap around her, holding her close, their bodies still trembling as the aftershocks of their shared climax ripple through them.

"Jesus, Harper," his voice hoarse, lips brushing her temple. "You're going to be the death of me."

She laughs softly, her cheek resting against his chest, her heart still racing.

"Not if you kill me first." Her wolf quiets again, but this time, it's a satisfied calm. For once, the voice that's always been critical and restless is at peace. Lucas isn't just her mate—he's her everything.

AFTER HEARING HIS NAMED SCREAMED, grunted, and the holy spirit entered Harper's body four times, Lucas is looking into the multi-colored eyes of his mate. He wonders if she realizes the power she has over him.

Music is playing from the speakers strategically placed throughout the enormous backyard. The pool and grotto takes up a good portion of it.

Spencer looks ridiculous standing behind the tiki bar with a round straw hat on playing bartender with a cheesy smile. Lucas has never seen him smile this much. Spencer has always been an easy-going guy, but this is pure bliss. The sweet little timid, Avery, is the reason for his newfound happiness.

It seems the Fates have finally found these two packs. Three mated pairs in a month is crazy.

"Lucas." She says into his chest.

"Hmm."

"What are we going to do about our packs? It's been so hard to be away from you and now that we've gotten more nights together, I don't want to give it up."

"I know, baby. We will need to talk with our alphas."

Lucas let his fingers trace the faint scarred ridges along Harper's back, his touch light but lingering. Some are old, nearly faded, but a few ran deeper—deliberate, intentional. His brow furrows. "These aren't just battle scars."

Harper doesn't lift her head, just lets the words hum against his skin.

"No, they're not."

His chest tightens at the quiet weight in her voice. "Ok, so what are they?"

Letting out a slow breath, her fingers move lazily, making lines up and down his forearm. "Charlotte, Jade, Luna and I created a..." Harper shrugs, "I guess you could call it a permanent commitment. A branding of sorts."

His grip stills on her back. "Branding?"

Harper tilts her head just enough to glance up at him. "Not like cattle, dumbass." Her touch never stops, tracing an absent-minded pattern against his skin.

"The four of us made a choice. We each took a mark— equal parts given and received."

The thought of someone cutting into Harper, even if it was her choice, twists something in his chest. "You're saying you let them carve into you?"

Smirking, though not with mockery, "It wasn't like that. It was mutual. We each took a mark, a reminder that no matter what happens, we're bound by more than just a pack bond. We're bound by a choice."

Lucas studies the scars again, something unspoken settling between them. The Red Rocks weren't like other packs. Loyalty wasn't taken—it was given freely, reinforced by something deeper.

The obnoxiousness that is Kai, stops their conversation dead.

"I must find my beauty." Kai is balancing at the peak of the grotto mountain, pounding on this chest like King Kong.

"What the fuck is he doing?" Harper lifts herself off his chest, making his wolf respond with a low growl.

"I don't know, but I think I will bleed him for distracting you. My chest felt better with you against it." Lucas hears a teeny voice behind him.

"I'm here."

He sees little waves as Luna bobs up and down in the shallow end of the pool. The spinning disco ball is making her stark white hair glitter. "Save me Kong."

Harper is giggling and shaking her head. "Oh my god, that females antics have always made me laugh, but I think she may have found her shenanigans match."

"Oh, he's a hoot alright. Some of the scars he carries are payback for the pranks he's pulled back home." Taking Harper's hand, Lucas leads her to the tiki bar.

"Hey barkeep. How about a beer?" Lucas slams his palm down the bar, feeling bad when he sees Avery jump in her seat behind Spencer.

Without even turning around, Spencer reaches behind him, pats her knee, then wipes down the already clean and dry bar with a white towel. With the other hand, he easily grabs a beer and a hard seltzer, setting them down on the brown shiny surface. "What troubles you, strangers?" Spencer plays along.

Lucas looks around the backyard. "Is everyone into role-play tonight?"

"What. No imagination Williams?" Luna yells from her perch on Kai's shoulders.

"Don't you worry about his imagination." Harper defends.

"Thanks baby." Kissing her forehead.

"Wait. Where's Charlotte?" The panic can be heard in Harper's voice.

"Relax second. She's in the grotto. Trust me, no one needs to check on her." Jade flips the throwing ax, finding her target attached to the white fencing she built.

"Chicken fight!" Lucas feels the cool water surround him after he cannonballs into the pool. Popping his head out of the water, he yells to Harper. "Come on babe. Let's show them which couple rules this pool."

Her nerves still show in her eyes, but she manages a smile and runs to the pool, diving in. He prepares as she torpedo's under the water coming right at him. As she is resurfacing, he feels the pressure from her mouth run along the front of his shorts. *Holy shit.* The smile on her face as she opens her eyes sets him on fire.

"Woman, if you do that again, we'll be forfeiting this match and I'll be taking you right back to your room." In one swift movement, he ducks under the water, putting his head between her legs, one of his favorite spots, by the way, and lifts back out of the water.

"Game on Williams." Kai cuts through the water with his powerful body, Luna perched on his massive shoulders to get to Lucas and his defender, Harper.

Both ladies are pushing and pulling at each other.

Laughter is filling the entire backyard. Words like; purple donkey tits, holy mother of all that is yellow, cockfoam, are echoing off the walls of the house. Maddy is calling points for good moves from the orange and teal lounger.

"Kick their asses, Harper." Avery's small, high-pitched voice stops everyone dead. "What? I put my money on Harper." Shrugging her shoulders up.

"I got you Avery." Harper goes at her opponents so fast it throws both Luna and Kai off. Hell, it almost threw him off balance, but he held it. Luna slamming the water, now ties up the game.

"10 out of 10" Both Maddy and Avery yell from the sidelines.

"No way. That was cheating." Luna is still wiping the water from her face.

"How?"

Between, Harper's voice and having her beautiful soft thighs squeezing his neck, Lucas is not really caring if it was cheating or whether they win. He has to stop looking up because he gets distracted by her very large tits every time.

Damn, this female intoxicates him. He always knew he would find her. The one. But he never imagined she would be this beautiful. He can't wait to get that dirty blonde hair wrapped around his fist again. He didn't know his very breath would depend on her proximity to him.

Jaxson pushes back from the table where he'd been talking with Isabell, his chair scraping against the pool deck, cutting through the low hum of conversation. He strides toward Maddy, all confidence and something else—something harder to name. There's always been something different about Jaxson, a quiet intensity beneath the easygoing charm.

He stops in front of her, lowering his big hand, palm up,

just inches from her face. "Will you be my defender, Maddy?" His tone is light, but there's a challenge in his eyes. "I think it's time we show these fools what it really means to play Pool Chicken."

Lucas can see the uncertainty on her face.

"I've never played before." Maddy tells him while slipping her hand into his.

"That's alright. We'll have beginner's luck."

The look that Jaxson shot Lucas told him they *would indeed* have beginner's luck. Lucas pats Harper's thigh and meets her eyes. She gives the nod of understanding. Kai and Luna have reset, and they both also acknowledge. Luna shoots Harper a wink.

All three couples are now set and facing each other in the water.

"Ok Avery. You start us." Lucas's looks over his shoulder giving her a nod.

Everyone settles quietly, knowing they won't hear her little voice if they don't.

"Ready. Set. Chicken."

All three ladies immediately push and pull at each other. Maddy's laugh is addicting. Lucas can't help but laugh with her. Her giggles become harder so everyone else's get louder. Avery and Spencer are cheering her on from the sideline.

Spencer's booming voice encourages her. "Give them hell Maddy!"

Luna takes the plunge first. Falling sideways and taking Kai down with her. Maddy is pushing Harper to the left. To the right. Then Lucas sees the opportunity and falls backwards.

"Eeeeee. We won Jaxson! We have beginner's luck."

"Will you look at that? I'd take you into battle any day

Little wolf." Jaxson sets her down in the water in front of him and pats her shoulder.

Suddenly a crash spins Lucas so quickly it causes water to push over the edge of the pool. He sees small brown feet flailing in the air.

Isabell's indiscernible kicking and screaming is echoing off the grotto.

"I got her." Jaxson says as he climbs out of the pool. "Come on Mamacita. It's time for bed."

"How the fuck did that happen?" Lucas laughs.

"She was making her own margaritas, so I have no idea. She said something about how we are pussies, and she would show us how to drink real margaritas."

"Yeah, I guess she showed us." Feeling the warmth of Harper's touch on his arm, she once again shows her kindness in a small way. "I'm going to follow and get her ready for bed. Jaxson won't be comfortable doing that part."

"Good call babe. I'll be here when you get back." And he kisses her lightly on her plump pink lips.

SHIT, that lady is small but mighty.

Harper finally got the drunk teeny latina in her tie-dye blue muumuu tucked into bed. Isabell kept saying a name over and over. *Litzy.* Harper has never heard her talk about a Litzy so she'll have to ask who that is tomorrow. Maybe once the hangover settles.

Standing in the doorway of Isabell's room, Harper looks back to check on her friend once more. Luna hired Isabell to help with the cleaning and cooking but she has become so much more than that. She may not be a wolf but she is pack.

Making her way through the sliding glass door, Harper

hears everyone saying their goodnights. She has to admit she is relieved. Lucas was going back to his own territory in the morning and Harper needs to be a greedy bitch. She will take every alone second she can before she has to say goodbye.

"Ok, Williams. My room. Now." Harper points towards the multi-slide doors.

"Yes, ma'am." Lucas grabs both of their towels and heads to the door.

After playing grabby asses all the way up the stairs, Harper closes the door on her den. The designers did a great job of capturing her taste. Walking past the large round bed, with black and white bedding, Harper stops in front of the large windows to admire her beautiful desert.

"Hey, Sheridan. What are you thinking about?"

Keeping her eyes on the pink, sun painted sand and sagebrush.

"I love my pack, Lucas. Charlotte is my Alpha. We have gone through hell together. I left a loving, well mostly, loving family to protect her. I don't know if I can leave her, but I can't live without you. You are now the oxygen in my lungs. Once you leave tomorrow, I don't know how I'm going to breathe."

Lucas, coming up behind her, slides both arms around her middle. His tall stature allows him to rest his chin on her head.

"Don't worry about it, baby. I'm going to talk to Spencer on the way home. Assuming Charlotte will accept me as a full pack member, it only makes sense that I come to your pack. Mine has the numbers already. It will be hard for me to leave Spencer. We've had quite the past too, but I won't live without you."

"You sound so sure." Harper grabs his hand from her

waist to move it over her heart knowing it will calm her wolf.

"I *am* confident. I will not live without you, Harper. Do you understand what I am saying?"

She hears the seriousness in his tone.

"I always knew I would find you. I used to dream what it would feel like to have my mate in my arms just like this."

"Am I everything you imagined?" Harper looks up with a flirty smile.

"Oh, Princess." He sweeps a chunk of hair out of her eyes.

"You are so much more than my imagination could come up with. Your passion for...well...everything, turns me on. Your body," with a moan and sniffing her hair. "Your body is the most beautiful thing I've ever touched."

She feels the tightness he uses as he squeezes her back tighter to his chest.

"Harper Sheridan. I love you and I will not let *ANYONE* or *ANYTHING* stand between us." He turns her around to face him. "Do you hear me? Not Spencer. Not Charlotte. Not even Isabell." He smiles, cupping her cheeks. "Nothing will keep me from you."

"You love me?" Her smile is a mix of happiness and hope.

"Yeah, I love you. You are the light in my dark, Princess. Whenever I had to leave you in those hotel rooms, my wolf tore me up. Now that we aren't a secret anymore, he has settled, well, until we talk about me leaving tomorrow. He has my chest on fire right now."

"I get it. My wolf is going nuts. I keep thinking she'll tire of howling, but she's pissed, so she keeps finding more energy." Harper slowly looks up to make eye contact. "I'm sorry.

I'm so freaked out. I think I just need some normal. Some routine."

"We'll figure it out. I need to go home to pack up the house and close out a few things. We'll have a solid plan by then. I will be back, and we will be together for the rest of our lives." Lucas places one hand on her ass while he surrounds the back of her neck with the other.

"I wish I would've found you twenty years ago." Harper rises to her tippy toes to place a kiss on his lips.

"I know, baby, but we had things to learn first. I was beginning to think the fates had forgotten the Humboldts' altogether, but look, Spencer found Avery. We found each other, and what's up with Kai and Luna?"

"Oh, don't get too excited about them. This is what Luna does. I don't know Kai, but I've seen this a hundred times with her. She's a love 'em and leave 'em type. Her trauma runs even deeper than Charlotte or Jade's. It's not just fear— it's survival. She builds walls like they're armor, and love doesn't get through easy."

Harper flinches as the words fall out of her mouth, a flicker of guilt for saying anything about her story flashing in her eyes before she schools her expression.

"Well, as I've noticed, *you* haven't said 'I love you' back," he says, his voice low and teasing, but his eyes holding hers like he's peeling back her defenses one layer at a time. "So, I guess I'll just have to fuck you until you scream it."

WHAT ARE WE GOING TO DO?

The next morning, after breakfast, the Humboldts are saying their goodbyes. The thank you's and see ya's are echoing off the foyer walls.

Lucas has Harper caged against the wall, one arm above her head, resting his forehead to hers.

"We'll figure this out, baby. I promise. I will talk to Spencer on the way home. It only makes sense I come to your pack. My pack is much larger, and the Red Rocks need the numbers. I won't be away for long."

"Ok. I hope Charlotte and Spencer both give their blessing. I love you, Lucas Williams, and I can't wait until we can wake up together every day."

"Me too, baby. Like I said, I *won't* be away from you for long."

With that, Lucas crashes into her mouth with a desperation she's never felt from him before. Hot. Sharp. Final. Like he's trying to leave something behind inside her.

Then he's gone.

The kiss breaks. Lucas shoves off the wall, grabs his duffle, and walks out the front door without looking back.

The howl that tears through Harper's wolf feels unbearable.

She sinks onto the bottom stair. Her arms lock around her middle as she curls inward, trying to hold together something that already feels shattered.

A second later, Luna quietly lowers herself beside her.

"This sucks." Harper rests her head on Luna's shoulder. Liam climbs the stairs behind both ladies. She feels his hand palm over her shoulder, calming her wolf slightly. Harper stares on the floor, allowing her mind to wander back to the day that Lucas pushed his way into her life.

"Miss. Hey Miss."

Turning, her breath hitches, seeing the hottest guy she has ever seen standing in front of her.

She's heard people say they get butterflies, now she knows what that means. Her breath hitches when his scent hits her.

He's a wolf. His light brown crew cut matches the color of his three-day stubble beard, except for the small patch of grey on his left cheek just below the sexiest 'oh shit' dimple.

"Yeah?"

"You dropped this." The beefcake holds out his hand, locking his dark brown eyes to hers.

Looking down at the piece of paper with a phone number on it, she suspiciously shakes her head. "No, I didn't. I haven't received a phone number in a while." 'Why did she just admit that, and why is her wolf being so quiet?' There is a strange male in front of her. Weird.

"Oh, I thought I saw it drop from your hand."

He inches closer.

"But." The gorgeous man takes another step closer. "Maybe I just wanted to make sure it made it into your hand."

That dimple cannot possibly go any deeper...can it?

"Yeah. I forgot." The *sexiest, most mischievous* smile slowly takes over his face. "That's what it was."

Harper opens her mouth to say something, but she can only manage to get a "squeak" to surface.

Deciding to go a different route, she finds her protective side. It was harder than it should be, though. What the hell is going on with her around this stranger? Very. Very hot stranger.

"What are you doing in my territory, wolf?"

"Oh, I'll be gone soon. I just followed a friend here, but he's an idiot, so I parted ways with him. I didn't know this was a taken territory until recently. I'll be leaving, but after seeing you, I thought maybe I would take a huge risk and ask you to dinner."

"That IS a huge risk stranger," Harper growls low. She knows she needs to get this guy out of town. "I will only give you one warning. Get. Out. Of. My. City."

The male drips sex appeal and confidence. Throwing up his hands up in surrender, Harper blinks hard, watching each muscle ripple beneath his warmly tanned skin.

Harper can't help but notice the definition in his forearms. Those would look good on either side of her head, holding her steady as— Oh my God, where did that come from?

"Ok she-wolf, I will leave but can I do one thing first, and I'm going to preface this with, I know it's an even bigger risk." He looks her up and down. "It might get my throat ripped out but." He tips his head with indifference.

Harper pauses for a split second. "Should I be concer..."

Her words are cut off when his mouth crashes into hers. Shock stops her from killing him, then her brain finally kicks.

He is walking them backwards as his mouth is making hers fire. Her back hits the side of her car. Harper is conflicted, but her wolf is licking at her insides, enjoying everything this stranger is giving them, but she knows she should kill this male for touching her without permission. But, fuck, this kiss is too damn hot.

Just as she reaches up to push him away, he runs his tongue along her bottom lip. Her... "always have a plan, plan" is thrown out the window. Instead, she parts her lips and deepens the kiss. Grabbing his neck and pulling herself up on her toes to give him even more of her. He is a good seven inches taller than her. This is the most impulsive thing she has ever done. Harper is not the impulsive type. This certainly was not in her "plan", but holy shit, he smells, tastes and feels like pure lust.

Giving in, she pushes her chest deeper into his. This man radiates sex. Her wolf wants every part of him. She wants him inside her now. She breaks the lust quickly.

"So, do you have a hotel?"

Resting his forehead on hers, grabbing a few quick breaths,

"Yeah, just up the road."

Suddenly, something soft hits her face, pulling her back to the now. "It smells like Lucas. His hoodie?" She immediately pulls it over her head.

"What? His bag was open... sorta." The thief in Jade's clothing stands there, shrugging like she's been caught jaywalking, her face the picture of unbothered.

Harper doesn't feel any better, but the faint trace of him lingering in the fabric steadies her, holding her together just enough. She swallows the lump in her throat, silently adding this to the growing list of debts she owes Jade.

THE TEXT

Harper drops onto the couch beside Charlotte in the game room, trying to ignore the gnawing nerves in her stomach. She fidgets with her fingers, a habit she hasn't shaken since childhood.

Lucas is on his way back to Vegas. Just the thought of him makes her chest tighten—not with fear, but with longing. He promised her she'd love the Humboldts, and she believes him—most of the time.

Still, the weight of what Charlotte and Spencer had negotiated sits heavy on her shoulders.

Dual pack membership. It sounded simple enough, but the cost was steep: she and Lucas would have to give up their Beta statuses. Harper had agreed—hesitantly— because being with him mattered more than a title. But now, with the prospect of seeing Lucas again, the enormity of the decision feels suffocating.

Across the room, Jade lounges against the pool table, her sharp eyes following Harper's every twitch. The glare is less judgment and more exasperation, but it still slices through Harper's fragile confidence like a razor.

"Fuck you, Jade. I was talking to Char, not you," Harper snaps, unable to keep her mouth shut any longer.

Charlotte raises an eyebrow, clearly unimpressed. "And here I thought you were trying to win people over, not start another fight," she says, her tone dry but laced with amusement.

Jade smirks. "Relax, Harper. You're the one making a big deal out of it. I don't care if you join, leave, or marry the guy —just don't mess up my pool shot next time."

Harper clenches her jaw, her nerves threatening to bubble over into something uglier, but Charlotte places a calming hand on her knee. "You've got this," Charlotte says quietly. "The packs will figure it out. Just remember, this isn't about titles—it's about what makes you both stronger together."

The words settle something in Harper, but only just. She exhales, leaning back into the couch, the thought of Lucas still looming large in her mind.

Charlotte barely glances up, her tone sharp but even. "And Jade, stop with the Second Alpha shit. It's just annoying. He's fine being called Liam."

Harper grins and high-fives Charlotte just as Liam saunters into the room. His timing, as always, is impeccable.

"I don't know, Alpha. I kind of like it," Liam quips with a mischievous smirk.

Jade rolls her eyes. "Well, shit. Now I have to come up with something el—"

Her voice fades like a distant echo. Harper's body stiffens as the air thickens around her, turning suffocatingly heavy. The sunlight streaming through the window dims, swallowed by an unnatural darkness. Her fingers tremble as her wolf surges forward, tearing at her insides like a hurricane caged within her skin.

Her vision blurs, her wolf's howls drowning out every other sound. It's primal. Relentless. The couch beneath her is gone, replaced by nothingness. Pain lashes through her chest like jagged claws, her breath catching in her throat. Her phone buzzes in her palm, but her hand feels detached, foreign. She looks down, and her stomach drops.

The screen displays Lucas. Bound. Bloodied. Barely recognizable.

Charlotte's voice slices through the fog, distant but firm. "Harper? What the hell?" She snatches the phone from Harper's trembling grip.

The message is simple.

> We will trade. Williams for Barlowe.

Harper stares at her hands, her vision tunneling. They're trembling violently now, her wolf clawing to the surface. Her skin burns, her chest heaving as her world narrows to one thought, *They touched him. They hurt him.*

Charlotte's voice anchors her, barely. "Luna, get on the computer. Find his car. Now."

Her skin ripples with the threat of a shift, her claws aching to tear free. The air around her grows thick, suffocating, like the walls are pressing in. Every sound—Charlotte's commands, Luna's typing—fades into the background, replaced by the pounding of her heartbeat and the primal roar of her wolf.

They will pay.

Harper grips the couch, the fabric tearing beneath her nails. If she moves, even an inch, she will lose control. Her wolf will take over, and there will be no stopping the bloodshed.

"Liam, call Spencer. Find out what he knows. Jade—

Jade! Where the fuck are you going?" Charlotte's voice is sharp, but Harper barely registers it. Her ears ring with her wolf's fury.

Tears blur her vision as she whispers into the chaos, her voice breaking. "Lucas, where are you?"

I FUCKED UP

"I'm sorry Harper. I fucked up. I let my guard down." Lucas feels cold concrete below his feet and ass. He sees her sitting there, leaning against the damp wall. She's not saying anything. *Why isn't she talking back?* Her face looks sad. *Why is she sad?*

"Shut up, you fucking idiot. She's not there. You're hallucinating, dumbass."

Looking over his shoulder, Lucas sees a male about his size. Six foot three, a large chest, short blonde hair, and a face that would scare his own mother.

Looking back to the wall, "It's ok Harper. I'll find a way to get us out of here."

"Ha! The only way you're getting out of here is in a body bag, Williams. Do you really think Ethan is going to let you live?"

Ugly face has turned his back to Lucas, so his voice echoes off the back wall.

WHOMP "Shut the fuck up Eli. Don't talk to him."

Lucas turns his body to see the only face he knows with

certainty. Ethan is standing over a tucked male that he assumes is Eli. *Why does that sound familiar?* The clanking sound shoots pain through his head as Ethan unlocks the chain wrapped around the rusty bars of his twelve by twelve steel prison. Reaching up, Lucas runs his fingers over his left eye, feeling dried blood on top of a partially healed gash. He's putting effort into trying to open it but can't see anything or even feel it.

"I told you, this wasn't over, Williams. Miles trusted you." Spit falls from Ethan's raging mouth. "He brought you into our pack because he knew you when you were kids. He believed your sob story."

An excruciating pain hits Lucas in the side, reminding him of the cracked rib... or two. "I never believed you. I warned Miles you would betray us. I was ready for it."

Ethan lifts his foot to kick him again, but Lucas was ready for it this time. Grabbing his foot mid-air, Lucas twists so hard Ethan's body follows and slams hard on the wet concrete.

"Fuck you, asshole. My pack will find me and you will die a slow death."

Pop. Lucas feels the dark close over his mind again.

Filling her lungs, Harper gains just a small amount of control over her wolf. The walls feel tight as she follows her alpha into the small room Luna claimed shortly after moving in. Quickly glancing at the sign next to the door that reads; *"Say Hi To Monty"*, she can't help but wonder what the hell does that mean?

Fully inside, the now amber-colored eyes of her wolf, scan the entire room. It looks nothing like it did when they bought the house. Little did Harper know there was a command center much like NASA's buried in her house. The four monstrous TVs mounted above five large computer monitors are playing different TV shows. She can't help but stop on the middle monitor, seeing the screen filled with a map of Nevada. *Where the fuck are you Lucas?*

Walking towards the hot pink chair that surely swallows Luna's tiny body, Harper can't imagine what wrongs Luna has righted in this room. Harper pushes on her chest, but it doesn't slow her wolf from biting, scratching, swatting her claws, ready to kill everything. She will take the throat of any creature, human or shifter that gets in between her and her mate.

Liam steps into the room but stops suddenly to survey the high-tech room that has been a secret. The purple and green LED lights create an even more mystifying feeling.

"This is the first time I've been to the dragon's lair."

"Wolf, Liam. I'm the smartest motherfucking wolf on the planet, and right now, I need to find my sister's mate."

Luna's next words are barely audible over the pounding of her pink keyboard. "Where are you, Lucas? Hang on, brother. We're coming."

The screen to her right streams with white numbers and letters, moving almost too fast for Harper's eyes to follow.

Liam places a palm gently on Luna's shoulder, his voice

carrying genuine remorse. "Sorry, Luna. That was insensitive. Let me know what I can do to help."

"It's alright." Luna's voice softens just slightly before a small smirk tugs at her lips. "I kind of like the lair, though."

Harper notices Luna's shoulders relax ever so slightly as she tilts her head, letting it briefly touch the top of Liam's hand. Wolf shifters are tactile creatures, and even a fleeting connection like this helps soothe their internal beasts.

Not moving his hand, he turns to Charlotte. "Spencer said he knows nothing. The last time he talked to Lucas was right before he left. He felt sadness in their bond roughly an hour ago, but he didn't think much of it. Lucas has been sad since they left here last week."

Standing behind Harper, holding her shoulders as if to hold her pieces together, Charlotte asks, "Does he have any idea where Ethan would take him?"

"I asked him and he said no. Lucas was the one that knew the ins and outs of the Cascade's and their patterns."

Luna breaks into their conversation as if they weren't even having it.

"Ok Alpha, I found his car in some campground next to a Walker Lake. It's about five hours north of here."

"Well, that makes sense. Harper, didn't you say Lucas told you he was about five hours out?"

Harper can only shake her head. She's afraid if she opens her mouth, her wolf will break free. And there are only two things that will let the human side have control again. Charlotte's alpha command. And that shit hurts. Or Ethan's dead body laying in front of her feet.

"It seems Ethan is as dumb as we thought." Charlotte walks up to the monitor with the map of Nevada pulled up. "Luna, send that to all our phones. Where the fuck is Jade?"

"I'm here, Alpha." Jade is strapped for war. "All our bags are packed and loaded in my truck. Let's go get our brother."

LIGHT. *Dark. Light. Dark.* Feeling both eyes opening and closing. The dim light causing knife cuts in his brain. Lucas leans up on his right hand, but stops, seeing two of his fingers bent in the wrong direction.

"Fuck!" Looking around the room as fast as his pain filled head will allow. He sees a figure in the shadows. "Hey! What the shit, man. Where am I? What the hell did I ever do to you?"

"Shut the fuck up, Williams. Your girlfriend will write. Your pain will end soon enough." Ugly face guy says.

Girlfriend? Who the fuck is this guy and where am I?

LOOKING AROUND THE GREAT ROOM, the gigantic mural of the Red Rock Canyon on the back wall begins to come into focus. The blur of shock letting go of its hold. Harper watches as her pack is preparing to hunt their prey.

Get your shit together, Sheridan. Our mate needs us.

"What's the plan?" These first words taste like fire and apparently they sound like it too because everyone turns to look at her.

Crossing to Harper, Charlotte hugs her tight. Harper doesn't move.

While still holding her, Charlotte whispers, "I called Willamina. She owes me one, so the coven is going to watch the territory until the guys can get here."

Breaking the hug, Charlotte cups Harper's cheeks,

ensuring eye contact. Harper still hasn't moved. Standing stiff, she knows the others cannot understand how hard it is to keep her wolf from breaking her skin and going on a killing spree. There would be no differentiating between friend or foe.

Charlotte is still working to maintain eye contact. "Kai, Jaxson, and Ryan are already on their way. They'll keep Maddy, Isabell, and our home safe until we get Lucas and bring him home."

Breaking free from Charlotte, Harper twists towards the front door. "What are we waiting for?" Anger has now taken over. "I have some wolves to kill."

OUTSIDE IN FRONT of their beautiful mansion, the five Red Rocks are throwing bags under the tonneau cover of Jade's blue F-250 Black Widow. There isn't a truck large enough for the tension these five shifters have built up, but Jades truck makes the most sense.

Giving a proper scolding, Isabell hands Liam the cooler full of road food, and energy drinks. "You bring my Lucas home."

After smacking Liam's stomach, she walks to meet Maddy standing in front of the wrought iron and glass gothic style door. Maddy is clutching her favorite purple shawl tight to her chest. Worry is heavy on her fine features.

Charlotte hollers at the closing door. "Jaxson will be here as soon as he can."

Harper and Charlotte don't make a move, waiting for the locks to click and the alarm system to beep.

"It's showing it's activated." Luna shouts from the backseat.

Harper climbs in the passenger seat, while Charlotte and Liam squish the teeny Luna between them in the back.

Luna flips her laptop open. She hasn't stopped monitoring Lucas's phone, hoping it will turn back on so she can pinpoint his location. "Ethan must have shut the phone off as soon as he sent the text. They were somewhere around this Walker Lake."

Harper twists in her seat. "I know the council won't do anything, but did you call Jase? This involves his inmate?"

"Yeah, I called him. He said to keep him posted. A trade is not an option. The COPS will never let Miles free, but he also gave me his super secret cell phone number. He said he would tell a little white lie to trick the fucknuts. It may buy us time if needed."

"I've always liked that guy...NOT." Jade curls her lip.

The rustling from the bag of Flavorblasted Goldfish Charlotte is struggling to open is rubbing on Harper's already very close to the surface nerves. She can't help the growl that rumbles deep in her throat.

Luna ignores it. "Once we get to Walker Lake, I would think it'll be easy to track Lucas down by his scent. Harper, you'll know it best, so we're just going to follow your lead."

Harper doesn't even need to see Charlotte's face to know how concerned she is. The pack's bond is electrified.

"Hold on! Lucas's phone just came online." As if Luna had sent the text herself, she snaps and points to the phone sitting on the center console.

"Harper phone."

With a shaky voice, Harper reads the text aloud.

> I haven't heard from you red rock bitch am I killing this asshole or what

As those words push the small pieces of shock and

doubt out of her body, Harper takes complete control. Even her wolf has pulled the anger into a fiery sphere within. This control is not like anything she has ever felt before.

With the steadiness of a surgeon, Harper hits play on the attached video. The screen is dark, but she can see Lucas's body tucked on a concrete floor. Bruises, shreds in his skin, and dried blood from head to toe. The scarring she sees tells her he has healed, then beaten again, many times.

"Leave me alone. Why are you doing this?" The voice has a hint of Lucas.

"Tell your girlfriend you want to live. Tell her to bring my Alpha and we'll trade."

"Please. I don't have a girlfriend. I just want to go home."

The video ends.

Charlotte clears her throat, but it doesn't help to mask her wolf being so close to the surface. "This has the COPS powder written all over it. Harper send that to Jase."

Thumbs tapping her screen, Harper hits send.

The moment Harper hits send, her phone lights up with Jase's name. He doesn't even wait for her to say hello before launching into his tirade.

"What in the fuck is wrong with these guys?" His earsplitting frustration makes her recoil, the volume forcing her to pull the phone slightly away from her ear.

"Yes, Harper, that *is* the powder. The council discovered a few years ago—by accident, mind you—that overexposure would start to... what's the best way to put it?" He exhales sharply, the sound crackling through the line. "Melt the brain. Individuals would start losing their memories, but worse—far worse—their animals would begin to... disappear."

"WHAT THE FUCK!" all five Red Rocks yell simultaneously.

"Accident, my ass," Charlotte growls. "They wouldn't get to that point unless they were experimenting, Jase. How do you sleep at night?"

"I sleep fine, Charlotte," Jase says, but his voice carries a sharp edge, the kind that hints at something far from restful. He pauses, dragging in a slow, deliberate breath like he's steadying himself. "It's easier to keep an eye on the monster," he continues, his tone dropping lower, almost a whisper, "when you're the one sharing its bed."

The words hang heavy between them, laced with a bitterness that feels like it's been simmering for years.

Harper can't help the fury building even more. "So what you're telling me is my Lucas may be lost forever?"

Jase exhales deep. "If you don't get to him soon, yes. I'm sorry, Harper."

Harper can hear the regret in his words. "From what I can see on that video, Ethan is giving him large doses and not waiting between. If Lucas already doesn't know he has a mate, it means his mind is..."

The pause hangs too long.

"Jase!"

"His mind is losing its compass. You are his compass, Harper. He won't know what is right or wrong. It won't be long and he won't even know who he is anymore."

"It's only been a couple of hours, Jase. This shit works that fast?" Harper's wolf is so close to the surface that she has no high tones to her voice anymore. It's more growl than English.

Jase figured out what she said, and his response comes with a lot of defeat in it.

"Absolutely. If he's receiving high doses, the descent will be rapid,"

Jase fills his lungs, followed by a short pause. Harper is

feeling the wariness that Jase has. There must be a lot more to his story than any of them have ever thought about.

"The poison was initially developed to aid field agents in controlling unruly shifters. Especially ones that are larger than us, like bears, silverbacks, lions. Hell, there could be a pterodactyl out there for all we know. We are still finding shifters all the time. Hiding is all we've really ever known until more recently."

"Sorry about that."

Harper glances to the backseat, where Luna is curled into herself, looking smaller than usual.

Before Harper can say anything, Jase's voice cuts through the silence, sharp and unrelenting. "Luna, don't you ever apologize for that shit. You did what you had to."

Harper's eyes flick to the phone in her hand as Jase's tone shifts, his voice morphing from weary to something unhinged.

"Those sick fucks exposed us, not you," he growls, the edge in his voice sharp enough to make her stomach twist.

Looking to the backseat again, Harper watches as Luna's back sits straighter.

"The drug was created because the council didn't want to resort to killing every shifter that lost control. Sometimes, we shifters' just need a little... time out."

"This is way more than a little time out. This is fucked up." Charlotte's irritation can't be hidden.

"I will say, the Council is far from perfect, Charlotte. We rewrote the vetting process after we found out research was being conducted off the books. That research is what revealed this extremely atrocious side effect. Right now, I'm putting all my time into finding the source of the Cascades' supply. It appears I have a problem in my own house."

"Yes, you do. Once we find Lucas, how do I dispose of

the powder?" Harper is trying to make her words under-
standable, but her wolf is making it difficult.

"Fire."

"Say no more." Harper ends the call.

"Why am I here? Why am I bleeding?"

"Shut the fuck up, Williams. God, I can't wait to kill you."

A man with a familiar face, brown greasy hair, and scar
down the left side of his face is yelling at him.

"Who is Williams? Is that my name? Did I do something
to hurt you?"

"YES! Yes, you fucking did. You betrayed our pack. You
took my Alpha from me!"

The stranger is standing over him, legs on either side of
his crumpled body. The pain is everywhere. He rubs his
thigh, looking for the knife that must be sticking into it, but
there is nothing but pain. He is sure his head is split open
from above his left eye to the right side of his neck, although
blood doesn't seem to be flowing from it.

"What can I do to make it right? I just want to go
home."

The strange man cracks an evil smile. "Where is home,
asshole?"

Closing his eyes, digging deep into his memories, he gets
nothing but black. He feels a low, faint growl. "What is
that?"

"What is what, crazy man?"

"I feel something in my chest? What is that?"

"That is your dying animal, fucker. Like I said, you took
something from me, so I'm going to take something from
you. I'm taking your animal *and* even if you don't remember

who she is, I'm taking your bitch. I will rip her heart from her chest."

Not even understanding why, he suddenly lunges at the strange man, but the pain that comes from the sudden movement drops him right back to the cold, wet ground and everything goes dark.

"STOP THE TRUCK!" There is no stopping the change.

Jade veers the truck into the desert shoulder and slams on the brakes. Just as Harper gets the door open, her white and black wolf breaks the human form.

Liam slowly slides out of the truck, followed by Luna. Charlotte's pure black wolf stalks around the back of the truck.

Harper responds by taking an aggressive stance, hackles raised, teeth bared. She would rather not bleed her alpha, but she will, if that's what it takes. This little road trip is taking too long. They must find their mate.

The salt and pepper turns to run, but Charlotte's warning yip echoes off the desert dirt, forcing the very pissed off animal to stop. Her alpha's scolding power forces her body to stiffen, causing pain points. Little clouds of dust surround her white paws.

Standing next to the open passenger door, Luna is holding her hands up in a surrendering pose. "Harper, we know you want to find him. We do too. We have to stick together, though."

Liam positions himself just behind Charlotte's left shoulder. The sound of Jade dropping the tailgate draws Harper's eyes to the truck.

"No. No Harper. Look at me. It's ok. It's just Jade getting us some water. Isabell packed us good eats. If you run ahead of us, we won't be there for backup. You know Alpha isn't going to let you go by yourself. Can human, have her body back? I will personally ensure you get the kill, Harper. I pinky promise," Luna holds out her tiny little pinky. "But we can't do it right until Harper has a pinky."

Charlotte's deep bark, grabs everyone's attention. Giving another yip, the black wolf looks back at Harper and takes off in a run. Harper follows, with Liam's giant black wolf on her left flank.

Jade and Luna jump in the truck, slamming their doors behind them and the chase is on.

Wolf growls as Harper pushes her to run harder. Knowing if she helps her wolf find some calm, it will benefit them both. They need to fully converge in order to become stronger than they ever have been. Harper never thought they would find a mate bond, and now the feeling is like a drug. She will allow nothing to take it from her. Finding Lucas before the powder takes hold, pushes her.

Her alpha slows the pace after many miles. Pushing her fear into the earth through her strong paws, is just the release both her and her wolf needed. Harper watches as Charlotte's pure black wolf turns and pads back to where Harper has stopped. The powerful wolf rubs her snout up and all over her face. Giving her little yips and whimpers of affection.

Liam is one of the biggest wolves she has ever seen. The monstrosity brings a stick and drops it at her front paws. As she reaches down to grab it, he snatches it back up and runs. Harper follows, jumping on his back, snapping to try to get the stick from him, but Liam's wolf is twice the size of her. She slides down and lands on her paws without the stick. The three wolves wrestled and bite at each other for a few more minutes while Jade and Luna fish out bottles of water, sandwiches, and clothes.

The last to change back into her human form, still as naked as a newly singled woman dancing around her house, Harper throws her arms around her alpha's neck.

"Thank you Char. My wolf couldn't take it anymore. She needed to do something. Running helped. Her and I are one now. We're ready. We need to find Lucas."

Jade's smokey voice draws Harper's attention towards the truck. "Ok but eat up first and for fuck sakes, put some clothes on before someone drives by and sees you three lunatics standing here naked eating a sandwich."

The water bottle she is drinking from makes the annoying cracking sound as she sucks down the clear liquid. "I have to answer the text."

Harper pulls the stolen hoodie over her naked chest. She pulls the neckline to her nose and breathes deep. Thank god, she had taken it off earlier. Otherwise, it would be in the pile of shredded clothes that Liam is tossing into a black plastic bag.

"Thanks Liam."

"Of course." Giving her a quick squeeze of her forearm as he walks by.

"I agree with Harper. She needs to answer him." Liam ties the bag closed.

Harper walks to the open passenger door, grabbing her phone off the floorboard and looks for any cracks. "What do I write back?"

"Tell the fat-cell that his death will finally allow him to do something productive for the earth. Once you kill him, he'll decompose and even his skinny body will bloat because enzymes leak, causing gasses to build. He'll turn an ugly color of green because of the sulfur-containing compounds that the bacteria release. The insects will take care of him from there. They eat the soft tissues first. That means his eyes. The smell will probably be as bad as it is now, though."

"Fuck Luna! That's a picture I didn't need." Shaking her sandwich in front of Luna's face, Jade scolds, "Damn, girl. I mean, I know I'm an animal, but I am trying to eat meat. You almost ruined meat for me."

Charlotte brushes the top of the hand holding the phone. "Say what your gut tells you to, Harper. We got your back, no matter what."

Turning towards the mountains in the distance, Harper walks away from the truck, phone in hand. Breathing in the desert, the setting sun is painting pinks, purples, and oranges to take over the blue sky. The sagebrush in bloom colors the desert in a bright gold and yellow color. This is a brilliant contrast to the normal browns and patches of green. Harper loves the desert. When she was younger, it was hard to leave the plains of Montana, but now, she could not imagine her den anywhere but the desert. She needs her mate to be with her.

Hold on Lucas, I'm coming.

Opening the messenger app, the text that is turning her

into an assassin is lit up. Thumbs speeding across the screen.

I am coming for you, Ethan. You. Will. Die. Do you understand you took something that belongs to me? You touched my mate. I will cut off your hands for that. Then I will take your eyes for daring to look at him. Next will be your throat for talking to him. I hope this is clear enough for you.

Stopping just above the send button, instinct tells her to stop. Harper walks back to her pack. Talking over the noises of Luna collecting empty water bottles while Liam is rearranging the items in the cooler.

"I think I need to make him think we have Barlowe. Don't you?" Eyes moving back to her screen, her thumb rests on the back arrow. "I think he'll stop bargaining if he thinks for a second that we can't deliver Miles." She watches as the letters disappear one by one. Anger washes over her as the words her heart wants to say vanish, but she knows her logic needs to lead on this one.

The click of seat belts now fill the cab of the truck as the pack all sit in the same seats. Luna pulls the GPS back up as Jade pulls the truck back to the highway.

> It took a minute, but I have Barlowe. Where are we meeting?

Right after she taps send, it hits her. Ethan is slow, but he is going to want proof.

She hurries and texts Jase.

> He's going to want a picture or something of Miles.

The responses from Jase come so fast she wonders if his phone is ever out of his hand.

The video he sent reveals Miles sitting in the backseat of

somebody's car. Knowing it's not Jase's truck by the grey upholstery, Harper can't help but wonder why Miles would be in a different vehicle. The blue jumpsuit he's wearing shows the video was filmed after Jase took Miles from the warehouse. Miles looks different. Smaller. Pale. Cheeks sunken in. His deep blue eyes move to the camera, devoid of any emotion. The sound has been cut out. Just as the video saves, Ethan responds.

I want to see him.

Harper immediately sends the video and waits.

MY LIGHT IS SO DARK

Turning just past the brown and white sign confirming they reached Walker Lake, Jade reaches over and turns off her headlights.

"Let's avoid any unwanted attention."

The sun has completely faded from the horizon, leaving only the light from the spanning Milky Way above.

Her inner animal gives Harper super powered eyesight, so really the headlights are just for the humans they passed on the road.

"There!"

Harper has no doubt that the car parked with the drivers door still open, is Lucas's. The older red Toyota Corolla, with a huge dent in the passenger side cannot be mistaken. The night before he returned to California, Lucas told her the story of how the dent came to be.

"Jaxson and Kai are complete douchebags. I was making a grilled cheese and I could hear them arguing off in the distance, but that's pretty normal for our place. Kai's trailer is the closest to mine, so I hear shit all the time. Even when we were kids, he never shut up. Anyway, Kai fucks with everyone, but it's hard to

get any reactions from Jaxson, so naturally, Kai plays the most pranks on him."

"Naturally." Harper's relaxed body is draped over Lucas's chiseled chest, stroking the top of her hand that is placed over his heart with each sentence.

She could've stayed like that forever.

"I guess that time the asshole pushed too far because I heard cussing, then full on wolf aggression that is getting closer to my place, so "naturally" I wanted to see Kai get his ass kicked."

"Naturally."

"But just as I made it to the deck, those fuckers rolled into my car. My Cora was hurt! Those fuckers! She was no match for those two ogres. Poor Cora. She's still a beauty, though."

"What was the prank?"

"Kai broke into his place. Now, mind you, this is a feat. Because Kai has broken into everyone's place so many times, Jaxson had a security system put in his trailer, plus multiple locks. But Kai still managed to get in and he took the last can of Spaghettios."

Harper pops up off his chest to be face to face. "What the fuck is with you people and the damn Spaghettios?"

Flying out of the truck's passenger side, Harper skids to a halt beside Lucas's abandoned Cora. The door swung wide like an open wound, a silent invitation for her to piece together what happened. Her breath comes in short, sharp bursts as she dives in—digging through the clutter on the passenger seat, prying open the center console with trembling hands. Lucas's scent clings to the air, wrapping around her like a fraying thread. It's not enough. It's never enough.

Her rational mind screams that this is pointless, that whatever clues might have been here are long gone, but instinct drives her forward, primal and unstoppable. Her wolf howls beneath her skin, desperate to sieze control, but

Harper holds the line—for now. This is her role. She has to find him.

Lucas. Hang on baby. I'm coming.

She takes a deep breath, forcing it past the tightness in her chest, grounding herself in the sharp mix of oil, dust, and the faint trace of him. Her lungs ache with the effort, her wolf straining against her resolve.

There's no blood. No torn fabric. No sign of a struggle. Relief and dread battle for dominance, leaving her unsteady. What the hell happened here? The absence of clues feels like a taunt, and the silence presses down on her like a weight she's not sure she can carry.

"Here!" Jade whisper yells, knowing Harper will hear her just fine.

Joining Jade at the edge of the parking lot, Harper sees the freshly disturbed dirt and broken cactus arm.

"This must be where they got him down. I don't see paw prints." Jade's voice has defeat. "He must not have had time to shift."

Watching Jade's eyes go from her normal light grey to the dark grey of her wolf, Harper knows she is not the only one on the edge.

"Wait." Luna whispers. "I've been digging into the local history and there is an old ghost town with a small mine. It's not on any maps, but from what I can find, it's close." Luna turns the laptop towards Charlotte and Liam. "That has to be where Ethan would go."

"How far away is it? They'll hear the truck out in the middle of nowhere like that." Jade is walking towards the others.

Harper hasn't moved. Staring into the darkness of the lake, she whispers. "I'm coming Lucas. Please hang on a little longer. I will find you." She pushes as much energy as she dare into the bond with each whisper.

"Not being on a map, I'm totally guessing here."

"Luna." Harper says with sincerity, still not turning around. "I have more confidence in your guessing than I do in most people's facts."

Looking up from the keyboard with watery eyes, "I flove you, Harper."

Finally, turning to her pack. "I flove you too. Now how far?"

"I'm going to say five miles or so."

"Yeah, we need to leave the truck. Even if they are deep in the mine, they'll hear this truck." Jade quietly closes the driver's door. "Hey Alpha, we might want to buy a car that makes zero sound."

"If this type of fuckery is going to happen, then yes. We probably do." Standing in front of a dark brown bulletin board, Charlotte asks "Is it this way Luna?" Pointing at the map with evenly spaced green dashes from the... "YOU ARE HERE" to a dot on the other side of the lake.

"No. It's here." Luna joins Charlotte at the water stained corkboard posters, phone in hand with a topo map on the screen. She points a few inches away from the dot.

Single file, the Red Rocks make their way down the trail, through the desert. The pedometer app she started on her watch at the trailhead, tells Harper they've gone 3.8 miles.

"There." Hearing Charlotte's voice, Harper brings her eyes back to the front of the trail. Just another few yards in front of them, there is another corkboard. The board reveals information about the lake and the end of the trail.

"We need to go this way."

Looking down, Harper sees both of Luna's tiny hands

holding phones. One with a topo map and one with a compass.

Charlotte's pleading tone sinks in. "Harper, please stay close so we can do this as a pack. We are stronger together."

Harper doesn't respond. She can't make that promise. Once she feels the bond get stronger or picks up Lucas's scent fully, any control may leave her completely.

Listening to Luna's commands. *Turn here. Go down that ravine. Climb over that boulder.* Just ahead Harper sees the outline of a small mountain that has some type of man made equipment protruding up. As they get closer, the small ghost town takes shape and her skin begins to burn.

"This is it. I feel him. He's in there somewhere. It's faint, but he's here." Her wolf is again snapping, teeth bared, and barking.

"We don't have a lot of time. They will pick up our scents soon." Liam crouches to his knee.

"Jade, go recon the town. I don't hear anything but make sure there isn't anybody on watch in any of these buildings." Charlotte instructs Jade, then crouches down with the other three Red Rocks.

Harper's control is hanging by a thread. She feels her teeth breaking the gums. Her clothes are getting tighter. This is always a sign that her body is taking on a larger shape. This sitting around planning is pushing her over the edge. Talking isn't killing, and killing is what she should be doing.

"We need to stay together. We need to hunt as a pack. It's how we've stayed alive time and time again. Harper! For fuck sakes, listen!" The alpha power stunning all of them.

"Liam, you haven't been with us long enough to know our movements, so I'm going to have you stick close to Luna. Luna, you need to stay in human form to lead us all out quickly as soon as we have Lucas. I would like to limit the bloodshed if possible."

Charlotte's orders come out with confidence Harper has heard during so many battles. What she doesn't know is, Harper has no intention of limiting the bloodshed.

"Harper, you lead. Dig into your bond. He may not know it's there anymore, but you do." Charlotte tips her head towards the entrance to the mine.

Harper can only nod her head. She is tighter than a spool of thread.

Jade stalks up behind Liam. "All clear. It doesn't appear they spent any time in the town."

"Ok. Harper. Are you ready?"

Harper stands to her full five-six height. "Don't forget Ethan is mine."

The five Red Rocks enter the dark mine shaft. Luna didn't tell them the history of the mine, but time has caused some of the support boards to fail. Stepping over the broken and splintered timbers, Harper then navigates the rubble that fell with the timbers.

Making their way further into the shaft, she's struggling to pick up any scents besides stale air and moisture. Goose bumps cover her arms. Even her shifter warmth can't stave off the colder it gets with each step she takes. Hearing a noise other than the water drips, Harper stops and throws up her hand to signal the pack to stop. Concentrating on the noise. It's voices.

She steadies her breathing and slowly strips off her clothes, folding them neatly before setting them aside. Her fingers linger on the hoodie, giving it a gentle pat as she whispers, "I'll be back."

Looking back, all but Luna are stripping off their clothes

and throwing them into a pile. They don't seem to be as concerned about getting them back.

Taking a deep breath, Harper steadies herself, knowing the shift must be silent. Her body trembles with the transition, muscles rippling and bones reshaping with a muted crackle that echoes faintly in the stillness. Her wolf emerges, larger than the average female shifter, her broad shoulders and thick frame built for raw strength rather than speed.

Her salt and pepper coat glistens faintly in the dim light, the darker streaks along her back blending with the shadows of the tunnel. Her ears flick forward, sharp and alert, while her yellow-gold eyes glint with a feral, focused rage. The low rumble of a growl vibrates through her chest, but she suppresses it, baring her teeth in silent fury instead.

As Harper stretches, her massive paws sink slightly into the soft ground beneath her, the slight splash of water muffled. She glances back as one by one, Charlotte, Liam, and finally Jade shift. Their transformations are unusually deliberate—monsters emerging with a quiet intensity that fills the air like the weight of an oncoming upheaval.

Harper's wolf has always been a force to be reckoned with, but tonight, there's something different. She feels her wolf's power coursing through her veins, the primal instinct to protect and destroy warring within her.

She turns toward the sound in the distance, every muscle coiled like a spring. Creeping forward, her steps are slow and measured, her paws barely splashing in the puddles of water that line the dark tunnel. The tension in the air is thick, every movement calculated, every sound amplified in the suffocating silence.

Her claws scrape against the stone floor as she presses closer, her heavy frame moving with surprising stealth for her size. The predator in her is unleashed, but her human mind stays tethered, barely.

Harper, still leading, comes to a cross section. There are three choices. One is dark but the other two have faint light dancing off the moisture on the rock walls. Stopping to concentrate on Lucas, the bond tingles her senses.

She picks the right entry, the light ahead growing brighter. Slowing her steps, she lets her eyes adjust, every muscle coiling in preparation. The unknown waits just beyond that glow, and when the moment comes, she'll have to pounce. She doesn't know how many Cascades are inside. Doesn't know if Lucas is there—or somewhere else entirely.

Harper can feel the breath of Charlotte on her right hindquarter now. This is a war tactic they perfected years ago. Even without looking, she knows Luna would've guided Liam to be on Charlotte's hindquarter and Jade will be on Liam's. Their closeness allows their wolves to protect from all sides once they can spread out.

Getting closer to the light, Harper pushes the pack as close to the wall as possible, staying in the shadows. Coming to the entrance, she examines a large room. The stench is awful. Rotten food, cheap whiskey, and males that haven't showered, fills her nostrils. It takes all control not to gag. Harper notes the eight males sitting at a table playing cards. She hears "Go fish."

Are you fucking kidding me? There are sleeping bags scattered throughout the room, lit by kerosene lanterns. The empty bottles and red cups scattered throughout, help explain some of the putrid smell. She feels a pull to the dark entrance on the other side of the room. *Lucas!*

Feeling Charlotte's pure black wolf brush against her shoulder—a subtle signal—Harper instinctively slinks back, her powerful frame lowering to the ground with practiced precision. Her wolf blends into the muted shadows of the tunnel, muscles taut but still, her ears swiveling to track the faintest sounds.

Charlotte moves forward, silent as a shadow, her jet-black coat absorbing the dim light. Her steps are deliberate, each paw placed with calculated care, avoiding puddles and loose debris. Harper watches as Charlotte's sleek frame vanishes momentarily into the darkness ahead, her every movement a reminder of why she is Alpha—a predator honed by countless battles, her presence commanding without needing words.

Behind Harper, Liam and Jade fall into formation. Liam's massive wolf shifts slightly to the right, his bulk providing a silent yet imposing backup, while Jade's lean, wiry frame slips to the left, her grayish-brown coat blending into the wet stone walls.

They move as one, each step synchronized, their wolves communicating in a language far deeper than words. This wasn't just instinct—it was skill, honed through years of training together. A single misstep, a splash of water, or a careless breath could ruin the element of surprise.

Harper takes her place in the formation, her heavy paws brushing over the ground with surprising grace for her size. Her nostrils flare, scenting the damp air, searching for any trace of their target. The pack's unity is palpable, the silence between them brimming with purpose and focus.

Ahead, Charlotte pauses, her head lowering as her sharp yellow eyes scan the path. Without a sound, she motions with a slight flick of her tail—a signal Harper recognizes instantly. Harper's wolf creeps forward, her heavy frame coiled like a spring, ready to strike when the time comes.

This wasn't just a hunt. It was a mission. And the pack

moved like a well-oiled machine, each wolf falling into their role with flawless precision.

"Did you hear that?" one of the males at the table asked, his voice low and sharp. The scrape of a chair against rock echoes off the walls, the sound unnervingly loud in the tense silence.

Harper freezes, her ears twitching, her wolf's instincts on high alert. Her body vibrates with the need to move, to act, but she waits, eyes darting toward Charlotte for a signal.

Charlotte's wolf shifts slightly beside her, muscles coiling, but before the Alpha can react, Harper feels a surge of panic ripple through her bond with Lucas. It's faint—so faint it feels like it could vanish entirely. Her wolf snarls in response, the sound rising from deep in her chest, clawing at her control.

She doesn't wait for permission. Logic gives way to raw instinct, and with a low, guttural growl, Harper pushes past Charlotte, stepping out of the shadows. Her hackles rise, her massive frame bristling as she lowers her head, baring her teeth in a warning that shakes her chest with its ferocity.

"What the fuck!" one of the males shouts, his voice cracking as chaos erupts around the table.

Seven of the males shift almost instantly, their wolves snarling and snapping, the confined space amplifying the noise to a deafening roar. The last male bolts, disappearing into the tunnel entrance that's already holding Harper's focus.

Her wolf's rage surges, and without hesitation, she follows, her powerful paws striking the ground with purpose. Behind her, the pack leaps into action, their growls and movements blending into the chaos. Harper doesn't need to look back; the trust in her pack is absolute. They'll handle the others.

Her attention is singular now. The bond with Lucas is fading, flickering like a weak flame, and the panic in her chest becomes a white-hot urgency. Her claws scrape against the damp stone floor as she barrels through the dark passage, the scent of fear and blood growing stronger with every step.

The tunnel opens into a dimly lit room, and Harper skids to a stop, her claws digging into the wet ground. There he is. Ethan stands at the center, surrounded by four massive wolves, their growls rumbling in perfect unison, shaking the walls like distant thunder.

Lucas. His crumpled body not moving. Broken bones protruding through his skin. Blood covering every inch of skin. She knows he's alive, but just barely.

"You stupid bitch. It could've been an easy exchange. I just wanted Miles back!" Ethan shouts.

Harper shifts into her human form, knowing the risk, but the *why* overcomes logic. Standing there naked as the day she was born with all the confidence of a woman that is about to kill her enemy, she asks. "Why? I just want to know why would you follow a psychopath like him. Why go to this length when you know he was in the wrong?" She hears her voice getting louder with each question. "You've killed my sisters. You know the atrocities he has done. Why still follow him?" She is full out yelling now. "Why want revenge for a man that doesn't care about you? Any of you!"

"He cares! He loves me!" Ethan's face flushes crimson, the veins in his neck bulging as his voice rises. Harper can see it—the raw nerve she's struck, exposed for all to see. The bond he's lost is tearing him apart, just as Charlotte warned it would. "I would do anything for him!"

"Why?" Harper presses, her tone sharp and unrelenting.

"Take this opportunity to build a better life for your pack. Get away from the violence, from *him*."

"You raggedy bitch. You know nothing." Ethan's growl rumbles through the space, but Harper catches the briefest flicker of hesitation in his voice. It's subtle, but it's there.

Her wolf bristles as Harper narrows her eyes, studying him. His fists clench so tightly his knuckles whiten, his broad shoulders trembling—not with rage, but with something deeper, something raw and fragile. This isn't just about loyalty to Miles. It's something far more personal.

And then it hits. Ethan drops his chin, his face contorting into something feral and unhinged. His voice drops to a guttural growl, his words landing like a blow.

"I will never give up on my mate."

For a moment, Harper says nothing, the weight of Ethan's confession crashing over her like a tidal wave. "Mate," she repeats quietly, the word tasting bitter on her tongue. Of course, it all makes sense now—the lengths he'd go, the fury, the desperation. "You really believe he loves you, don't you?" Her voice is softer now, almost pitying.

Ethan's face twists into something monstrous, his lips pulling back to bare his teeth. "He's mine," he growls, the sound low and guttural. "And you? You're nothing. You think you can take him from me? You think you can change me? I will never give up on my mate."

His voice drops, each word dripping with venom. "I'd tear apart every pack on this earth if he asked me to."

Harper doesn't have time to process Ethan's words before his massive grey wolf explodes from his human form, muscles rippling as he lunges for her. His snarl reverberates through the cavern, sharp and unrelenting.

She's ready. The conversation had a purpose beyond words. While she demanded answers, her sharp eyes assessed every inch of the room—its corners, its shadows, its potential battleground. Harper's wolf bursts free, her thick, powerful body coiled like a spring.

Ethan underestimates her, like they all do. They see the short legs, the stocky build, but they don't know the raw strength she wields. Built like a powerlifter, Harper's wolf is all muscle and precision. She leaps for the boulder to her left, claws scraping against the rough stone, and uses it as a springboard.

With a powerful push, she sails through the air, a blur of black and white. The five enemy wolves whirl, snapping their jaws, but they're too slow. Harper lands behind them, a shadow at their backs, and immediately pounces on the hindmost wolf. Her back claws dig deep into his haunches, anchoring her as she twists her body. Her jaws clamp around his throat, crushing down with unrelenting force.

The taste of copper floods her mouth, and her wolf howls with the thrill of the kill. She doesn't let go until she feels the wolf's body go limp beneath her. One down. Four to go.

As the first wolf's corpse crumples to the floor, the black wolf to her right lunges. Harper whirls, ready for the attack, but Jade's lithe wolf crashes into him like a battering ram. The impact sends the enemy tumbling into the wall with a sickening crunch, giving Harper room to move.

She pivots to her next target, her claws ripping through fur and flesh with surgical precision. The wolf snarls and bites, but Harper is faster, her strength overwhelming him. Her jaws find his shoulder, and she tears downward, shredding muscle and sinew. He falls, blood pooling beneath him, his cries silenced by Harper's final strike.

Two down.

Harper's eyes dart to Jade, who's in a whirlwind of fury.

Jade's wolf is a blur of claws and fangs, ripping through her second opponent with savage efficiency. With a final snap of her jaws, she splits the wolf's throat, sending a spray of crimson across the stone floor.

The two wolves stand together, panting, adrenaline coursing through their veins. Harper's ears swivel, catching the faint echoes of movement. Her sharp eyes scan the cavern. The copper tang of blood fills the air, but something's missing.

Ethan.

"Where the fuck did the coward go?"

Harper shifts back to human form in one swift motion, her breaths ragged. "Liam!" she screams, her voice breaking as she throws herself at the chain wrapped around the bars, tugging with everything she has. The metal bites into her palms, but she doesn't care. She has to get to him.

Liam's massive black wolf barrels into the room, his yellow eyes blazing. Without hesitation, he clamps his powerful jaws around the chain. The metal groans under the force of his bite before snapping with a deafening crack. Harper frantically pulls away the remaining pieces, the jagged links cutting her fingers as she works.

The second the way is clear, she stumbles forward, collapsing beside Lucas's broken body. "Lucas... Lucas, baby, please wake up," she sobs, her voice raw with panic. Her trembling hands reach for him, her fingers brushing his face as gently as she can, afraid of causing him more pain.

His chest rises and falls in shallow, uneven breaths, but he doesn't stir. Tears spill freely down her cheeks, splashing onto his face. "Baby, please don't leave me," she whispers, her cries growing louder, more desperate. "Lucas, open your eyes, asshole. Please. I need you."

Her fingers trace the bruises and cuts marring his skin,

her touch featherlight. "We have this great life planned, babe," she pleads, her voice cracking with each word. "Pleeeeease wake up."

His swollen eyes open slightly.

"Charlotte, get your ass in here!" Liam shouts.

Charlotte runs in with Luna following close by. "Did you find..." Her words stop when she sees the mess that is before her.

"Alpha's heal him." Luna yells from behind Charlotte.

Charlotte yells back. "How? Luna. How do we use this power?"

"Touch him. Hold him. Sing Kumbaya for all I fucking know. Try something." Luna's panic is bouncing off the walls.

Charlotte slides next to Harper. Putting her hand on Harper's thigh and Lucas's cheek. Liam covers her hand. Lucas' eyes close again. Harper feels the bond fading. "He's fading. Luna, what do we do? You're the one that said you read something about true alphas being able to heal others." The tears running down Harpers' cheeks are creating white streaks through the blood that had painted her.

"I don't! It didn't come with a damn instruction manual."

Jade, coming out of nowhere, in one motion, flips her butterfly knife open, grabs Lucas's hands, cutting open each palm, then flips the handle directly in front of Charlotte's face. "Cut yourselves and give him your blood, Alphas."

Harper watches as Charlotte and Liam cut into their palms, then lock their hands with Lucas's. Once Liam and Charlotte lock their uncut palms together, a burst of light fills the room. This is exactly what it looked like the day that Liam vowed fealty to Charlotte. The Alpha blood bond was instantaneous. As Harper looks at the light surrounding her mate, she fills with hope. *Please let this light heal him.*

"Fuuuuuuck." Charlotte is clearly getting weak. The light is fading. Slowly, this time. Not like the first time they saw this in the game room at the mansion.

Charlotte's body trembles as the bond pulls her energy away, her breath coming in short gasps. The light surrounding Lucas pulses with an almost violent intensity, and she clenches her teeth, refusing to break contact.

"Hold on, Red," Liam growls, his voice strained but steady. His face is pale, sweat dripping down his temples, but his grip on Lucas's hand doesn't falter.

Harper feels it too. "Our bond is growing. I feel him. He's getting stronger."

The light is all but gone now. Liam and Charlotte both drop their hands. Jade catches Charlotte while Luna slides in behind Liam for support.

"Holy shit." Jade is pulling Charlotte's jet black hair off her face. "I don't know what made me think to do that."

The Red Rocks are all looking at each other with eyes the size of plates.

"Oh, fuck me." Harper's heart clenches as she watches Lucas's body repair itself. The sounds of bones snapping back into place make her stomach churn, but she can't tear her eyes away. For the first time since they found him, she feels the bond between them strengthen, a faint spark growing into a steady flame.

"Please, baby," she whispers, stroking his face as gently as if he might shatter. Her fingers tremble against his skin, warm now but still too pale. "Come back to me."

Lucas doesn't stir. His breathing is steady, but each shallow rise of his chest feels like a fragile promise—one she isn't sure will hold.

"Okay, let's get out of here. The Alphas need water," Jade says, reaching down to pull Charlotte to her feet.

"Plus, it's weird that I'm the only one with clothes on. I feel like we're in some twilight zone," her sharp look confirming her discomfort.

Jade takes the lead, her head snapping toward every shadow as she moves, her senses on high alert. Ethan escaped, but the memory of that powder lingers like a threat hanging in the air.

Harper and Luna lift Lucas together, each of his arms draped over their shoulders. His legs drag uselessly across the rock floor, and Harper winces with every jolt, afraid it might undo the fragile healing process. She adjusts her grip, her fingers curling tighter around his wrist as though sheer willpower could pull him back to her.

The silence in the cavern is suffocating, broken only by the shuffle of feet and the occasional drip of water echoing off the stone walls. The scent of blood and battle clings to Harper like a second skin, the metallic tang sharp in her nostrils.

Harper glances down at Lucas's face, his features still and slack. She leans her head against his shoulder for just a moment, her voice a whisper only he can hear. "Stay with me, Lucas. Just stay."

His weight feels heavier with each step, the exhaustion creeping into her bones. But she doesn't care. It's a burden she'd carry forever if it meant keeping him alive.

As they near the exit, faint moonlight spills into the cavern, casting jagged shadows that stretch like claw marks across the walls. The fresh air feels sharp and cold, but it does little to ease the tension coiled in Harper's chest.

Her eyes drift to Lucas, his body limp between them. His breathing is steady but shallow, each rise and fall of his chest taunting her with its fragility. He feels so heavy, his silence deafening.

What if this wasn't enough? The thought claws at her, sharp and unrelenting. *What if the powder created scars we can't see. And those are the ones that break him?*

"Wait," Jade says suddenly, her sharp tone cutting through the quiet. She stops near the cavern wall, crouching low. Her fingers brush the dirt, and a faint glint catches the moonlight. "What the hell is this?"

She lifts a small vial between her fingers, the glass cracked but still holding traces of glittering white powder. The residue sparkles faintly in the dim light, eerie in its beauty.

"Is that...?" Charlotte's voice trails off as she steps closer, her gaze locked on the vial.

"I wonder if it's the powder," Jade says, her voice tight. She turns the vial slowly, inspecting it. "The stuff Jase warned us about."

Harper shifts Lucas's weight on her shoulder, her wolf bristling as unease courses through her. "If this is the powder, it's bad news. We need to get it to Jase. He'll know for sure."

Charlotte nods, her expression grim. "We'll secure it when we're back. Whatever this is, Ethan didn't want us near it. That much is clear."

Luna leans closer, her eyes narrowing. "So he's either sloppy or wanted to scare us." She glances at Harper. "Either way, this stuff needs to be out of our hands and into Jase's before it causes more damage."

Jade slips the vial into her pocket with a sharp motion, her eyes darting around the cavern. "Got it. But if this is the powder, we've already been exposed. What if it's airborne?

What if we've already inhaled it?" Her voice is low but urgent, the question hanging heavy in the air.

Charlotte stiffens, her gaze snapping to the vial. "We don't know enough about it," she says, her voice grim. "That's why it has to get to Jase as fast as possible. If it's already affecting us..." She doesn't finish the thought, but the unease in her voice is unmistakable.

Harper adjusts Lucas's weight on her shoulder, her wolf bristling at the idea. Her voice comes out in a growl. "Whatever this stuff does, we'll figure it out. But not here. We need to move. Now."

Jade glances at Charlotte, who nods for her to take the lead.

Harper glances down at Lucas as they step back into the faint moonlight, his body slack but breathing. Her fingers tighten around his wrist, her throat constricting. The vial's presence changes everything. This powder isn't just a threat —it's real. And whatever Ethan has planned isn't over.

Her wolf growls low in her chest, her rage simmering beneath her skin. Ethan got away this time, but it won't happen again. Harper swears to herself that she'll hunt him down, drag him to his knees, and make him pay for everything he's done—for Lucas, for her sisters, for the blood spilled.

He'll die. The promise rings loud and clear in her mind. She'll paint the desert red with his blood, and she won't stop until he's gone.

As they walk into the clearing, the silence feels heavier than the darkness they left behind. The fight isn't over. And Harper can't shake the feeling that the next battle won't just be with enemies they can see, but with the ghosts now buried inside her mate.

AFFIRMATIONS

Harper has never hated a road trip as much as this one. The miles stretch on endlessly, even though Jade is driving like the devil himself is chasing them. Every bump in the road makes her heart clench, her eyes darting to Lucas's still form.

From the passenger seat, Luna keeps checking on Lucas. The quiet murmur of her reassurances is a lifeline Harper doesn't know she needs. But it doesn't stop the chaos in her head.

All Harper can think about are the nights she and Lucas have spent together. How many times had she tried to deny they were mates? How many times had he come back, relentless, knowing she couldn't fight it forever? His demanding presence burns in her memory, an inferno that consumes her every time. And now... now, the thought of never seeing their future unfold grips her chest like a vise.

When they made it out of the mine, Ethan was already gone. There wasn't time to track him. They hadn't even tried. Jade had made the call, her voice steady but firm:

"We'll deal with him later. Getting Lucas to the den is all that matters right now." Harper had agreed, though it hadn't stopped the bile from rising in her throat.

Jade glances in the rearview mirror, her eyes flicking between the road and Harper cradling Lucas in the backseat. Her jaw is tight, her hands gripping the wheel with an intensity Harper has only seen once before.

The memory hits Harper like a punch, sharp and unforgiving. It was years ago, when they were still in their teens. Jade had heard Harper's screams and found Steve—her brother Ryder's best friend—pinning her down. Harper's wolf hadn't grown yet; her first shift was still months away. But Jade had shifted, and her wolf had revealed its true strength.

Harper shivers at the memory, her fingers brushing against Lucas's shoulder for grounding. Jade's wolf had been a whirlwind of fury and violence, a killer Harper didn't recognize in her best friend. By the time Ryder arrived, it had taken everything he had to pull Jade off Steve. The sight of blood dripping from Jade's fangs and her wild, unrelenting rage was seared into Harper's memory.

And now, as Harper watches Jade drive, she sees that same protective fire simmering just beneath the surface. Harper doesn't need to ask—she knows. Jade would go to war with the entire world before letting anyone hurt Harper again. And by extension, Lucas.

The car jolts over a pothole, snapping Harper back to the present. She squeezes Lucas's hand, willing him to wake up, even though she knows it's too soon. "Hang in there, baby," she whispers, her voice barely audible over the hum of the tires.

Jade's voice breaks the silence, calm but sharp. "We'll get

him there. He's not going anywhere, Harper. Not on my watch."

Harper swallows hard, her gaze shifting between her unconscious mate and her fierce, unwavering friend. For the first time in hours, she allows herself a sliver of hope.

The pack makes it back to the mansion just after dawn, the sky streaked with the soft pinks and oranges of morning. Harper sits silently in the car, her body pressed against Lucas's as if proximity alone could keep him tethered to her. Charlotte and Liam follow close behind in Lucas's car, their headlights bouncing off the towering stone façade of the mansion.

As the SUV pulls into the horseshoe driveway, Harper catches glimpses of the elaborate wrought iron and stained glass doors through the tinted window. The familiar sight does little to ease the knot of tension in her chest. The car stops, and Harper's breath hitches.

The door swings open, Kai, Jaxson, and Ryan are there in an instant, their faces set with grim determination. Harper shifts to let them take Lucas, her fingers lingering on his shoulder before she forces herself to let go. She can feel their emotions through the bond—an undercurrent of pain, anger, and desperation that mirrors her own.

Kai cradles Lucas's upper body while Jaxson and Ryan support his legs. The three of them move as one, careful but swift, carrying their injured brother toward the front doors. Harper steps out of the car, her legs trembling beneath her, and follows close behind, her eyes fixed on Lucas's still form.

The front doors creak open, and Isabell freezes in the foyer, her sharp eyes widening at the sight of them. Her usually composed expression falters, and she whispers something rapid and low in Spanish, her voice trembling with what sounds like a prayer or plea.

Harper's gaze flickers downward, catching sight of the massive compass inlaid in the marble floor beneath Isabell's feet. Its intricate design, a blend of polished stone and metal, gleams faintly in the early morning light spilling through the stained glass above the doors.

The compass has always been a centerpiece of the mansion—a symbol of the pack's unity and direction. Harper's wolf stirs uneasily as she watches the pack cross over it. The north point seems to glint brighter, almost as if guiding them forward.

Isabell's voice, soft and reverent, breaks through Harper's thoughts. "El Norte siempre guía," her gaze lifting to meet Harper's.

Harper's gaze flickers down as she steps over the lines of the compass inlaid in the marble floor. She barely registers the rest of the foyer as her focus shifts entirely to Lucas, his still body cradled between Kai, Jaxson, and Ryan as they ascend the grand staircase. The ornate compass fades from her thoughts, replaced by the steady rise and fall of Lucas's chest, each breath both a relief and a reminder of how fragile he is.

Every step feels like an eternity, the echoes of their movements bouncing off the high ceilings. Harper's wolf paces restlessly inside her, snarling at the scent of blood clinging to Lucas like a dark shadow. Her fingers twitch at her sides, the urge to shift and carry him herself almost overwhelming. But she stays human, her focus locked on her mate as the pack carries him farther from the compass and closer to whatever hope their den might hold.

They reach the door already open as if anticipating their arrival. The Humboldt's move carefully, carrying Lucas inside, but Harper lingers in the doorway, her feet rooted to the floor.

She can't move. The sight of him steals the air from her lungs. His body, battered and bloodied, tells a story of violence she can barely bring herself to imagine. Cuts mar his skin, some so deep they haven't fully closed despite the Alphas' healing. Dirt clings to his hair and face, and the scent of blood still lingers around him, sharp and metallic.

"Harper," Jade's voice cuts through the haze, low but firm. "He needs you."

Harper doesn't respond, her feet glued to the threshold. She watches as Ryan, the newest face among them, gently adjusts Lucas's position on the bed. When he steps back, he pauses, then makes his way to her. Harper barely registers him until his arms wrap around her in a brief but firm hug. The gesture startles her, but she doesn't pull away.

Ryan doesn't speak, but his actions speak volumes—a quiet offering of strength when hers feels like it's slipping away. He releases her and steps back, their eyes meeting for a brief moment before he disappears through the doorway.

Kai approaches next, his movements deliberate. He stops beside her, wrapping his large hands gently around her shoulders. His lips brush her forehead, a grounding touch. "Our brother is strong," he says softly. "We've fought many battles together. He recovers fast. But..." He pauses, his lips quirking into the faintest smile. "He'll be pissed off —so be ready, she-wolf."

Harper exhales shakily, managing a faint nod as Kai leaves the room. Her gaze drifts back to Lucas. She feels like she's watching from a distance, the scene too surreal to fully process.

When her eyes refocus, she finds Jaxson kneeling beside the bed. His hands rest on Lucas's forearm, his head bowed as he whispers something Harper can't quite hear. She tilts her head, straining to catch the words, but even her wolf's sharp hearing picks up nothing.

Jaxson's stillness unnerves her, but she doesn't move. Less than a minute passes before he rises, his face unreadable as he turns toward her.

"Lucas says, 'Hang in there, baby.'" Jaxson's voice is calm but firm, his steady gaze holding hers. "He just needs more time for his body to heal. He'll be back soon. You know he will."

Harper stiffens, her wolf stilling inside her. She blinks, unsure if she heard him right. "What do you mean, *he says*?"

Jaxson strides toward her, his steps slow and purposeful. Stopping directly in front of her, he locks his fingers behind his back. He leans down, pressing his forehead gently to hers.

The moment their foreheads meet, Harper feels a pulse. It ripples through her bond with Lucas, faint but unmistakable. Her breath catches, and light blooms behind her closed eyes—not harsh, but warm, like a spark of life reigniting.

"He knows you're here," Jaxson's voice steady and low. "He needs to feel you. Go to him."

Still frozen in place, Harper doesn't notice Jaxson slipping out of the room. The quiet click of the door closing behind him goes unheard as she stands there, caught between the weight of what just happened and the sight of Lucas lying motionless on the bed.

Her chest feels tight, her lungs burning, until she finally draws in a huge, shuddering breath. The sound snaps her out of her trance, and her gaze locks on Lucas's chest, rising and falling with each labored breath. Relief and anguish hit her all at once, the dam inside her breaking as tears spill freely down her cheeks.

Without thinking, she moves. She rushes to the bed, her movements frantic. Her hands tremble as she strips off her clothes, letting them fall in a forgotten heap on the floor. Sliding into the bed beside him, she curls into his side, wrapping her body around him as if her warmth could shield him from the horrors he's endured.

The stench of blood, dirt, and the foul remnants of his captivity clings to him, sharp and nauseating. But Harper doesn't care. She buries her face against his chest, her hand resting over his heart, feeling the steady, fragile rhythm beneath her palm. "Lucas," she whispers, her voice breaking. "Baby, I'm here."

Her fingers trace gently over his broad chest, avoiding the worst of his wounds as her tears fall onto his skin. "You just rest, okay? Let your body heal." Her voice is soft but insistent, like a lullaby meant for both of them. "I cleared out part of the closet for you," she says, her words tumbling out in a nervous ramble. "And I bought new towels for us. Jade made fun of me for it, but I didn't care. They're his-and-hers towels." She lets out a shaky laugh, brushing her thumb over a faint scar on his collarbone. "They're green and pink—because, you know me, I love pink."

Harper keeps talking, her words a steady stream of small, everyday details. She doesn't know if he can hear her, but she needs him to know she's here. She'll always be here. The sound of her voice fills the room, a fragile barrier against the silence that threatens to consume her.

"I love you," she whispers after a while, her voice barely audible as her tears soak into his hair. "I've got you, Lucas. Just come back to me."

She talks until her words grow softer, her sentences

trailing off as the heaviness in her eyes begins to win. Her body curls tighter against his, her breathing slowing to match his as sleep finally overtakes her.

HARPER WAKES WITH A JOLT, her heart racing until her eyes land on Lucas, still fast asleep beside her. His chest rises and falls steadily, and the tension in her wolf eases slightly. Glancing at the clock, she blinks in disbelief—she's slept almost twelve hours.

Carefully, she crawls over Lucas, pausing to press a soft kiss to his lips. Her wolf growls possessively, but it's more a signal than a warning, a reassurance that their mate is safe. Harper's bare feet touch the cool floor as she stretches, a sense of duty pulling her upright. *He'll be awake soon. I need to be ready for him.*

Padding into her large en suite bathroom, she takes a deep breath, letting the familiar beauty of the space settle her nerves. The white two-person soaker tub sits gracefully in the center of the room, its presence framed by the elegant crystal chandelier above it. Little rainbow prisms dance across the walls, a dazzling effect that once made her fall in love with this room.

Harper's gaze shifts to the floor-to-ceiling grey cabinetry with etched flowers and vines decorating the mirrored fronts. It's girly and stunning, a reflection of a life she once thought would remain uncomplicated. Grabbing a plain towel—she refuses to use the new ones until Lucas is by her side—she moves toward the open shower in the corner of the room.

The screen on the shower's control panel lights up with a soft blue glow as she taps a few buttons. Water bursts to life from all seven showerheads, cascading down in warm streams. Harper steps in, testing the temperature with her wrist before letting the heat soak into her soul.

As the water drenches her blonde, shoulder-length hair, she lets out a soft moan of relief. But when her gaze drops to her feet, her body stiffens. The water swirling around the drain is dark red.

Blood.

She hadn't even realized. Between the chaos of getting Lucas into bed and collapsing beside him, she hadn't thought about the dirt and blood still clinging to her. The sight sends a chill through her, but she quickly grabs the handheld showerhead, twisting and turning to rinse herself off completely.

Grabbing her body wash, she squeezes an overabundance onto her pink loofah and scrubs with frantic determination. Her strokes become harder, faster. She switches hands to scrub her arms, her belly, her legs—rubbing so fiercely the loofah leaves scratch marks on her skin.

Tears stream down her face, mingling with the water as the last thirty-six hours crash over her like a tidal wave. Ethan's words resurface, slicing through the emotional fog.

"I will never give up on my mate."

Harper shudders, the memory clawing at her mind. She hasn't told anyone about his admission yet. It wasn't something she'd ever considered before—the Cascades having mates. To her, they were the enemy. Monsters. But those words had made Ethan seem... human.

The empathy that creeps into her chest feels like betrayal, and she hates it. She scrubs harder, tears slowing as she wrestles with the confusing swirl of emotions. She understands the feeling of never giving up on your mate, but she refuses to let it cloud her judgment. Ethan's confession doesn't change who he is—or what he's done.

Harper finally drops the loofah, her hands trembling. The water pounds against her skin, washing away the last traces of blood and dirt, but it can't cleanse the chaos inside her. She stands motionless under the waterfall showerhead, focusing on the steady rhythm of the droplets as they cascade over her body, willing them to quiet her racing mind.

A scream bubbles in her throat, raw and desperate, but she presses her lips together, forcing it down. Her wolf claws at her insides, demanding release, but Harper won't give in. She doesn't want to alarm the rest of the packs—not when so much is already on the line.

Instead, she lets the scream out silently, her mouth opening as her chest heaves, the sound trapped inside her like a wild animal in a cage. The force of it rips through her, leaving her knees weak and her breaths ragged. Her tears fall harder now, mixing with the hot water as it streams down her face.

Minutes pass before her breathing evens out, the weight of her anguish easing just enough for her to move again. Harper reaches for the soap, her motions slower now, methodical. She finishes washing away the blood and grime, letting the scalding water carry the last remnants of the chaos swirling inside her down the drain.

Turning off the water, she steps out, wrapping herself in the towel, she avoids the mirror, unwilling to face the reflection of her tear-streaked face and red-rimmed eyes. Instead, she focuses on the small rituals that keep her grounded—blow-drying her short dirty blonde hair, pinning the front back in a neat crisscross, and slipping into clean clothes.

The faint smell of food catches her attention, and her

stomach growls in response. Following the scent down the stairs, Harper's bare feet hit the cool white marble tiles, grounding her further. She hadn't thought to check the time, but the soft hum of voices from the dining room tells her all she needs to know.

It must be around six o'clock. Isabell, the four-foot-nothing Latina firecracker, has made it clear that dinner happens at six sharp—or else. Harper smirks at the memory of her threats. The little ball of sass had once declared she'd quit if the pack didn't start using the dining room for proper meals together. Nobody wanted to imagine the mansion without her, so they'd made it a priority to gather every night. Tonight, clearly, is no exception.

Harper strolls over the dining room threshold, her heart lifting at the sight of the pack gathered around the oversized round dining table. The lazy Susan is spinning, dishes of mashed potatoes, green beans, and—was that meatloaf?—circling the table as everyone takes their share.

Harper blinks in surprise. She hasn't had meatloaf since she left Montana. Her mom used to make the best. For the first time in what feels like days, a small, genuine smile pulls at her lips.

"Harper!" Luna jumps up so fast her chair crashes to the floor behind her.

"Oomph," Harper grunts as Luna wraps her arms tightly around her neck.

"We were just talking about you and Lucas. How's he doing?" Luna asks, pulling back to look Harper in the eye.

"He's still sleeping," Harper replies softly.

"Well, Alpha," Luna says, pulling a chair out and motioning for Harper to sit, "you need to do that cutty thing again. Give him more of your blood."

"Will that even work?" Harper asks as she sits down, tilting her head back to meet Luna's gaze.

Luna shrugs. "How am I supposed to know? I didn't even know about the cutty thing in the first place. How did you know, Jade?"

Jade, busy pouring gravy over her plate, shakes her head. "I didn't know. It just... felt right."

Liam pats Jade on the shoulder. "Well, it was a damn good call, Jade."

The clink of Harper's fork hitting her plate silences the room. She looks up, tears already streaming down her face. "I'm sorry, everyone. I didn't even thank you for helping me find him and for... for killing to bring him back." Her voice cracks as the tears come harder. "You're the best pack any female could ever want to be a part of."

The sound of chairs scraping against the floor echoes off the cream-colored walls as the pack stands, surrounding Harper. Charlotte, Jade, Liam, Maddy, and Luna place their hands on her shoulders, their presence grounding her. Across the room, Kai, Jaxson, and Ryan exchange glances, unsure of the ritual unfolding before them.

"You are strong and creative. You are the rock that holds us together."

"You are the second-best cooker person I know."

"You are cunning and a visionary."

"I can't wait to get to know you better."

"You aren't a pussy. Keep it together, sister," Jade says before walking back to her plate, scooping a giant spoonful of green beans, and shoving them into her mouth. "Now eat before it's cold, and Isabell comes in here and yells at us again."

Harper laughs through her tears, grabbing a napkin to blow her nose. "Second-best cooker person?"

"Sorry, Harp. Isabell makes comfort food. If I'm in my favorite pair of Louboutins, I want your food. When I've got my..." Luna lifts her Croc-covered foot into the air. "Crocs on, I want meatloaf."

"Fair. I have to agree with that. But I can make a mean meatloaf, too," Harper says, pouring herself a glass of lemonade. She takes a sip and pauses. "Is this fresh-squeezed?"

"Sí, señorita." Isabell appears seemingly out of nowhere, her small frame somehow commanding the room. She takes Harper's hand in her own. "Estoy contenta de que estés en casa." She kisses the top of Harper's head. "Now eat. Lucas needs your strength."

"She says she's glad you're home," Jaxson translates to the group. "You got the other part."

Harper looks at Jaxson, her eyebrows raised. "Jaxson, you sure are full of surprises."

"Oh, you have no idea," spinning the lazy Susan until it stops on the apple pie.

Jaxson's gaze sharpens as he looks across the table at Harper. "Going back to what Luna said earlier—I agree. Maybe the blood bond could help again. His mind is still very dark. He needs all the light he can get."

Charlotte glances at Liam, then back to Jaxson. "I'm not sure what that means, but yeah, we can do it again."

"Absolutely," Liam says firmly. "Let's finish eating and drink tons of water. Last time took it out of me, but if we think it'll help him, darn tootin', we're going to try."

Harper looks to Kai and Ryan. "Actually, before they do that, will you help me get Lucas into the shower? He's still filthy, and I want to wash those memories off him."

"Of course," Kai says with a bow of his head.

As Harper looks around the table, her heart swells. The

more time she spends with the Humboldt's, the more she falls in love with them. They're good men—protective, respectful, and loyal. How did she get so lucky? Not only to have one incredible pack of strong, independent, and brilliant women but to be part of a second pack filled with brave, powerful, and honorable men?

Life has a cruel way of tearing things apart, but sometimes it has a funny way of mending what's broken—piece by piece, with the strength of a pack.

(UNCONSCIOUS) LUCAS

Miles is such an asshole. Why is he always pushing Spencer's buttons? Lucas has wondered this a hundred times, especially during moments like this. It can't be easy for Miles—being the runt of the pack has to sting—but that doesn't mean he has to pick a fight every time they play dodgeball.

"Miles, leave him alone. You know he hit you. Why can't you just play the game right?" Lucas's voice cuts through the tension, firm but weary, as if he's said it a dozen times before.

"He didn't get me. I'm faster than any of you!" Miles's whine is like nails on a chalkboard. He leans down, clutching the red rubber ball so tightly his knuckles turn white, his frustration palpable.

Spencer rolls his eyes, brushing dirt off his pants. "I've heard that one before. A million times. It wasn't true then, and it's not true now."

Lucas catches the flicker of anger in Miles's expression, a sharp contrast to his usual bravado. He steps forward, planting himself between the two. "Come on, Miles. Let's just play the game like we used to. Don't start a fight again."

Miles glares, his lips curling into a sneer. "Fine," he spits, his voice trembling with barely contained rage. "But if Spencer cheats again, I'm taking him down."

Lucas exhales heavily, the weight of the moment pressing down on him. It's always like this. Miles's small frame practically vibrates with anger, while Spencer stands calm and immovable. Spencer has never feared Miles—why would he? Every fight between them ends the same way: Spencer holding back, Miles throwing everything he has, and walking away battered but never humbled.

The boys reset for another round of dodgeball, tension crackling in the air like a live wire. Spencer keeps his eyes trained on Miles, reading him, waiting for the inevitable attack.

"I hit you, Miles. You know it," Spencer says, his voice steady, but Lucas hears the edge creeping in. "You're just trying to start a fight again."

Lucas watches as Miles shifts uncomfortably, his posture defensive yet brimming with misplaced confidence. "I'm the fastest, the strongest," Miles always brags. But Lucas knows better. Miles's arrogance is a fragile mask, a defense against insecurities that gnaw at him like a hungry wolf.

"You're just scared of me, Spencer," Miles snaps, the words laced with venom.

Spencer towers over the group, his height making him seem older than he is. But his presence isn't intimidating. It's steady, grounded—Alpha material, even as a boy. He meets Miles's glare with calm composure. "Scared of you?" he repeats, his tone almost pitying.

Miles sneers, his grip tightening on the ball. "When are you going to admit you cheat? Your whole family cheats. That's the only reason your dad's Alpha. Your stupid family stole everything from the Barlowe family. You think you're so tough."

Lucas steps forward, placing a firm hand on Miles's shoulder.

"Miles, enough," he says, his tone low but commanding. "Don't drag this into something it doesn't have to be. Let's just play the game."

But it's already too late. Miles throws the ball, his anger fueling its speed as it hurtles toward Spencer's head.

In a blur of motion, Spencer's hand shoots up, catching the ball midair with ease. The force sends a dull thud reverberating through the clearing, the sound louder than any of their words.

"Miles, why do you do this?" Spencer's tone is calm, almost disappointed. He tosses the ball to Kai, nodding for the game to continue. "Let's play."

THE AWAKENING

"Ok baby. The guys are going to come and carry you to the shower." Peeling the blanket back from her mate's blood covered chest. "I love you, but you stink. I'm going to..." Harper squeals and suddenly finds herself flipped on her back, looking up into the eyes of a deranged Lucas.

"Where am I?"

Harper doesn't even recognize the voice. Trying to answer, only a squeak comes out of her. That's when she realizes he has tightly wrapped his hand around her throat, cutting off her air. "We're in our den, baby."

Harper's voice is scratchy and airy from the lack of oxygen.

"Lucas, you have to let me go." Harper reaches up and runs her hand down his cheek. "You are safe, Williams." Feeling the grip ease off her throat slightly. "It's ok baby. You are home."

"Yeah, let's get this ugly fucker into the shower, so I can ask Luna if she wants to pet my penguin."

Harper's eyes dart towards the door, hearing Kai's voice carrying through the hallway.

Just as quickly as Lucas had pinned her, he lets go, spinning towards the now opening door.

"Woah buddy." Jaxson throws his hands up in surrender. "It's just us. We need to get you cleaned up."

"Williams. Stand down." Ryan's command sends shivers down Harper's arms. Lucas must have given his fealty to the now Beta of the Humboldt Pack.

Lucas crouches, growling at the three large males now standing in the room, ready to defend themselves if needed.

"Move!" Charlotte pushes through Kai, Ryan, and Jaxson. "Williams, that's enough. Stand down." The power she puts behind her command fills the room with static electricity, raising the short hairs on the top of Harper's head and stunning Lucas. For a split second, Harper saw *her* Lucas.

"You can't control me, she-wolf. Lucas Williams died in that cage. You are not my Alpha."

"Who are you then?" Harper's voice wavers, the words shaking as they leave her lips.

The question stops him. Lucas turns slowly, almost as if her voice tugged at some hidden thread inside him. Their eyes lock, and for a fleeting moment, she sees it—the man she loves, buried beneath the rage and confusion. His expression cracks, the pain etched across his face cutting her deeper than any blade. "I... I don't know."

The words gut her. A tear escapes her left eye, slipping free before she can stop it. Harper brushes it away quickly with trembling fingers as she takes a cautious step forward. "Lucas..."

Before she can reach him, a blur of movement takes

Lucas to the ground. Liam moves so fast that even Harper's heightened senses don't have time to process. The sound of their bodies hitting the floor echoes in the room, sharp and sudden.

Kai and Ryan are there in an instant, pinning down a snarling Lucas as he thrashes against their grip. Liam plants a hand on Lucas's chest, his weight anchoring him to the ground. "Stay down!" Liam barks, his tone sharp but not unkind.

Charlotte steps forward, the steel glint of a blade in her hand. She slices into her palm without hesitation, her eyes locked on Lucas as Liam raises his hand to signal Kai. "Hold him steady!"

Kai forces Lucas's arm into the air, his grip unyielding.

Charlotte presses her bleeding hand to Lucas's, her blood mingling with his as the now-familiar light bursts from their joined hands. The glow spreads rapidly, engulfing Lucas, Liam, and Kai in a blinding brilliance. The room fills with warmth, an energy.

Harper can only stand and watch, her breath caught in her throat. The light bathes them, pulsating like a heartbeat, and she clings to the desperate hope that it will bring Lucas back to her. "Williams!" she yells, her voice raw and scratchy. "Come back to me!"

As the seconds stretch on, Harper sees the change. Lucas's thrashing slows, the tension in his body easing as the light works its way through him. His face softens, the hardness giving way to the Lucas she knows—the one she loves.

The glow fades as quickly as it appeared, leaving the room dim and quiet. Lucas's body goes limp beneath his pack mates, his breathing shallow but steady. Harper feels her knees weaken as relief floods her, but she doesn't dare move, her eyes locked on him.

"Holy fuck! I've fought him for as long as he's been alive. He's never been that strong before." Kai is now sitting on his knees next to his lifeless childhood friend with a look of confusion and worry.

"What the fuck happened, Harper?" Charlotte's eyes lock with Harper's, sharp with concern. Without waiting for an answer, her gaze drops to Harper's throat, her expression darkening as she examines the angry, already-healing marks.

Behind her, Ryan steps closer, his stance protective and his eyes fixed on Harper's neck as if assessing the damage for himself.

"I don't know. He was sleeping, then he wasn't. It happened fast. His voice didn't sound like him, but there were moments of the Lucas I know that came through." Harper pushes past Charlotte and kneels next to Kai. Leaning down to put her cheek on Lucas's chest. "He's still in there. We just have to keep talking to him. He'll come back."

"Ok, let's get this foul-ass stench fixed first." Ryan bends down and lifts one side of Lucas while Kai follows suit on the other side. Legs dragging behind him, Harper watches as a streak of dirt forms from each foot and thinks, *Isabell is going to kill him when he wakes up,* which brings a small smile to cross her lips.

Harper hears Kai warn, "Okay, buddy. This is going to shock you, but you stink. Please don't kick my ass if you wake up again." He grabs the handheld showerhead and turns the water on, testing the temperature with his hand. "Ryan, don't you leave, man."

Ryan, already halfway out of the bathroom, groans and

turns back toward the shower. "I'm not washing him. I'll grab clean clothes. You can wash his balls."

"Ew, man. I'm not washing his balls!" Kai snaps, his voice echoing off the tiled walls.

Just as Harper steps into the shower, she gets a faceful of water."Kai!" she yelps, sputtering as she swipes at her face.

Kai grins sheepishly, holding out the sprayer toward her. "Here, you do it."

She takes it, laughing despite herself. "What's the matter, Kai? Intimidated by his size?" she teases, her grin widening as Kai's face twists in mock disgust.

"Ew, Harp. No! I don't look at his junk," Kai protests, stepping back out of the shower. "I mean, I've glanced a few times—who hasn't?—but let's be real. Mine's way prettier than his. So, no, I don't need to look at it, wash it, or do *anything* with it. That's your job."

Harper doubles over laughing, the sound echoing off the walls as Kai, now soaking wet, retreats through the open shower doorway. "Why are you rambling, Kai?" she asks, still grinning.

"Fuck this shit. I could be getting laid right now," Kai complains, throwing his hands up as he stomps out of the bathroom, clearly pouting.

Harper runs the handheld showerhead over her mate, his body propped up awkwardly in the corner of the shower. Brown and red streaks swirl down toward the drain, the sight dragging her back to the chaos of the night before. Her instincts remain razor-sharp, her wolf on high alert, watching for any sign that the water might rouse him again.

"Are you sure, Kai?" she asks, her tone low and even as she keeps her focus on Lucas. "Have you talked to Luna since you've been back?"

Kai leans casually against the doorframe, though his

voice betrays a hint of uncertainty. "No. Why? Does she not like me anymore?"

Harper spares him a quick glance, sighing softly. "I don't know, Kai. Luna isn't the type to stick with one person for long. You probably shouldn't assume her bed is always open whenever you come to town."

"Oh," Kai sighs clearly deflated.

Before Harper can say anything else, Lucas's voice breaks the tension, soft and raw. "I'm sorry, Harper," he mumbles. "I fucked up. I let my guard down. They grabbed me."

Harper freezes, her heart lurching at the sound of his voice. His lips move sluggishly, but nothing else stirs. "It's okay, baby," she whispers, crouching to meet his eyes. "You're safe now. I'm going to finish getting you cleaned up, then it's back to bed for healing. Okay?"

"Okay," Lucas replies, his voice barely audible.

Harper glances at Kai, her eyes wide with a mixture of disbelief and exhaustion. "Wash his balls, Kai, and let's get him back to bed."

Kai groans dramatically, throwing his hands up in mock protest. "Why do I always get the worst jobs?"

It takes half an hour and what feels like 200 gallons of water, but by the time they're done, Lucas smells more like himself. Yet, something lingers—a faint, smoky scent that wasn't there before. It clings to him like a shadow, subtle but unsettling. Harper's wolf bristles at the unfamiliar odor, pacing within her, but she pushes the thought aside for now.

"Thanks, guys," she says, draping a towel over Lucas's waist as she looks at Kai, Ryan, and Liam. Their clothes cling to them, damp and wrinkled from the effort, their faces showing equal parts exhaustion and relief.

"No problem, Harp," Liam replies with a small, reassuring smile. He pauses in the doorway, his tone gentle. "Holler if you need anything. Rest. You need to heal too."

"Yeah," Harper replies softly, brushing damp strands of hair from Lucas's forehead. Her fingers linger for a moment longer than she intended, as if reassuring herself he's really there. "I just want to stay with him in case he wakes up."

"Of course." With a soft click, the door closes behind them, leaving Harper alone with her mate.

She moves with quiet purpose, careful not to disturb Lucas as she climbs into bed beside his unresponsive yet warm body—a stark contrast to the cold fear still gnawing at the edges of her mind. Her breath catches for a moment as she takes in the steady rise and fall of his chest, grounding herself in the small reassurance of his presence.

Once he's settled, she pats the bed around them, her hand brushing over the soft fabric as she searches for the remote. Her fingers finally close around it at the foot of the bed, the cool plastic a small victory in the midst of her restless thoughts.

With a press of a button, the large TV rises smoothly from its concealed box at the end of the bed, its screen flickering to life. The room is immediately filled with the comforting hum of her favorite cooking show, the familiar voices of chefs defending their dishes to the judges.

Setting the remote behind her, Harper curls into Lucas's side, resting her head against his chest. The rhythmic rise and fall of his breathing begins to calm her frayed nerves, a quiet reminder that he's still with her.

The low chatter from the TV and the steady warmth of his body lull her into a rare sense of peace. Her eyelids grow heavy, and she fights to stay awake, unwilling to miss even a moment of his presence.

But exhaustion is relentless. As the chef with the risotto wins his argument, Harper's eyes flutter closed, her body finally surrendering to sleep.

LOST TO AN HDMI CORD

The dining room hums with the soft scrape of forks and the lazy chatter of the pack. Sunlight spills through the tall windows, pooling golden light over the oversized round table where the lazy Susan spins with its bounty of Isabell's magic. The smell of bacon, eggs, and buttery toast is enough to make Harper's stomach rumble as she steps into the room.

Heads swivel toward her instantly, all conversation grinding to a halt.

"How's Lucas?" Charlotte asks first, her calm, a quiet force in the room.

Harper tucks the loose strands of her blonde hair behind her ear and tries to smile, but it doesn't quite reach her eyes. "Still out," she says softly, voice just above a whisper. "But he's breathing steady."

There's a collective exhale, like the pack has been holding its breath.

"You need to eat," Jade says bluntly, pointing a fork at her. "Sit your ass down before you fall over."

Harper raises her hands in mock surrender and pulls

out a chair, sinking into it as the lazy Susan comes to a slow stop in front of her. She stares at the food for a moment, letting the quiet reassurance of her pack ground her, before noticing the empty chair at the far side of the table.

"Where's Luna?"

"Upstairs," Charlotte answers, spearing a sausage with deliberate intent. "Kai, go get her. She's been at it all night."

"No, wait," Harper cuts in, glancing toward the frowning hollywood pretty-boy. "I'll get her. I need to stretch my legs anyway."

Kai's fork hovers midair. "You sure? Because I'd *love* to go drag her off those damn computers. I didn't see her *once* last night." He throws a dramatic glare toward Charlotte. "You know what she told me? 'Kai, you're blocking my screen. Move.' Like I'm a piece of furniture!"

Ryan snorts into his coffee, shaking his head. "Poor guy. Replaced by a laptop."

"Damn right I was!" Kai says, stabbing his bacon like it personally offended him. "I'm a mother-fucking wolf damnit, and I lost to a HDMI cord."

Jade rolls her eyes, smirking. "You lost to someone with better focus, *Ken*."

Kai's head snaps up, clearly offended. "Kai. My name is Kai."

"Yes, but you *look* like a Ken doll," Jade shoots back, her grin widening.

Kai's jaw drops. "Ken? Ken?!" He flexes his arms, muscles bulging as he strikes an exaggerated pose. "Ken doesn't have *this*. I'm way too jacked to be a plastic toy."

Jade snorts, unimpressed. "Sure, Ken. Keep telling yourself that."

Harper can't help but smile faintly as she stands. "I'll

bring her down. She probably just got in too deep to realize how long it's been."

Liam calls after her. "Tell her she needs to come help us hide all the HDMI cords."

"Keep it up, Liam," Kai teasingly cautions, as Harper disappears into the hall.

Harper steps into the foyer, pausing, her bare feet skimming the edge of the compass. The familiar sight should bring her comfort—stability, direction, a reminder that they're still standing despite everything. But today, the air feels heavier. The weight of last night's chaos lingers, pressing down on her chest.

With a quiet exhale, Harper steps over the compass, careful not to scuff its gleaming surface. The golden points of north and south seem to glint as she crosses, a whisper of reassurance—or warning. She shakes off the thought and heads toward the hallway that leads to Luna's office.

The door is slightly ajar, a faint bluish glow spilling into the dim hallway. Harper pushes it open, her brows furrowing at the familiar hum of machinery. Inside, the air is cool, the scent of stale coffee and electronics filling her nose.

Screens line the far wall, their lights flickering like an artificial heartbeat. Satellite maps, lines of code, and data feeds flash across them, the constant movement a testament to Luna's sleepless dedication.

Luna sits at the center of it all, her slim figure dwarfed by the oversized desk cluttered with empty coffee mugs, half-eaten snacks, and pens sticking out of random places. Harper's eyes zero in on the pens holding Luna's long white hair in a messy bun, each topped with a brightly colored penis. The fluorescent tips wobble as Luna tilts her head, completely absorbed in the screen in front of her.

"Luna," Harper calls softly, but the other woman doesn't stir.

Harper steps closer, crossing her arms as she leans against the desk. "If Kai saw you like this, he'd probably cry. Those pens are getting more attention than he is."

Luna's pale face turns slightly, her glowing purple eyes narrowing. "Kai cries when the wind blows too hard," her voice flat but edged with amusement.

"He's pouting," Harper replies, straightening. "You've been up all night, haven't you?"

"Maybe." Luna spins her chair halfway, the pens in her bun wobbling dangerously. "But I'm onto something, Harper. Ethan's trail—it's faint, but it's there. He's being very careful. I just need more time."

Harper steps forward, her expression softening as she takes in Luna's appearance. Her friend's alabaster skin glows faintly in the light from the monitors, the dark circles under her eyes betraying just how long she's been at this.

"Luna," Harper says, her tone firm but gentle. "You need to stop. Come eat. Get some sleep. You're no good to anyone if you collapse."

Luna's lips twitch into a faint smile. "You sound like Charlotte. Since when did you get so bossy?"

Harper shrugs. "Since you stopped taking care of yourself. Now, come on. Isabell made bacon, and Kai's threatening to write sad poetry if you don't show up."

With an exaggerated sigh, Luna finally pushes her chair back. She grabs an oversized hoodie from the back of her chair and pulls it on, the fabric swallowing her small frame. "Let's get this over with before Isabell hunts me down with a spatula."

As they leave the room, Harper glances back at the glowing monitors. The maps and markers feel like a ghostly trail, a breadcrumb path leading somewhere dark and dangerous. Her wolf stirs, ears perked and teeth bared, sensing the hunt before it begins.

She doesn't know where that path ends yet, but she *will*. Luna will tell her—*when the time is right*. Harper won't wait for the pack to come up with a plan. She'll get the information out of Luna herself, one way or another. Ethan dared to touch her mate, dared to harm what was hers. *And for what?*

Her teeth grit, the memory of his words echoing in her mind. *"I will never give up on my mate."*

Harper's lips curl back in a silent snarl. Ethan's loyalty to a psychopath like Miles doesn't excuse what he's done. Mate bond or not, he *chose* this path. He chose violence. And now, she'll make him regret it.

I'll find you first, Ethan, she thinks, her eyes narrowing. *And I'll kill you.*

Pushing the thought down, Harper steps back into the hallway, the faint hum of Luna's computers fading behind her. When she reaches the foyer, her gaze flicks briefly to the compass in the center of the floor, and for the briefest moment, it feels like it *sees* her.

It's just a design, she reminds herself. A symbol of direction. But as the light catches its surface, the familiar shimmer takes on an ominous edge, and a chill settles in her chest.

Harper tears her gaze away and moves forward, determined. She has a promise to keep—one Ethan won't live to see fulfilled.

STARVING

Harper sits curled up in the oversized chair by the window, her knees tucked beneath her and a dog-eared paperback clutched in her hands. The title reads *I'm Not Your Mate, You Oversized Lizard,* with an absurdly shirtless dragon shifter smoldering on the cover. She snorts quietly as she turns the page, shaking her head.

"Dragons. Seriously," she snorts. "Vampires running a burlesque club in Vegas? That tracks. Dragons? That's just reaching."

The pack library has a few of these guilty pleasures scattered around, and Harper's always had a soft spot for dragon shifter romances. Probably because dragons are just far-fetched enough to not feel *real.* And that made them safe— unlike the rest of her reality.

Still, as ridiculous as it is, she can't deny it's entertaining. The heroine is currently arguing with the brooding dragon alpha who *just* happened to land on her balcony in human form, all muscles, scales, and ego. Harper smirks at the dramatic dialogue.

"I'm your mate, and I'll burn the world down for you!" the dragon alpha proclaims.

"Sounds like someone needs therapy," a small grin tugs at her lips. She stretches her legs out with a groan, the sound echoing in the otherwise quiet room.

Lucas hasn't stirred all day. His breaths remain steady, the slow rise and fall of his chest reassuring her that he's here, alive, and healing. She glances at him, tucked into their bed, the faint crease of his brow the only sign that his mind isn't completely at rest.

"Burn the world down for you," she repeats sarcastically, flipping the page. "Lucas would roll his eyes so hard at this crap."

The sunlight streaming in through the window shifts, casting long shadows across the room. Harper's own eyelids begin to droop as the quiet wraps around her like a blanket. She leans back further in the chair, her book slipping slightly in her hand as her breathing slows.

Just as her head lolls to the side, a sharp gasp tears through the room.

Harper jolts awake, the book tumbling to the floor with a *thud.* Her heart leaps into her throat as Lucas shoots straight up in bed, his chest heaving, golden eyes wide and wild.

"Lucas!" Harper scrambles out of the chair, her pulse pounding in her ears. She reaches his side in an instant, placing a trembling hand on his arm. "Lucas, baby, it's okay. You're safe. You're here. With me."

His gaze snaps to hers, unfocused at first, but then recognition dawns, and some of the tension in his shoulders eases. He swallows hard, his breaths still ragged.

"Harper?" His voice is rough, hoarse, as if it hasn't been used in weeks.

"I'm here," she whispers, brushing a damp curl from his forehead. "I'm right here."

Lucas collapses back against the pillows, his chest rising and falling as he tries to catch his breath. Harper stays close, her hand never leaving his arm.

"Was I... dreaming?" he rasps, his eyes flicking toward her.

"Maybe," Harper says softly, though the look in his eyes tells her it was more like a nightmare. She forces a small smile, needing to lighten the moment for both their sakes. "You missed a thrilling day of me reading about overly dramatic dragon shifters. They're very real, you know. Apparently, they'll burn the world down for their mates."

A faint smirk twitches at the corner of Lucas's lips, though it's brief. "Sounds exhausting."

Harper huffs a quiet laugh, her heart finally beginning to settle. "Tell me about it."

She studies him closely, her wolf still pacing restlessly inside her. He's awake now, but that lingering darkness clings to him like smoke—subtle, insidious.

Harper exhales, letting herself ease down onto the bed beside him. Lucas's arm instinctively curls around her, pulling her closer, and she lets him. The steady rhythm of his breathing, slow and even now, steadies her own heartbeat.

Her wolf growls softly in the back of her mind, uneasy still, but Harper ignores the warning. She presses a soft kiss to Lucas's chest, savoring the warmth of him. "You're here," she whispers, more to herself than him.

Lucas doesn't respond—he's already drifting again, his body still heavy with the need to heal. She curls her body into his side, letting her arm drape over his chest, her fingertips brushing against his skin. Her mind settles, if only slightly, lulled by his nearness, and once again Harper feels her eyelids growing heavy.

The room feels *too quiet,* though. The air, *too still.* Harper shifts slightly, her ears straining as though listening for something just out of reach, but all she hears is the gentle hum of the house around them. *It's fine,* she tells herself. *You're just tired.*

She closes her eyes. The last thing she remembers is Lucas's hand resting at the curve of her waist and the faint scent of smoke lingering in his skin

HARPER JOLTS AWAKE, her wolf snapping to attention so violently that it leaves her breathless. For a moment, she's disoriented—the room is dark, bathed in silver moonlight pooling through the curtains—but then she feels it.

The energy has shifted, sharp and electric, as if the air itself is alive with tension.

Lucas shoots upright in bed, his sudden movement jolting Harper fully awake. The golden glow of his wolf's eyes cuts through the darkness, but it's not the warm amber she knows. This is darker, edged with something primal and untethered.

"Lucas?" Harper whispers, her voice hoarse with sleep and worry.

His breath is ragged, his shoulders heaving as though he's fighting off invisible chains. For a moment, he doesn't seem to see her—until his gaze locks onto hers, and something clicks.

"I need you," he growls, the words rough and desperate, a plea tangled with a command.

Her heart stumbles, her wolf straining toward him,

feeling the desperation rolling off him in waves. But there's something off-kilter in the hunger on his face—a wild edge that makes her pulse spike.

"Lucas, hey, I'm here," she whispers crawling closer. Gently, she cups his face, forcing him to look at her. His skin burns under her touch, trembling with barely restrained tension. "You're safe, baby. I'm here."

Lucas shudders against her palm, closing his eyes as if grounding himself. "I'm sorry," he whispers, his voice breaking. "I let them take me. I couldn't stop them, Harp. I—"

She silences him with a kiss—soft, certain—pouring every ounce of her love into it. "You didn't let me down," she breathes against his lips. "You're here now. That's all that matters."

For a heartbeat, his body sags into hers, a moment of fragile vulnerability. But then he's kissing her back—harder this time, the edge of desperation returning.

"I need you," he says again, softer now but no less urgent.

Harper doesn't hesitate. "Then take me," she whispers, steady and sure. "I'm yours, Lucas. Always."

Something flickers in his eyes—recognition, maybe—but it's fleeting, swallowed by the raw need stretching between them. His hands trace the curves of her body, rough palms igniting every nerve as he presses her back against the bed. His weight settles over her, warm and grounding, the heat of his skin chasing away the last remnants of doubt.

His mouth finds hers, desperate and claiming, as his hips press between her thighs. The hard length of him brushes against her, teasing, testing, sending a shiver down her spine. He groans against her lips, the sound raw, almost pained.

Harper tilts her hips, inviting him in, needing him just as fiercely. Lucas's breath shudders as he sinks into her, a slow, aching stretch that steals the air from both their lungs. A gasp slips from her lips, swallowed by his kiss as he stills, buried inside her, his body tense, shaking with restraint.

"Fuck," he rasps against her mouth, forehead pressing to hers. "You feel—" His words break off into a low growl as Harper tightens around him, urging him to move.

And then he does.

The first thrust is deliberate, testing, as if he's relearning every inch of her. Then another, deeper this time, pulling a moan from her throat. The pace builds, the need consuming them both, tangled in breathless gasps and whispered names.

Her nails scrape down his back, his muscles tensing beneath her touch. Their bodies move in sync, a perfect rhythm forged from longing and desperation, the bond between them thrumming with each roll of his hips. He grips her thighs, holding her open for him, pressing deeper, chasing that place where pleasure and connection blur into something infinite.

The world outside this moment doesn't exist. Just them. Just this.

Lucas shudders as the last waves of pleasure crash over him, his forehead pressing to hers, breaths ragged and uneven. His body still trembles, but his grip on her doesn't falter—like letting go isn't an option.

Rolling to his side, he pulls her against him, locking her in place with the full weight of his arms. He buries his face in her neck, inhaling deeply, his breath hot and uneven against her skin.

"I missed you," he murmurs, voice rough, frayed at the edges.

Harper smooths a hand over his back, fingertips tracing along his spine. But beneath the warmth, beneath the lingering aftershocks, she feels it—something dark, like smoke curling beneath the surface, waiting.

For a while, they say nothing. Lucas traces lazy patterns on her skin, his touch gentle now. Harper listens to the rhythm of his heartbeat beneath her cheek, savoring the sound she thought she might never hear again.

"Don't leave me again," she whispers, the plea escaping before she can stop it.

"Never," Lucas replies, his voice resolute. He presses a lingering kiss to her temple. "No one will ever take me from you again. I promise."

Harper exhales slowly, letting her body melt into his, but even as her eyes drift shut, her wolf stirs restlessly. Something isn't right. The smoky scent lingers faintly in the air, a dark undercurrent beneath the familiar warmth of her mate.

Lucas chuckles softly, breaking the silence. "You're awfully quiet, Sheridan. Thinking about round two already?"

Harper snorts softly, the sound muffled against his chest. "I'm trying to make sure my legs still work, thank you very much."

Lucas grins, his teeth grazing the sensitive skin of her neck in a playful nip. "Good. I like it when you can't walk straight after."

"Cocky wolf," she teases, though she can't stop the smile curling at her lips.

"Yours," the simple word sending a flutter through her chest.

For a moment, everything feels right again—the warmth of him, the weight of his arms around her, the steady rise and fall of his breathing. Harper shifts slightly in his embrace, tilting her head to look at him. "Lucas," she begins softly, brushing her thumb along his cheek. "Are you hungry? Isabell's been dying to make you whatever you want."

"I'm fucking starving," he replies, his voice softer now, more like the Lucas she knows. But as the faint smoky scent reaches her again, that dark thread beneath his familiar warmth gnaws at the edges of her relief. It lingers like a whisper of something unfinished, something lurking.

"Okay," she says with a small smile, trying to push the unease aside. She begins to move, but before she can get far, Lucas flips her effortlessly onto her back, pinning her beneath him.

"Damn, Williams, give a girl some warning before you flip her like a pancake," she huffs, her heart stuttering at the devilish grin that spreads across his face.

"You're not going anywhere yet," brushing his lips against hers in a kiss that's both tender and possessive.

Harper's breath catches as his touch shifts—soft, then demanding—igniting sparks across her skin. "Lucas..." she whispers.

"I missed you, Sheridan," his lips trailing along her jaw, his deep voice sends tingles straight to her nipples.

"But right now, the only thing I need to eat is you."

Her body melts into the bed, anticipation thrumming through her veins. "I fucking missed you too, baby," she breathes, her voice low and husky. "Now eat your pussy. Make me scream your name."

Lucas doesn't hesitate. His golden gaze locks onto hers as he moves lower, his tongue dragging slowly, deliberately along her. "Oh, you'll scream my name," he promises, his voice dark and full of heat.

Harper gasps as his fingers join the rhythm of his mouth, the slickness of their earlier release making every stroke smooth and unrelenting. Her back arches, but when her head tips back, Lucas growls—a low, possessive sound that sends shivers through her.

"Don't break eye contact," he commands, his dominance simmering beneath the words.

Harper obeys, forcing her gaze to stay on him, even as pleasure coils low in her belly, winding tighter with every teasing flick of his tongue. Her breaths turn ragged, her body trembling as his other hand cups her breast, thumb grazing over her nipple in perfect time with his movements.

"Lucas..." she moans, his name spilling from her lips like a prayer. "I love you. Never leave me again."

Her release crashes into her, violent and unstoppable, a wave of pleasure that tears a cry from her throat. Her body shakes beneath him, his name echoing through the room as the climax consumes her.

"Holy shit, baby," Lucas growls, crawling up her body to rest against her. "You taste so damn good."

Harper exhales shakily, as her heart begins to slow. "I need you, Lucas," she whispers, her voice soft but resolute. "All of you."

Lucas lifts his head slightly, his lips curving into a small, satisfied smile. "You've got me, Sheridan. Always."

But as Harper breathes him in, her wolf stirs uneasily. That faint, smoky scent is still there, just beneath the surface—an ominous whisper in the warmth of her mate.

And though her body is still humming from his touch, her heart can't shake the feeling that whatever darkness lingers hasn't finished with them yet.

LUCAS DANA WILLIAMS

L ucas grips the edges of the granite countertop, his knuckles stark white as he stares at the stranger in the mirror. His reflection mocks him—his shoulders slump in defeat, his pale skin drawn tight over tense muscles. But it's his eyes that cut the deepest: wild, haunted, darting like a trapped animal.

You're pathetic, the thought sneers, and his wolf growls low in agreement, pacing restlessly inside him. Memories assault him—chains slicing into his wrists, laughter echoing in the dark, and the cold stone floor slick with his blood. He squeezes the washcloth in his hand until it twists like a noose, the fabric bearing the brunt of his spiraling rage.

The door creaks slightly, and Harper's voice floats through. "Liam brought your bag up. Do you want to put your stuff away?" Her tone is light, unaware of the war raging behind the bathroom door.

Lucas closes his eyes, her voice grounding him. *You didn't die for her. Now you have to live for her.* But the thought feels hollow, tainted by doubt.

"Yeah, baby," he replies, his tone too smooth to be real.

He straightens, shoving his inner turmoil into the deepest recesses of his mind. His wolf snarls in protest, but Lucas shuts it out. *Not now.*

He steps out of the bathroom, his bare feet sinking into the soft carpet. The sensation is foreign, almost jarring. He wiggles his toes, staring down in brief distraction.

"You okay, babe?" Harper calls, and he looks up just in time to see her bounding out of the closet like a burst of sunshine.

For a moment, Lucas forgets how to breathe. She's stunning, her blonde hair falling loose around her shoulders, and her barely-there outfit leaves nothing to the imagination.

"Damn, woman," he rasps, his voice rough with want. "Could you possibly be any hotter?"

Harper glances down at herself, and he doesn't miss the flicker of self-consciousness in her eyes. The sight stirs something primal in him—protective and unrelenting. He strides toward her, closing the distance between them in three steps.

Before she can speak, he takes her hand and presses it to his chest. "This," he says, his voice low, roughened with emotion. "This is what your body does to mine, Harper Jane." His heart thunders beneath her palm, uneven but steady.

Her lips part, but she doesn't speak. Instead, she lets her hand linger, her touch grounding him in ways his wolf never could. For a moment, the turmoil inside him quiets.

Still looking at her hand, Harper breaks the silence. "Did you know hugs are healing?" she says softly. "There are studies that show a twenty-second hug every day can add a year to your life."

Lucas tilts his head, his brow furrowing. "Is that true?"

Harper nods, a small smile tugging at her lips. "Yup. So, technically, if you hug me for twenty seconds every day, we'll live forever."

Lucas's mouth twitches into a grin, his wolf letting out a quiet, pleased rumble. "Forever, huh? Then I guess I'll have to hug you twice as long—just to be sure."

He pulls her closer, his hands settling on her hips, his thumbs brushing against the soft curve of her waist. The feel of her beneath his touch is everything—familiar, grounding—but he doesn't miss the way her laughter falters, her breath catching. Her body stiffens, just slightly, but it's enough for him to notice.

His wolf stirs, uneasy. "What's wrong?"

Her gaze drops, her smile slipping away like sand through his fingers. "You know," she begins softly, her voice quieter than before, "growing up, my father didn't abuse me like Charlotte and Jade endured. But I had my own kind of torture."

The words hit him like a sucker punch, but he keeps his grip steady, his hands firm on her hips, silently telling her: I'm here. I'm not going anywhere.

"The entire pack bullied me," she continues, her voice trembling, each word slicing through him. "The women were the worst. My brother wasn't much better. I was the pity friend, Lucas. Jade and Charlotte took me in because they felt sorry for the fat girl."

A low growl builds in his chest, reacting to the pain in her voice, but he reins it in. This isn't the moment to let his fury show. Instead, he lets his hands do the talking, shifting slightly to anchor her, his thumbs tracing slow, deliberate circles against her skin. He's steady, grounded—everything she needs him to be.

"You're not her anymore, Harper," his voice low and

sure, cutting through the shadows of her doubt. "And you were never just a pity friend. You were their strength, even back then. And now? You're mine."

Her laugh is soft, almost hesitant, but it's there, and it's enough to make his chest loosen, just a little. He hooks his finger under her chin, lifting her gaze to meet his. The movement is slow, deliberate, and when her wide multi-colored eyes lock onto his, the vulnerability and intensity in her stare nearly undoes him.

"Listen to me, Harper Sheridan," he whispers, his voice thick with emotion, both a plea and a command. "I will kill anyone who has hurt you—past, present, and future. You are mine. Mine to protect. Mine to keep happy. And make no mistake..."

He pauses, his words hanging heavy between them, his grip on her firm yet tender. He inhales deeply, taking in her scent, her warmth, her presence. "You are everything I never knew I needed. And I will spend every second of my life making sure you believe that."

But even as he speaks, the weight of his own insecurities presses down on him. *Mine? You couldn't even protect yourself. What makes you think you can protect her?* The memory of his failure claws at him, but he buries it beneath his desperation to be what she needs.

"Lucas," Harper says softly, her hand still steady on his chest. "You don't have to carry everything alone. We protect each other. That's what mates do."

The sincerity in her voice hits him like a wave, washing away the doubt—if only for a moment. "You're mine, Harper," he repeats, his voice softer but no less resolute. "And I'm yours. For Infinity."

She smiles, leaning up to press a gentle kiss to his lips. "Infinity," she echoes.

They stand there, wrapped in each other's presence, the weight of the world outside their room fading into the background.

Lucas exhales deeply, his forehead resting briefly against Harper's before he steps back, grounding himself in the sight of her. The tension in his chest eases a fraction, but the lingering darkness doesn't leave completely. *Will it ever?*

As he ties the drawstring on his black lounge pants, something catches his attention. A strange but enticing scent drifts through the air, curling into his senses and tugging at his instincts. His wolf stirs, intrigued, and Lucas's stomach growls in loud agreement.

"What is that smell?" he asks, his brows scrunching as he glances toward the door. The hunger hits him all at once, sharp and insistent. "Holy shit, I'm fucking starving."

He turns back just in time to see Harper tugging his hoodie over her head. It isn't oversized on her—it fits just right, snug enough to show her curves while still swaddling her in his scent. His wolf quiets for a fleeting moment, a pleased rumble echoing in his chest.

"Is that my hoodie?" he asks, raising a brow, his tone hovering somewhere between accusation and amusement.

Harper looks up, feigning innocence. "Oh, this old thing? Found it lying around... somewhere."

"Somewhere?" Lucas narrows his eyes, stepping closer. "I've been looking for that. Thought I lost it."

"Well, technically, you *did* lose it," Harper teases, tugging the hood over her head and adjusting it like it's a crown. "It was abandoned and lonely, sitting on top of your bag when you were leaving last time so *Jade* gave it a better home."

Lucas chuckles, his hands finding her waist as he leans in, his voice dropping to a playful growl. "You know that counts as theft, right?"

She shrugs, unfazed. "Call it a rescue. Besides, it smells like you, and I like that. So, no, you're not getting it back."

His grin widens as he steps back, admiring the way the fabric hugs her frame. "You know, it looks way better on you than it ever did on me."

"Obviously," Harper quips, flashing him a cheeky smile. "Now, are you coming to eat, or are you just going to stand there sulking over your poor, mistreated hoodie?" Harper turns towards the door. "We better get down there or Isabell will kill me for keeping you wasting away up here."

Giving her ass a gentle swat. "Ok. Go give her a hand and I'll be down in a minute, babe."

"Everything ok?"

"Yeah, I just need to shit."

Scrunching her nose, "Hmm, I guess the honeymoon is over?"

Lucas watches as his very reason for breathing walks across the room, the soft click of the door barely audible over the maelstrom brewing inside him. Her absence leaves a hollowness in the air, a stark contrast to the fire raging in his chest.

Taking a deep breath, he clenches his fists. The fury swirling inside him is a living thing, sharp and unrelenting. He presses his palms to the cool surface of the wall, trying to ground himself. "I know, wolf. I know," he growls through gritted teeth.

His wolf snaps back with a growl, the bite of its frustration gnawing at his mind. Lucas pulls his fist back, ready to punch the wall, but stops just before impact, the tremble in his arm a testament to his fraying control.

"Let me get some fucking food in me and talk with Luna, alright?" His voice is low, growling, as if reasoning with the beast inside him. "We can't leave without getting as much info as possible. Fuck! Stop biting at me, you bastard. We'll get our revenge. I swear it."

After splashing his face with cold water, the icy sting doing little to cool the fire roaring in his veins, Lucas strides down the stairs. He stops when the little hairs on the back of his neck prickle, a warning that grips him with an uneasy edge. His wolf growls low, a menacing rumble in the pit of his stomach. The sharp tang of an unfamiliar scent hits his nose, foreign and unwelcome.

Frustration flickers through his bond with Harper, her emotions rippling across the connection like a sudden gust of wind. Lucas's jaw tightens, his wolf prowling beneath the surface. Something's off.

HARPER IS about to ask Isabell if she needs more plates when it happens. A faint but unmistakable scent hits her— the scent of pine and smoke, intertwined with something deeply familiar and yet completely out of place. Her wolf stirs, recognizing it instantly. And then she hears it—Lucas's heavy footsteps thundering down the stairs. Her pulse spikes.

Harper moves swiftly through the doorway, her pulse quickening as the tension in the air thickens. The faint scent clings to her senses, fueling the unease already brewing in her chest. She pushes open the door to the dining room and freezes.

Charlotte stands near the far end of the table, her arms crossed and her jaw tight. Liam is beside her, his posture guarded but calm, though his eyes flick to Harper as soon as she enters. Ryder—her brother—is standing by the door, his broad shoulders squared, looking like he's trying to keep his ground but failing under Charlotte's scrutiny.

"What the fuck, Ryder?" Harper's voice slices through the air, her frustration bubbling to the surface. Her eyes dart to Charlotte. "What the hell is he doing here?"

Before anyone can answer, heavy, rapid footsteps thunder down the stairs. Harper's stomach drops. She knows that sound—Lucas. He stomps into the room, his expression dark and unyielding, his wolf practically radiating off him in waves.

The moment he sees Ryder, Lucas's fury ignites. In a flash, he crosses the room, grabbing Ryder by the throat and slamming him against the wall with enough force to make the windows tremble. "I don't need to know your name before I kill you, but you will know mine. I am Lucas Williams, mate and shield to Harper Jane Sheridan," he growls, his voice more wolf than man.

Harper's heart races as she moves closer, trying to assess the situation. There's something unsettling in Ryder's eyes.

She doesn't need the bond, to feel the fury rolling off Lucas. His wolf is too close, and she can see it in the sharp lines of his face, the tension in his muscles.

"Lucas!" Harper shouts, her heart racing as she steps forward. "Stop! He's my brother!"

Lucas tilts his head, his grip loosening slightly as her words register. His wolf still lingers too close to the surface, his chest heaving as he stares into Ryder's eyes. Harper doesn't wait for him to fully process. She closes the distance, her voice firm. "Williams. Let. Him. Go."

Harper feels a sharp pang through their bond, like a string vibrating with her fear. "Let him go... Williams!

She steps closer, keeping her voice firm, though her heart is pounding so loudly she's sure everyone in the room can hear it. Finally, Lucas shakes his head, the fury receding just enough for him to loosen his grip and let Ryder drop to the ground, coughing and sputtering.

"Your brother?" Lucas asks, his tone still rough and disbelieving.

Harper exhales shakingly, feeling the tension in the room shift but not dissipate.

Her relief is short-lived when she catches the satisfied smirk tugging at Lucas's lips. It's enough to make her snap. Without thinking, she balls her fist and punches him in the chest—not hard enough to hurt, but enough to make her point. "Lucas! Why the fuck are you smiling? I don't love the guy, but I don't want you to kill him right here in the dining room."

Before Lucas can respond, Charlotte's commanding voice slices through the heavy air. "Williams, whatever you're doing, knock it the fuck off. There's a scared little pup in the house. I don't need whatever you have going on making it worse."

Harper's attention shifts immediately. "A pup?" she asks, looking toward Ryder. Her voice softens, but her eyes remain sharp.

Ryder rubs his throat, still hoarse, but manages to answer. "Yeah, asshole. I need the Red Rocks' help."

Before she can process his words, the familiar voices of the Humboldt trio echo through the foyer. "Holy shit, that little tike is strong for his age."

Kai's tone tinged with quiet empathy. "The kid is going to be a monster wolf."

The suffocating tension in the room thickens as the Humboldts join them. Jaxson raises his hands in mock surrender. "Hey, brother. It's just us. You good?"

Lucas's response is automatic, his tone dripping with sarcasm. "Yeah, I'm fine, fucker. Why do you ask?"

Kai steps forward, glancing between Lucas and Ryder with a knowing look. "Because the air is thicker than a yeti's pussy, man."

Harper's lips tighten, but before she can comment, Charlotte takes control again. "For fuck's sake, Williams. Sit your ass down, and we'll explain everything."

Harper follows as everyone moves to the table. The scrape of chairs against the marble, grates on her nerves. Isabell's arrival is perfectly timed; the older woman sweeps into the room, placing dishes on the table while musing softly in Spanish. Harper watches as she turns to Lucas, her expression full of emotion.

"Señor Lucas. I so happy you home. Safe home. I worry. You are Miss Harper's very breath. You no do that again," Isabell says, her voice thick with tears.

Lucas straightens, his wolf quieting under Isabell's heartfelt words. "I'm sorry I worried you, Isabell. I'll try my damndest to never do it again." He hugs her tightly, and Harper feels a lump form in her throat. She knows how much Lucas needs this moment—how much he needs to feel grounded.

"Now eat. You small. Eat to get strong," Isabell says before retreating to the kitchen. Harper watches her go, her heart heavy with concern.

Charlotte's voice pulls Harper's attention back. "Let's do this before Jade gets home and all hell breaks loose again. What is it you want, Ryder?"

Her Alpha tone settles over the room, but Harper's focus remains on Lucas. The tension hasn't left him—his wolf pacing just beneath the surface—and she knows this is far from over.

Ryder leans back in his chair, his usual smirk plastered across his face like armor. "Charlotte, you know I wouldn't come here unless I was desperate. I had to get that pup out of Montana. That chick begged me to take her kid because some guys were chasing her. She came out of nowhere, already beat to hell."

Harper narrows her eyes, leaning forward. "And you're what? The hero now?"

Ryder snorts. "Hardly. I should've left her to fend for herself instead of getting mixed up in whatever shitstorm she's dragging behind her. But here I sit."

"Oh, typical Ryder," Harper snaps. "Always the victim. She's the one who was beaten."

"Yeah, well now I've got a couple more kills added to my already busting logbook because of it," Ryder fires back, his tone sharp.

"See? Again. It's all about you," Harper shoots, her fists clenching under the table.

"She didn't say much on the way here. Just sat quiet, holding her kid like her life depended on it. Hell, maybe it did." Ryder's voice dips, something almost vulnerable slipping through before he quickly masks it. "I don't know why they were chasing her. She didn't tell me, and I didn't ask. Figured it was safer not to know."

"Safe for who?" Harper's voice is ice.

Ryder's gaze flickers, something raw passing through his eyes before he recovers with a smug smirk aimed at Harper. "The kid's a handful, and I know nothing about kids, so..." He shrugs, locking eyes with her. "The little shit shifted in the drive-thru."

The sharp clang of Jaxson's fork hitting the floor echoes off the walls. "What do you mean he shifted? He's like... five."

"Thanks for the brilliant observation, asshole. I'm aware."

Ryder snaps, his tone dripping with sarcasm.

"He wanted chicky nuggs, and apparently, I didn't get them fast enough. He started crying, then it turned into this tiny little howl, and the next thing I know, there's a pure white wolf pup bouncing around the back seat. I've already gone through two damn car seats because the little fucker keeps shredding them."

The room falls silent, tension crackling in the air. Harper catches Luna's fork freeze mid-air, her knuckles whitening briefly before she sets it down.

"You've got to be kidding me," Harper says, her tone sharp. "Shifting before puberty? That's not—"

"Normal?" Ryder interrupts, his smirk widening. "No shit, Harp. I figured that out when he sprouted fur mid-meltdown."

Luna shifts in her seat, the movement subtle but enough to catch Harper's attention again.

"What?" Harper presses, her tone sharper now. "What is it, Luna?"

"Nothing," Luna says quickly, but her voice is too even, too measured. She sets her fork down carefully, smoothing her napkin over her lap. "It's just... unusual, that's all."

"He's going to need an Alpha, Charlotte. I knew my Alpha wouldn't provide sanctuary to them, after you threatened to take his balls if he brought any trouble to the Sidney pack."

"Well if he wasn't such a dumbass, I wouldn't have to make such threats. You were closer to the Black Canyon Pack. Why not take them there?" Charlotte asks.

"The farther away, the better."

Harper's wolf stirs uneasily beneath her skin, the undercurrent of Luna's discomfort prickling at her instincts. She files it away for later, but the knot in her chest tightens. Whatever this is, it's more than just a kid with bad timing.

Lucas's growl rumbles beside her, low and steady, vibrating through their bond. The protectiveness seeping through.

"Williams! Shut the fuck up!" Charlotte's voice cracks through the air, her Alpha power rolling over the table like a shockwave. The command makes everyone flinch—except Ryder, of course. He sits there, completely unfazed, his smirk lingering like he's just won some unspoken battle.

The statement leaves the room in silence, everyone pondering what they just learned about a young one shifting years before he should be, but the quiet shatters as Jade's sharp, agitated voice cuts through from the living room. 'What the hell was that for, Alpha?' The lingering echo of Charlotte's command must have carried through the house, low and resonant like a drumbeat demanding attention.

Heavy footsteps follow, deliberate and full of purpose, until Jade appears in the doorway. She stops dead, her eyes darting between the occupants of the room. Her expression twists into one of disbelief before she lets out a disbelieving scoff. "You have got to be fucking kidding me."

Before Harper can process, Jade lunges. Noodles go flying, and Ryder hits the ground with a satisfying thud. Jade straddles his waist, her hand gripping his throat with murderous intent. "Why are you here, Ryder? I told you, the next time I saw you, I'd kill you."

Despite the chokehold, Ryder grins, the smug bastard. "I missed our foreplay, Jade."

"Fuck you, Ryder. Get out of my house."

Harper stands, but Lucas is quicker, already halfway to

pulling Jade off. "He's here for a reason, Jade," Harper interjects, trying to keep the room from erupting.

Jade doesn't even look up. "What the fuck, Harp? Even
you told him never to come near us again. We agreed. You
could injure, and I could maim."

Jade's free hand waves theatrically before a blade
appears, hovering dangerously close to Ryder's favorite
appendage. "Like take his dick."

"Jade, stop!" Harper's voice is sharp, but it's Charlotte's
bored tone that cuts through the chaos.

"Let him go, Jade." Charlotte takes another bite of garlic
bread, clearly unimpressed. "I can't believe I'm saying this
again."

Jade reluctantly releases Ryder, growling curses under
her breath as she stalks to an empty chair. Isabell, unbothered as ever, begins cleaning up the scattered dishes and
food. "Senorita Jade, no more mess. Eat. Need strength to
protect pack," she chides, casting a glare at Ryder before
disappearing into the kitchen.

"Jade, please stop." Luna's voice comes from behind
Harper, soft but pleading. "There's a little nugget in the
house, and we don't need to scare him more than he already
is."

Jade freezes mid-step, her head snapping toward Luna.
"What did you just say?" Her voice is low, almost calm, but
Harper can feel the fury building behind it.

Luna takes a small step back, her hands raised defen-
sively. "There's a pup, Jade. He's upstairs, scared out of his
mind and he needs our help."

Jade's expression shifts instantly, the calm shattering as
she pivots toward Ryder. Her chair scrapes against the floor
as she spins, her glare cutting through the air like a blade.
"What does that mean—there's a pup in the house, and we

need to help? Help with what? What did you do this time, you piece of shit?"

Ryder leans back in his chair, the smirk on his face a perfect blend of arrogance and malice. His eyes flick to Jade, taking in her fury like it's a source of amusement. "Why don't you sit your ass down and shut the fuck up." he says, his voice low and laced with venom, each word dripping with disdain. "Then maybe, I'll bother telling you."

Harper feels her stomach twist, her wolf bristling at his tone. She knows Ryder well enough to recognize the cruelty in his words, the way he wields them like a weapon. The smirk he flashes is calculated, designed to rile Jade up even further, and Harper's hands curl into fists under the table once agian.

Before Harper can even process the exchange, a chunk of garlic bread sails through the air, smacking Ryder squarely on the forehead. He freezes, the smirk wiped clean off his face as the bread bounces to his lap.

Kai lowers his arm with the casual confidence of someone who knows he's made his point. His eyes narrow, his voice steady but razor-sharp. "That's enough," Kai growls. "You will pay proper respect to this house, and to Isabell, who cooked this meal for us. Quit being a prick. You're making my girlfriend nervous."

Harper's lips twitch despite herself, a flicker of amusement breaking through her frustration. Ryder's jaw tightens, his smirk slipping back into place, but Harper can see the glint of irritation in his eyes. For once, he doesn't have a retort.

"I'm not your girlfriend!" Luna snaps, swatting at Kai's arm.

Kai smirks, leaning back in his chair. "Not yet, but my dick is in love."

"Kai," Liam's calm voice cuts through the room, steady but firm.

Ryder doesn't even flinch, his focus unwavering as he addresses Charlotte. "I just need to know if they can stay here. I can't have them with me when I go after that last bastard I missed. I don't need to spend the rest of my life looking over my shoulder."

Charlotte folds her arms, her expression unreadable. "We'll talk about it and let you know. This one's different, Ryder. We've never taken in a kid, and it sounds like trouble could already be on its way here."

Ryder snorts, his tone carrying its usual edge of entitlement. "I'm not stupid, Charlotte. I made sure we weren't followed." His gaze shifts to Harper, his voice dipping into something almost earnest. "I'm not the same guy you all left behind ten years ago."

THE SOUND of the shower drifts through the open bathroom door, steam curling out like ghostly fingers to claim the edges of the room. Lucas is in there, scrubbing off the day in silence—this new way of coping. He doesn't say it, but she feels it. The weight of his recovery clings to him like the mist, heavy and unshakable.

Harper's wolf paces beneath her skin, unsettled. Ryder's sudden arrival stirs a chaos she can't pin down, and Lucas's silence only feeds her restlessness. Is he healed enough to handle the strain? The bond between them feels taut, stretched thin by everything they're trying to hold together —Lucas's broken pieces, the pack's shifting dynamics, her brother waltzing in like he owns the place.

Ryder always has a way of sticking... digging under her

skin like a splinter she can't reach. And Lucas? He's holding together with the same fragility.

She crosses the room and sits on the edge of the bed, her fingers tapping out a single message.

WTF Mom

> Oh no. Who died? Or is this just about you not liking your haircut again?

Mom! Ryder. He's here. I thought you kept track of him.

> Oh, that's where he went. I was starting to think he joined a commune or got abducted by aliens.

I'd rather deal with the aliens. You lost him?

> Yeah. I took my eyes off him for five seconds, and poof. Nothing. He's like a toddler in a china shop but with fewer apologies.

Well you raised him

So you don't know why he's here?

> If I had to guess? Probably money. Or a dramatic declaration of his misunderstood genius. Ryder loves a captive audience.

No. He brought a female and her son. He didn't call you and tell you about it?

> Nope but that sounds pretty dramatic. Last time something like that happened, he got a scar across his eyebrow. Maybe I need to call Charlotte and ask her to lock up the rolling pins.

One time, Mom. I used it one time, and I stand by my decision.

Of course you do. And I'm sure the dent in the countertop stands with you as well.

Seriously, why do you even keep track of him? You know he's the worst.

Because I'm his mother, Harper. It's in the contract. I bake cookies, give unsolicited advice, and keep tabs on your pain-in-the-ass brother. Deal with it.

Hang on. Mom!!! I didn't even think about it before. How did he know my new address?

Oh shit. Busted.

Mom. You did know about Ivy and the boy. You told him to bring them here, didn't you?

Of course I did, dear. Do you think your brother is smart enough to think of that?

Always the savior.

Yeah. Just call me Motherf'ing Theresa.

Fine. I'm kicking him out of my territory.

Just aim for his ego. It's big enough to absorb the impact.

IN THE SHADOWS

The office is a temple of luxury—floor-to-ceiling windows overlooking a glittering city, black marble floors so polished they reflect every glimmer of light, and a sleek mahogany desk that looks as though no one has dared to touch it.

A leather chair sits behind the desk, its back to the room. All that can be seen is the elegant curve of a woman's shoulders, perfectly framed by the glow of the city skyline. Her posture is unnaturally still, as though carved from stone.

The clock ticks. Tick. Tick. Tick. The only sound in the vast space.

The phone rings. A shrill, jarring tone that cuts through the silence. Her hand moves slowly, picking up the receiver with a grace that feels deliberate. Controlled.

"Speak," she says, her voice smooth as silk but colder than ice.

The reply crackles through the line, anxious and rushed. "We found her. She's with those bitches—the Red Rocks."

Silence.

Her fingers tap once—*click*—against the arm of the chair. For a moment, the only sound is the ticking clock, the tension stretching so thin it could snap.

"Good."

Her voice holds no triumph. No gloating. Just certainty, like she's already won.

She sets the receiver down with a calculated *click*, the sound echoing in the empty room. Slowly, the chair begins to turn, the glow of the city catching the edge of her face as she comes into view.

Her beauty is a cruel thing. Cold, sharp, and predatory. Pale skin, storm-gray eyes that seem to see everything—and a faint, jagged scar running from the corner of her jaw to just below her ear.

She stands, her movements liquid and controlled, the kind of grace that comes with absolute power. Moving from the desk, she trails her fingers across an untouched glass of bourbon, her nails clicking against the crystal as she pauses.

For a moment, she stares at the city below, her expression unreadable. Then, softly, she speaks.

"Run all you want." Her voice drops to a whisper, the faintest edge of venom lacing each word. "I always find what's mine."

GET THE FUCK OUT

"Having Ryder in the house feels weird," Harper whispers into Lucas's chest.

The blue flames from the water vapor fireplace in the game room dance in her eyes, casting flickering shadows that mirror her unease.

She squeezes his waist tighter, hoping the steady pressure might anchor her, might zap her stability back into place. But instead, she feels his wolf beneath the surface, growling and snarling, matching the wrath inside her.

The low hum of the wall-sized TV behind her barely registers. It's Lucas's heartbeat that holds her focus, steady and grounding.

She locks her fingers together behind his back, pulling him even closer. His small, involuntary moan sends a shiver through her, finally grounding her in the moment. It's the response she didn't realize she needed.

"I hope Charlotte decides soon so he can get the hell out of here," her voice low. The weight of her older brother's history presses down on her, dragging up memories she thought she'd left behind. Anger she believed buried years ago bubbles to the surface, sharp and fresh, simmering just beneath her skin.

Both human and wolf churn with restless energy, unable to let go of the need to find Ethan. But now, there's more. She can't leave—not with her untrustworthy brother in her territory. Not with a pup who needs protection and a mother who needs safety and assurance. Everything feels tangled, and the knots are tightening by the second.

"Babe, did you hear me?" Lucas's deep voice pulls her attention, though it barely registers.

"Yeah, I heard you," her gaze distant.

"Really? You heard me?" Lucas gently pushes her back, breaking her hold on him. His deep brown eyes pierce hers, unyielding. "Here's the thing, mate. You can't lie to me anymore. When you do, I literally feel it." His head tilts, one brow arching in challenge. "So, I'll repeat myself. What did that asshole do to make all of you hate him so much?"

Before she can answer her phone lights up.

"What the fuck, Harp? You good?"

Harper takes a deep breath, trying to find the answer. Should she be honest or should she hide it? Jade will know if she's hiding anything. They've gone through way too much together, especially when it comes to Ryder.

No but should I be? So much has happened. Him being here just makes all this harder.

Harper sets her phone back down and exhales sharply, the question hitting harder than she expects. Going back to Lucas's question.

"He's just that. An asshole. He was the worst big brother

anyone could have been stuck with. He tortured me, made fun of me, picked fights whenever he could. I just hate him."

The chime brings her eyes back to her phone.

> I could kill him in the backyard but you'll have to help me get rid of the body and clean up before Isabell finds out.

Kai's booming voice echoes off the walls, pulling her attention to the doorway. "Who's down for a Donkey Kong tournament?"

Kai—looking more like he should be on stage winning a Mr. Universe contest then walking into this room—peacocks through the doorway, followed by the other three mammoths. Ryan, Jaxson, and Liam.

The vintage arcade machine comes to life as Liam taps the buttons. *Boing. Boing. Boing.* "Sure. We could use a little lift in the mood around here."

Harper jumps when a high pitch scream rings through the room, quickly followed by little pattering footsteps and Luna's voice saying "I'm going to get you."

The cutest little curly blonde-hair bounces onto the couch and tucks into a ball, giggling, "Nooooo." More giggles. "I big and trong Una. You can't get me."

Harper watches as her friend tickles the little boy, his giggles filling the room like a melody. "I big an trong," he keeps repeating, his small voice brimming with determination. The sound is cathartic. Harper feels the black cloud that's been weighing on her lift, as if the boy's laughter has blown it away. She tilts her head back, her eyes moving to the ceiling as if she could actually see the shift.

Being a realist, she knows the relief won't last forever. But for now, she closes her eyes, takes a deep breath, and lets the warmth of the moment soak into her bones. With a playful slap to Lucas's chest, she grins. "Thanks for the hug, Williams."

"Hey, where are you going?" Lucas reaches for her, but she ducks under his arm with a quick skip and lands on the couch. "Who's your friend, Luna?"

"Oh, hi, Harp. This is Henry. Henry, this is my very good friend, Harper."

"Hi, Harpa!" The boy beams at her, his tiny voice radiating pride. "I eat broccoli so I can be big and trong."

The laugh that escapes Harper comes from deep within, bubbling up in a way that surprises even her. "That's a good plan. I love broccoli too."

"See, it works. I can tell you're trong. Grrrrrr!" He growls, his little face disappearing behind a flash of the whitest teeth she's ever seen.

Holy shit. Those tiny words boost her confidence a thousandfold. Her wolf, so restless and uneasy just moments ago, suddenly goes quiet. Harper realizes she's smiling—a real, genuine smile that feels foreign but welcome.

"Thank you, Henry," she says softly. The urge to hug him swells in her chest, but she hesitates, not wanting to overwhelm him. For now, she just watches him, her heart lighter than it's been in days.

"Henry?" Hearing a new voice come from the hallway. "Henry?"

The most beautiful women corners the doorway.

"There you are." The woman's yellow-blonde ringlets cascade down, framing her delicate, fine features. Her sunkissed skin, marred by fresh cuts and bruises, tells a story of recent violence. Defensive wounds. Harper's wolf growls low in her chest, the sight igniting a protective fire that drowns out everything else.

She clenches her fists, feeling the primal urge to track

down whoever did this. But it's not just revenge driving her —it's the overwhelming need to ensure this never happens again. Harper forces herself to focus on the present, watching as concern fills the stranger's glowing, glacial blue eyes.

"Hi, I'm Ivy. I'm so sorry. I hope he's not causing any trouble." The beautiful mother's eyes turn to the little boy with concern.

Whatever those animals did to her has slowed her healing. Wolf shifters have a naturally accelerated healing process—bruises vanish within hours. But these injuries linger, dark and raw. Harper's wolf growls low, agitated by the sight. Then something clicks, freezing her thoughts mid-spin. *Wait.* Harper fights to keep the confusion off her face. *She's not a wolf?*

"No, he's great! This house needs a little giggling," Harper says quickly, forcing a reassuring smile as she shifts her focus back to Henry. Her instincts hum, sharpening as she tries to make sense of the scent—or the strange lack of one. Kneeling, she gives Henry's tiny side a playful tickle, drawing another burst of his glorious giggle that fills the room. The sound soothes her wolf, easing the tension knotting her chest.

Rising to her feet, Harper moves toward Ivy her steps measured and calm. She extends her hand, slow and deliberate, careful not to startle the wary woman. "I'm Harper," she says, her voice warm and inviting.

Ivy hesitates, her round eyes flickering with uncertainty as they meet Harper's. After a moment that feels longer than it is, she finally takes Harper's hand. Her touch is feather-light, her grip tentative. She says softly. "Thank you for allowing us into your incredible home."

"Yes, absolutely. I'm so sorry you had to leave your home

and for everything you're going through," Harper replies, her voice soft with empathy.

"Thank you," Ivy's shutdown is almost immediate—her shoulders sink, her gaze drops to the floor, and she pulls the blue shawl tighter around her thin arms.

The movement strikes Harper like a blow. She's seen this exact motion a hundred times with her pack sisters—fragile, protective, trying to disappear.

Harper's jaw tightens as a familiar fire ignites in her chest. *Not here. Not in this house.* She keeps her voice steady, her smile soft, even as her wolf bristles under the surface. Ivy and her son would get the protection they needed—no matter what it cost.

"Henry, come here. You need a bath."

Henry climbs down, feet first, his cutest little jean-covered butt waddling over to his mother. He clings to her side before settling on her hip, the picture of contentment. Harper's smiles have been rare these days, but this little nugget has managed to bring a few back.

Her gaze shifts subtly to Ryan, who stands perfectly still, his piercing eyes fixed on Ivy and Henry. His stance is rigid, unyielding, like a silent sentinel.

The moment gives way when a gasp escapes Ivy. Harper's attention snaps back to the doorway, where Charlotte and Jade round the corner, their sudden appearance startling the nervous mother.

Ryan moves in a blur, stepping closer to Ivy and Henry with a quiet intensity. His stance is firm, steady—not aggressive, but undeniably watchful.

Ryan doesn't say a word, his focus unwavering, and she wonders briefly if it's simply his nature to guard others so instinctively.

"Woah. Sorry. We didn't mean to scare you, Ivy" Charlotte tries to find her most comforting tone. Then tips her head. "And thank you for protecting her, Ryan."

Damn, she's a good Alpha.

Harper watches Ivy move forward, eyes staying turned down to the hand she places lightly on Ryan's forearm. "Thank you. We're ok. I'm just a bit jumpy." Tucking Henry closer to her, she vanishes through the doorway.

The tension eases, the air in the room no longer feeling as heavy. "Luna, what did you find out about Ivy and Henry's past? Anything?" Charlotte asks as she moves toward her usual pacing spot between the fireplace and the floor-to-ceiling windows.

Beyond the glass, the Vegas skyline flickers to life, city lights blinking against the backdrop of the setting sun as it dips behind the Spring Mountains.

"Well, first, I found out that wolves don't have blue eyes. EVER." The tone is unlike Luna. Tucking her legs underneath her, she looks over her shoulder at their alpha. "Many domesticated dog breeds do, so there have been hybrids, but biologist have never recorded a pure blood wolf with blue eyes and there are no evidence of a domesticated dog shifter."

"She's not a wolf." Harper's voice stops the room. The only sounds are from the Donkey Kong game that Kai's hands are resting on. All eyes have shot to her. "Seriously. I can't be the only one that figured that out." Scanning the room, still looking for back-up. "Come on, guys. Tell me you smell wolf and I'm going crazy."

"She's a mystery, but," Charlotte looks around the room. "The Red Rocks will keep them here as long as Ivy wants to. I know we can protect her and the boy." Charlotte is still pacing. "If he is already shifting, it's going to take more than just his mom to keep him safe."

Harper is a little shaken that everyone has gone back to what they were doing, but didn't address the elephant in the room. The loud *crack* of pool balls slamming each other, draws Harper's attention to Jade standing next to the hot pink pool table that Luna just "had to have." "Yeah. We can't let that douche canoe Ryder teach him. The kid will be fucked for life."

Harper nods her head in agreement. "Plus, I heard Isabell come home earlier. Those bags sounded like she bought every toy a five-year-old boy could ever want."

Maddy seems to come out of nowhere. She must be learning from Isabell.

"Ivy's about my size, so I took a bunch of the clothes that Luna and I bought last week to her," Maddy says as she plops down next to Luna, her voice tinged with guilt.

Luna gasps, clutching her chest dramatically. "You *what?!* You gave away the clothes I painstakingly curated for you? The ones I wrestled from the jaws of mediocre fashion to transform you into the goddess you're meant to be?"

Maddy's eyes widen. "I-I thought... I mean, Ivy needs them more than I do. She's been through so much, and—"

"And you're over here playing Fairy Godmother with *my* magical wardrobe picks?" Luna interrupts, her tone mock-offended but with a mischievous glint in her eye. "Did I not say those sequins were sacred?"

Maddy flushes, glancing down. "I'm sorry. I just wanted to help."

Luna sighs loudly, throwing an arm over Maddy's shoulders. "Oh, sweet summer child. Don't apologize for doing a good thing. But next time, at least let me sprinkle my Luna-approved fairy dust over the decision first."

Maddy peeks up at her, the tension easing from her face. "You're not mad?"

"Mad? No. Offended that you didn't consult me? A little," Luna replies with a wink. "But let's face it, Ivy deserves some sparkle, and I'm always up for another shopping trip. It's a win-win."

Maddy lets out a small laugh, relaxing under Luna's arm. "Thanks, Luna. I'll ask next time, I promise."

"You better," Luna says with mock severity before grinning wide. "And Maddy, don't think for a second this gets you out of the new wardrobe I've been planning for you. Prepare yourself."

Maddy groans, but her lips curve into a smile. "Why do I feel like I'm doomed?"

"Because, darling," Luna says, flipping her hair with flair, "you've entered the Luna Wardrobe Experience. There's no turning back now."

"Hey, Charlotte, I think I'll take you up on that free day pass for your gym." Ryan says, his voice low as he drags a hand through his hair. The tension on his face is impossible to miss.

Charlotte nods, her tone calm but laced with curiosity. "Yeah, okay. I'll text the desk and let them know you're coming."

"You good, man?" Kai's concern cuts through the moment, his brow furrowing as he watches Ryan.

"I'm fine," Ryan says, though his clenched jaw and the tightness in his shoulders suggest otherwise. "Just wound up. I hate seeing a woman with bruises. My wolf is burning me up." He exhales sharply, pointing at Kai, Jaxson, Lucas, and then Harper. "Humboldts, pack run tonight."

Harper's eyes widen as she glances at the three towering men behind her. Her thoughts race, nerves and excitement tangling in her chest. This will be her first pack run as a

Humboldt. The realization sends a thrill coursing through her.

"Fuck!" Charlotte curses, tucking her phone back into the small pocket of her bra strap. Harper can't help but think, *I need to get me one of those bras.*

"What's up, Red?" Liam asks, already striding toward Charlotte with his usual focus.

"Jase is on his way here. He wants to talk to Lucas and Harper specifically." Charlotte replies, her tone sharp with irritation. "How does that fucker always have the worst timing?"

"Did he say why?" Harper's heart leaps at the possibility of news about Ethan.

"No. I'm guessing he caught wind of Ryder being in our territory and wants to know why I haven't killed him yet."

"Well, I guess I'll make it easy for him to meet me then," Ryder says, strutting into the room like he owns the place. He plops down on the couch right next to Harper, the cushions sinking under his weight. The woodsy smell of his cologne assaults her senses.

"What the fuck, Ryder? How the hell do you wear that shit?" Harper snaps, wrinkling her nose.

"Wear? What shit?" he asks innocently, flapping his black leather coat over his plain white t-shirt, deliberately wafting the smell toward her.

"I fucking hate you, Ryder," Harper hisses, crossing her arms.

Jade slams a pool stick onto the table, the sharp crack silencing the room. "We were just discussing how you can get the fuck out of our territory now. Ivy and the kid will stay with us."

Ryder swings his legs over the back of the couch and closes the distance between him and Jade in a heartbeat, leaning into her space. "I think I'll need to hear that from the Alpha of this pack. Not you."

Lucas shifts, stepping forward, but Harper sends a warning through their bond. *Stand down.* She shakes her head, and Lucas stops in his tracks. *Good mate.*

Simultaneously, Jade raises a hand, signaling Kai and Jaxson to stay back. Her lips curl into a dangerous smile as she inches closer to Ryder, their noses nearly touching. "You can leave, or—"

The tension explodes as Jase barrels into the room, his voice booming. "What the fuck, Charlotte? Do you just let any bastard into your territory these days?"

"Clearly." Her tone is the same every time when it comes to Jase. She acts like he annoys her, but they truly have a common respect for each other. "You're here, ain't ya?" The crooked smile tells her truth.

"Who the hell is this character and why hasn't Jade killed him for standing in her space?" Jase points to the couple, still standing nose to nose.

"Jase, this is my brother, Ryder. He was just leaving."

"Charlotte?" Ryder is the first to take a step back. "Are Ivy and the kid good to stay here? Under your protection?" Facing Charlotte and Liam now, his face isn't his normal, resting asshole face. He actually looks concerned. Ryder doesn't care about much, but he seems to care about what happens to Ivy and Henry.

"Yes. The Red Rocks will take them into our home. We will work with Ivy to heal and guide Henry into his animal on one condition."

"Of course there is," Ryder says, his tone sharp and cutting, sending a ripple of growls through the room like a symphony of discontent.

He glances around, his smirk unwavering. "Oh, come on,

I'm not the asshole here. There's always something in return." He leans back casually, locking his arms behind him on the edge of the table, his posture daring anyone to challenge him.

"Shut the fuck up. My Alpha is speaking." Jade tells him.

"Sure Ryder, there is something in return and this something...benefits everyone here."

"Fine. What do you want in exchange for keeping that woman and the boy safe?"

"You fucking leave and do not return. For nothing. I don't care if you rescue the Pope himself. Do not step foot in my territory again."

Charlotte's Alpha energy ripples through the room, a palpable force that demands submission. Harper's eyes flick to Ryder, catching the briefest flinch—too quick to be a reaction of fear. His jaw tightens, his arms locking stiffly at his sides as if bracing against something deeper, something unspoken.

"If you do," Charlotte continues, her voice cutting like a blade, "Jade has my full authority to not only complete that maiming she spoke about earlier, but to watch it heal—over and over—before splitting your throat."

Ryder's gaze lingers on Charlotte, unreadable but charged. For a fleeting moment, Harper wonders what it is about Charlotte's power that makes even Ryder falter. The thought sticks, persistent, as the tension in the room simmers.

"Fucking hell, what did I walk into?" Jase's voice carries over the room, casual but laced with curiosity. He grabs a small chair from the poker table, spins it around, and straddles it, resting his arms across the back. "I don't know you, man, but I'd run. I know these ladies pretty well, and they don't fuck around."

Ryder's lip curls as he steps in front of Harper, blocking her view of Jase. "Trust me, I know them better than you do."

Lucas moves in a flash, his wolf crackling under his skin, ready to strike. "Relax, man," Ryder says, raising his hands, "I just want to say goodbye to my sister."

Harper senses the hum in her bond with Lucas, the tension ready to snap. Lucas's eyes gleam with the color of his wolf, but Harper steps between them, her hand brushing Lucas's forearm. "It's fine, Williams," she says softly, sending a pulse of calm through their bond. She turns to Ryder, her tone cold. "Bye, Ryder. Do not come back."

Ryder smirks. "See ya, fuckers!" He spins on his heel and vanishes out the door, leaving behind his signature scent of pine and trouble.

Jase raises a brow, his shamrock-green eyes widening slightly. "Your brother? From up north?" His tone shifts, curiosity overtaking his usual cocky ease. "What the fuck is he talking about, and why is he here?"

"None of your fucking business, Jase," Charlotte snaps, stepping forward, her stance solid. Her hands plant firmly on her hips, her Alpha energy radiating. "You called me. I didn't call you. So if you don't have the intel I asked for, you can either leave, or for once, just act like a normal person."

"I'm not here to drop intel," Jase says, leaning back lazily. "I'm here to ask—nicely—for you to stay out of it."

"Stay out of what?" Harper's voice cuts through the tension, her fingers tightening around Lucas's hand as she braces herself.

"Ethan," Jase says simply, his gaze sweeping the room. His expression is calm, but Harper catches the sharpness in his eyes as they flick over each face. "I know you're thinking about going after him, but I need you to hold back on this one."

Lucas growls low, his body taut. "Why? If you've got a lead, why wouldn't we help?"

Jase sighs, dragging a hand over his neck, his easygoing demeanor slipping. "Because I need him in play, Lucas. If he's where I think he is, he's bait. And if I'm right, he'll lead me to the mole. I can't risk you two jumping in and spooking him."

Harper tilts her head, her wolf stirring uneasily. "How did you know Lucas was awake?" The question lands hard, cutting through the room.

Jase doesn't flinch, but his grin widens slightly, softening the tension. "I hear things," he says with a wink, his tone light but evasive. "What can I say? I've got my ways."

Harper's gaze darts around the room. *Who told him?* Her eyes lock briefly on Charlotte, who stands with her arms crossed, her expression unreadable. Then on Luna, who shrugs slightly, her lips quirking as if to say, *Don't look at me.*

Jase straightens, the teasing grin fading. "Look, I get it. You want answers, and you want justice. But I'm asking you to trust me on this one. You've got enough going on here. Let me handle Ethan. If I get anything solid, you'll be the first to know."

His gaze lingers on Lucas for a moment before shifting back to Harper. "Besides, the two of you have more important things to focus on. Like keeping this pack safe." He nods toward the door, his grin returning. "Now, if you'll excuse me, I've got to get back to work before Charlotte threatens to maim me for overstaying my welcome."

The room remains silent as the door clicks shut behind Jase. Harper watches his retreat, unease curling in her chest. *How does he always know exactly when to show up?*

"Well, that was cryptic as hell," Kai leans back on the couch with Luna comfortably perched in his lap. His tone is light, but his eyes glint with suspicion. "Does he ever just... tell you what's going on?"

"No," Charlotte answers bluntly, her arms still crossed. "And that's what bothers me the most."

Jaxson whistles low, shaking his head. "The guy's timing is too perfect. Always showing up just in time to dangle some half-truths and keep us on edge."

Lucas growls softly, his frustration barely contained. "Keeping Ethan alive might make sense for him, but it sure as fuck doesn't for me."

Harper exhales sharply, her wolf restless. "He said he knew Lucas was awake. How? Who the hell is feeding him that kind of detail?"

Luna straightens, her playful demeanor giving way to curiosity. "That's the question, isn't it? I mean, it's not like we've been advertising it."

Charlotte narrows her eyes, her voice measured. "No one in my pack would betray us like that. But the timing—" She stops, her words heavy with implication.

Luna tilts her head, her voice edged with thoughtfulness. "Maybe he's not working alone. If he's looking for a mole, maybe someone's feeding *him* just enough to keep the game going."

Harper's jaw tightens as her wolf snarls. "Or maybe he already knows who the mole is, and he's just playing us all."

Silence settles again, the weight of the thought filling the room. Lucas squeezes her hand, his voice low and firm. "Then we need to be ready. If Jase is hiding something, it's only a matter of time before it bites us."

Charlotte steps forward, her Alpha presence steadying. "No one makes any moves until we know more. Stay sharp. If Jase has an angle, we'll find it—and we'll deal with it."

A MYSTERY NAMED IVY

Lucas winces as the pain from his wolf claws through him, raw and unrelenting. It's not just the physical ache—it's the darkness riding beneath it, coiling in his gut and feeding off his fury. He drags his palm over his chest, his nails scraping against his shirt as if to confirm the flesh hasn't been ripped apart.

For a fleeting moment, he considers the mirror to his left but shakes his head. He knows what he'll see—golden eyes, seething with rage, staring back at him like a stranger wearing his skin.

The bastard is close. The knowledge pulses in his blood, more intoxicating than anything he's ever known. Ethan isn't just a target; he's a spark to the inferno brewing inside Lucas—a hunger for violence he's kept buried for too long. His human side fights to keep him grounded, but his wolf is already halfway out the door, snarling for freedom.

Lucas doesn't care about Jase's mole, the plan, or the fallout. All he cares about is the promise of blood—the release that comes with destruction.

Once Harper is asleep, I'll go. Alone.

He grits his teeth against the thought of her seeing this side of him. She can never know how deep the shadows run, how far he's already fallen.

His fingers curl into fists, the phantom weight of vengeance settling in his hands. The coming fight won't just be about justice—it'll be an outlet. A reckoning. His lips curl into a bitter smile at the thought of Ethan's screams, the way his body will give under the weight of every blow. He doesn't just want to end him; he wants to *break him.*

A low growl rumbles in his chest as he finally turns toward the mirror. The reflection meets him with a predatory stare, gold eyes gleaming with malice. His wolf isn't a silent passenger—it's an eager accomplice, urging him forward, whispering promises of pain and power. The lines between them blur, the darkness binding them together, feeding them both.

Lucas exhales sharply, the sound more snarl than breath. His grip tightens on the edge of the coach, his knuckles white with strain. There's no room for hesitation. Ethan is out there, and every second he waits is another second wasted.

The image in the mirror tilts its head in unison with his own, a perfect reflection of the monster lurking beneath the surface. A smirk pulls at his lips, cruel and satisfied. *There's no redemption in this. Only the promise of destruction.*

I'm sorry, Harper, but I'll be doing this alone.

Lucas blinks several times as Luna's high-pitched complaints pull him back.

"What the fuck Kai? You said you were good. I thought I was finally going to find someone that could beat his ass!"

Luna is bouncing around the Donkey Kong game like a baby kangaroo while Maddy and Liam stand behind a defeated Kai.

His mate is annihilating Jade at the pool table. Harper leans casually against the table, a smirk tugging at her lips as she lines up her next shot. Jade's muttered curses drift across the room, only adding to Harper's obvious satisfaction.

Lucas can't focus on the game. The pressure in his chest is mounting, his wolf pacing just as much as he is. He pops his knuckles one by one, the sharp cracks breaking the silence around him. It's movement at least, but it does nothing to calm his insides.

His hand brushes against the phone in his back pocket, the temptation to map out his route clawing at him.

Don't. Don't even think about it.

He knows the second he gives in, the bond will reveal his intent, and Harper will sense everything.

"Hey, Williams. I don't know about you, but I've got some pent-up energy. Wanna go for a swim before dinner?" Harper's voice breaks through Lucas's spiraling thoughts.

Too late.

"Oh, is that what you guys call it now?" Luna pipes up, making exaggerated air quotes. "Swimming? We call it..." She air quotes again, smirking. "Talking politics."

Kai turns, mock offense plastered across his face. "Hang on. Me? Talk politics? No fucking way!"

Jaxson snorts, his tone dripping with amusement. "Hey man, I don't know. Maybe you're branching out."

Kai grins, jerking a thumb at Luna. "Well, I *am* becoming a man of many talents. My beautiful genius over there is teaching me how to be more..." He pauses, glancing at Luna for confirmation. "Cultured?"

Luna gives a proud, soft, "Yes."

"Cultured," Kai repeats louder, his grin widening. "She's helping me be smarter. More polished."

Jaxson leans back against the wall, arms crossed, his rare smirk tugging at the corners of his mouth. "Polished? You?" He shakes his head. "Polished my ass."

Lucas feels a laugh bubbling up, surprising even himself. Seeing Jaxson—stoic, unflappable Jaxson—show a flicker of amusement is a sight in itself. But the idea of Kai, his lifelong friend, becoming "polished" under Luna's guidance? That's comedic gold.

"If Kai suddenly becomes polished," Lucas says, shaking his head with a rare grin, "I'm checking the sky for flying pigs. And if Luna's the one to make it happen, then hell's officially frozen over."

Kai throws an arm around Luna, looking entirely too smug. "You'll see, man. Next time you need to negotiate with a vampire, you'll be begging for my cultured ass to help."

"Yeah, I'll be sure to call you," Lucas deadpans, the tension in his chest easing just a fraction.

"Williams." Harper's voice pulls him back. She's standing in front of him now, her lips quirking into a smile as she tilts her head up. "Let's leave these *cultured* fools to be *polished*."

He doesn't have time to answer before Harper inches onto her toes, brushing her lips against his. The kiss drowns out the chaos in his mind, if only for a fleeting moment.

"Holler at us when Isabell's ready?" Lucas throws over his shoulder to Jaxson.

"Yeah, man, we got you," Jaxson replies, his usual monotone back in place.

Leading Harper through the doorway to the patio, Lucas slows his stride when he spots Ivy sitting on the edge of the pool, her legs dangling in the water. Her blonde curls glisten under the patio lights, and her shoulders are hunched like the weight of the world is pressing down on them.

"Should we let her be? We can go to our hot tub instead," Harper whispers, her breath warm against his arm.

Ivy starts to push herself off the pool deck, her voice hesitant. "Oh, I'll go back to my room."

Damn shifter hearing.

Harper steps forward quickly, her tone reassuring. "No, please don't. We want you to feel at home here. Honestly, I'm already in love with Henry. He brings an energy, this house desperately needs."

Lucas watches as Harper lowers herself onto the pool's edge beside Ivy, dipping her legs into the water and swishing them slowly in unison. The soft, soothing movement seems deliberate, a subtle way of encouraging the other woman to relax.

"I can't thank you enough for letting us stay here," Ivy says quietly, her gaze fixed on the rippling water. "It's been a hard few days. My head is spinning. I'm sorry I'm not more confident, like you ladies."

Lucas slips into the pool without a word, moving to stand waist-deep in front of them. The water's coolness calms the simmering tension in his chest, but it does little for the restlessness in his wolf. He watches Ivy closely, noting the way her shoulders stay tight despite Harper's warm smile.

"Oh, God, Ivy. It sounds like you've been through hell," Harper says gently. "I wouldn't expect you to feel confident right now."

Ivy shifts uncomfortably, her fingers clutching the edge of the pool deck. "I'm an Omega, so I'm not very strong anyway."

Lucas cups the water in front of him, letting it spill through his fingers in a steady rhythm. "I beg to differ. We've only heard bits and pieces of what happened, but you're still here," he says, his voice steady and sure. "That's strength."

"Thank you," her voice is hollow. "But I don't feel strong. Actually... I'm not sure I feel much of anything."

Lucas watches her squirm, her body language tight and guarded. He wonders if her animal is stirring uneasily inside her—or if Harper is right, and her animal isn't a wolf at all.

"I'm sorry if Henry gets in the way," Ivy says suddenly, her tone shifting. "He can be a handful sometimes."

Lucas furrows his brows at the abrupt subject change, but Harper answers with ease.

"Yeah, well, so can Kai, so we're not worried," Harper says with a grin. She lifts her leg out of the water and lets it splash back in, sending tiny ripples toward Lucas.

He catches the faintest smile tugging at Ivy's lips. Small, but it's there.

"Ryder told me we'd be safe here," she says after a pause. "Other than that, he didn't really talk much on the way."

"Ryder's never been much of a talker," Harper quips, rolling her eyes. "Unless he's being a dickwad."

A soft huff escapes her, fleeting but real. Her shoulders loosen, just a fraction—barely noticeable, but Lucas sees it. A crack in the wall.

He notes how Ivy's posture relaxes a little more with each of Harper's lighthearted words. He decides to just stay quiet and let the women talk, running his palms over the water's surface. The repetitive motion soothes him, just a bit.

He's noticed lately that water unsettles his wolf—something new since the mine. The memories of that place are dark and fragmented, but his wolf seems to remember enough to keep the unease alive.

"I've never seen two packs get along this well," Ivy says after a moment, her curiosity slipping into her tone. "How is it that the Red Rocks allow another pack into their territory so willingly?"

"Ohhhh, there's a story," Harper says with a soft giggle, tilting her head back. "I'll give you the short version for now. The Humboldts helped us with our second Alpha's sister, Maddy. She was in trouble, and Spencer—their Alpha—agreed to help. So, we got to know Kai, Jaxson, and..." Harper turns to Lucas with a sly smile that sends warmth straight through him. "I already knew Lucas though."

She throws her chin in his direction, and for the first time since Isabell's hug, Lucas feels his wolf go still. Pride swells in his chest, forcing him to stand a little taller in the water. Damn, that woman can do things to him no one else on the planet ever could. The thought makes him second-guess his decision to go after Ethan without her.

"We just met Ryan. He became the Humboldts' second, when Lucas had to step down to be with me," Harper continues.

"Hang on, woman. You had to step down too," Lucas interjects, smirking slightly.

Ivy's gaze flickers between the two of them, her expression curious.

"Yes, I did," Harper says, smiling. "Lucas and I have the best Alphas. They agreed to share us, so we're in dual packs now. Both Red Rocks and Humboldts."

"We were both second in command," Lucas adds, his voice steady. "But we had to step down because we're splitting our time between the packs."

Her brows lift, eyes widening. "Wow. That must be a first. I've never heard of that."

"Neither have we," Lucas admits. "We're hoping it works

out." Seeing the surprise still etched on her face, he adds, "Unfortunately, I was ambushed before we could fully set it in motion. I just got back here yesterday."

"Do you know who ambushed you?" Ivy asks softly, her voice laced with genuine concern.

Lucas's gaze hardens as the question cuts through the quiet. He doesn't hesitate, his voice sharp and venomous. "I know exactly who. Ethan and his packmates. The rest of them are dead—thanks to my mate and the Red Rocks." His jaw tightens, his hands curling into fists under the water. "But Ethan got away. He ran like the coward he is."

Ivy freezes, her knuckles white as she grips the edge of the pool. The energy around her shifts, subtle but palpable, her unease feeding into the tension already burning in Lucas's chest.

"Lucas," Harper warns firmly, her tone cutting through the haze in his mind. "You need to stop."

He turns toward her, his eyes flashing gold, his wolf pressing closer to the surface. "Stop what? Telling the truth?" His voice is low, dangerous, and crackling with suppressed fury. "The bastard's out there somewhere, and we all know he won't stop until—"

"Enough." Harper's voice slices through his words as she jumps into the water, her movements quick and deliberate. She makes her way to him, her fingers digging lightly into his arm. Her glare is sharp, commanding. "You're scaring her."

Lucas's gaze flicks to Ivy. Her wide eyes are filled with fear, and her legs churn the water in quick, nervous kicks. The sight sends a snarl rippling through his wolf—not at her, but at himself. He drags in a breath, the tension in his shoulders easing slightly as he forces his hands to unclench beneath the water.

"I'm not mad at you," he says, his tone softening but still raw. "This has nothing to do with you, Ivy"

She nods slowly, but her body remains rigid, her posture guarded. "I—I didn't mean to bring it up. I'm sorry."

"You don't need to apologize," Harper says, her voice smooth and steady. She shifts closer to Ivy, her warmth countering Lucas's earlier intensity. "He's just... carrying a lot right now."

Lucas catches Harper's brief glance in his direction, a silent reprimand layered with concern. His wolf growls low in his chest, but he lets the sound dissolve into the water, unwilling to escalate the moment further.

Ivy finally exhales, her movements slowing as the tension begins to fade. "I just... I don't want to cause any more trouble. You've already done so much for Henry and me."

"You're not causing trouble," Harper assures her with a small smile. She leans in, her tone turning playful. "And if Lucas ever gets out of line, trust me—I'll handle him."

The faintest laugh escapes Ivy, reluctant but genuine, and Lucas sees the smallest shift in her posture as the tension ebbs. Harper has that effect—bringing calm where he can only seem to ignite chaos.

But even as the conversation shifts and Ivy relaxes, Lucas feels the weight of his wolf's anger simmering just beneath the surface. Ethan's name sears through his thoughts, a constant brand of unfinished business. Harper had saved his body, but was it enough to keep him from slipping fully into the dark? Or was it already too late?

I'LL LAUGH OVER YOUR DEAD BODY

Harper hesitates briefly outside the thick wooden door, her knuckles poised midair. Luna's office isn't just quiet—it's sacred ground, a sanctuary of chaotic genius. The carved crescent moon etched into the center of the door gleams faintly under the soft hallway light. Harper lets out a steadying breath before knocking, her fist making three firm raps against the door.

"Enter," comes Luna's singsong voice, immediately followed by a dramatic sigh. "Unless you're here to complain about my methods, in which case, turn around and save me the headache."

Harper pushes the door open, stepping into a room that buzzes with energy and the faint hum of electronics. The walls are lined with shelves packed with mismatched books and binders, stacks of old computer towers, and tangled cords draped like spiderwebs. Neon lights pulse softly along the edges of three massive screens mounted above two smaller ones, casting a kaleidoscope of colors across the room. The air smells faintly of lavender mixed with something metallic, and a half-empty cup of coffee sits precariously on the edge of the desk.

Luna sits behind a sprawling desk cluttered with keyboards, USB drives, and a rainbow assortment of sticky notes. Her feet are propped up on the corner, one hand scrolling through code on a tablet while the other absently twirls a pen. On top of her head, a messy bun is barely held together once again by two pencils with neon-green dick erasers poking through her white hair, the whole thing looking like it might collapse at any moment.

A soft glow from the screens highlights the amused smirk she wears as she looks up at Harper.

"Harp," Luna greets, her voice light and teasing. "To what do I owe the pleasure? Here to watch me single-handedly save the world with caffeine and sheer brilliance?"

"Not even close," Harper replies, closing the door behind her and leaning against it.

"Good, because I didn't take a nap and world saving requires naps." Luna motions to the chair in front of the desk. "Sit. Spill. Entertain me, darling."

Harper takes the seat, her fingers gripping the edge of the armrest. "I need to know if you've found anything. On Ethan."

Luna's teasing expression falters, replaced by something sharper, more serious. She leans back, clasping her hands together. "Harper, you know I'm looking, but these things take time. I can't just wave a wand and—"

"Luna," Harper interrupts, her voice firm. "I need to know. Now."

For a moment, Luna studies her, the sharpness of her gaze cutting through Harper's determination. Then, with a small sigh, she reaches for the leather journal on the corner of her desk.

"I don't have much," Luna admits, flipping open a notebook and scrolling through her notes. "But something Jase mentioned led me to dig around northern Nevada. There's a motel off Highway 50 near Ely that caught my attention. It's the kind of place that advertises cash payments and rents rooms by the hour. If Ethan's trying to stay off the grid—no credit cards, no paper trail—it fits. That's all I've got. No movement, no additional intel. Just... that, for now."

Harper's heart pounds at the mention of a location, her wolf stirring with restless energy. "And you're sure he'd go there?"

"I'm not sure of anything," Luna replies with a shrug. "But if Ethan's predictable and we already know he's very fucking predictable, it tracks."

Harper's grip tightens on the edge of the desk. "Why didn't you tell me sooner?"

"Because," Luna says, leaning forward, her eyes narrowing with mock seriousness, "you're already running hot, and I didn't want you charging in half-cocked. And because I wanted to confirm it first, which I haven't been able to do yet. Besides..." She smirks, her voice taking on a mischievous lilt. "Do you really think *Mr. Shamrock-and-Smirk* left here without me tagging him? Please, Harper, I'm better than that."

Harper blinks, then tilts her head, a knowing smile creeping onto her lips. "Mr. Shamrock-and-Smirk aka Jase.?"

"What?" Luna shrugs, her expression innocent but her cheeks giving just the faintest flush. "It fits. He's got that whole cocky, 'I know everything, and you'll never guess how I do it' vibe. Don't tell me you've never noticed."

"I've noticed," Harper replies, her tone teasing. "But I didn't think *you'd* notice."

Luna rolls her eyes, her bun bobbing with the motion. "Oh, please. Just because I call it like I see it, doesn't mean I'm planning to hand him my heart-shaped keychain or something."

"Uh-huh." Harper smirks, crossing her arms. "So, when are you planning to make him your next project?"

Luna waves a dismissive hand, the flush deepening. "Never. He's too... Jase-y. Besides, I don't have time to fix that much cocky. I'm busy saving the world one hacker move at a time." She gestures grandly at her screens, a flicker of pride replacing the blush.

Harper smirks, shaking her head. "You're impossible." Her gaze flicks to the glowing monitors, her expression shifting as something clicks. "But you're also brilliant. If Jase really wants Ethan, he'll lead us right to him."

Making her way to the door, Harper pauses with her hand on the knob. "Thanks, Luna. Let me know if you get anything new. And, please, don't tell anyone I asked you. Especially Lucas. He needs to stay here and heal."

"How is his 'healing' going?" Luna's air quotes punch through the air like jabs.

Harper hesitates, then offers a tight smile. "He's good. I think he just needs more time. He'll be back to his old self soon." She knows Luna will sense the half-truth through their bond, but she hopes she'll let it slide this time.

Luna arches a brow, her playful tone slipping back in. "Oh, I'm sure he will. But do me a favor, Harper—don't burn down any motels without giving me a heads-up first. I'd hate to miss the fireworks."

A small smile tugs at Harper's lips as she steps out into the hallway. "No promises," she tosses over her shoulder before the door clicks shut behind her.

Making her way to the kitchen, the comforting buzz of

pack life settling around her like a warm blanket. Luna's voice lingers in her head, their earlier conversation still tugging at her thoughts. She's about to head for the fridge when movement in the corner of her eye catches her attention.

Jade stands at the sink, her back to the room, rinsing out a glass. Her long distressed locs pulled over one shoulder, exposing her back—and the bruises blooming across her umber-colored skin. Deep purples and greens smear across her shoulders, angry marks that scream of hits taken harder than any training session would allow.

Harper freezes, her stomach tightening. Her wolf bristles, growling softly, but it's not anger—it's protectiveness, a primal need to shield her packmate from whatever—or whoever—did this.

"What the hell happened to your back?" Harper blurts, louder than she intended.

Jade stiffens, the glass slipping slightly in her grip before she sets it down with a deliberate clink. She doesn't turn around. "It's nothing."

"Bullshit." Harper steps closer, her voice sharp. "That doesn't look like 'nothing,' Jade. Are you going to tell me what's going on, or do I have to drag it out of you?"

Jade turns slowly, her eyes guarded, the same steel Harper recognizes from every time Jade's trying to keep the world at arm's length. "Drop it, Harper."

"Not a chance," Harper snaps, crossing her arms. "Those bruises didn't come from sparring, Jade. Don't insult me. If they did, they'd be gone by now. Shifter healing, remember? Unless you've taken up a hobby that involves throwing yourself into steel pipes or wrestling with concrete walls, I'm guessing you've been up to something you don't want to admit."

Jade's silence is answer enough.

Harper takes a deep breath, forcing herself to steady her voice. "Are you fighting again? That's where this is coming from, right?"

Jade's jaw tightens, but she doesn't deny it. "What if I am?"

"What if you are?" Harper echoes. Her wolf growls, restless with frustration. "Jade, are you out of your damn mind? Do you have any idea what this could do to you? To us?"

Jade shrugs, her muscles flexing with the motion, but there's something in her eyes—something Harper doesn't like. It's the same look she's seen before, back when Jade swore she was done with this. "It's just a couple of fights. Nothing to get worked up about."

Harper's wolf snaps at that, her own frustration bubbling over. "Nothing to get worked up about? Jade, this is illegal! Do you want to end up in a cell—or worse? If the human cops don't catch you, Jase will. And what then? You think he's going to turn a blind eye because you're one of us?"

Jade leans back against the counter, her posture deceptively casual, but Harper knows better. "Relax," she says, her voice dripping with forced calm. "Nobody's caught me. Nobody's going to."

Why now? Harper's stomach twists. "Let me guess," she says, her tone sharp enough to cut. "You found a fight last night, after Ryder left?"

Jade's expression falters, guilt flickering across her face before she quickly shutters it. She doesn't answer, but her silence is louder than words.

"Unbelievable," Harper runs a hand through her hair. "You've been through this, Jade. You did the work to get past it. Why would you throw that away?"

Jade's gaze hardens, her walls snapping up like a steel fortress. "I'm not throwing anything away. I'm doing this because I want to."

"That's not an answer," Harper says, her voice softer now but no less firm. "You're risking everything—your safety, the pack—for what? To prove something to Ryder? To yourself?"

Jade's shoulders tense, and for a moment, Harper thinks she might open up. But instead, Jade pushes off the counter, her voice colder than Harper's ever heard it. "You don't get it. You don't know what it's like."

"Then tell me," Harper urges, stepping closer, her voice softer now but tinged with desperation. Her frustration has melted into raw concern, and her wolf paces with unease, its instincts screaming to fix this, to protect. "Help me understand, Jade, because all I see right now is you going back to a dark place. A place you fought so hard to climb out of. And I know that's not who you are."

Jade's jaw works, her muscles visibly tightening, but she doesn't speak. The silence between them feels like a chasm, growing wider with each second. She turns back to the sink, gripping its edge like it's the only thing holding her together. "What? You disappointed in me?" Her voice is low, almost a whisper, but the crack in it makes Harper's chest ache.

"I'm not disappointed in you," Harper says, her voice steady but heavy with emotion. "I'm worried about you. There's a difference."

Jade stays still, her back to Harper, her shoulders stiff as if bracing for a blow. The weight of her words presses down on them both, the room thick with unspoken pain. Harper waits, hoping for anything—a reaction, an explanation— but Jade doesn't move.

"Jade, you know I have to tell Alpha," Harper says, the

words tasting bitter on her tongue. "This brings danger to our pack. And with everything else going on around us right now, this adds another layer of concern we don't need."

Jade's fingers curl tighter around the edge of the sink. Her voice—when it comes—is low and cold, carrying the weight of something Harper can't quite touch. "Do what you have to, Harper, and I'll do what I have to."

The words land like a blow, sharp and unforgiving, and Harper feels the air rush out of her lungs. Her wolf growls faintly, a mix of frustration and pain, but even she seems to recognize that pushing Jade right now will only make things worse. Harper's muscles ache as she exhales, the lingering tension in her body refusing to fade—a reminder that her own healing isn't what it should be.

Her bruises from the last fight still sting, faint discolorations clinging to her skin longer than they should. Normally, they'd be gone by now, but the weight of everything—the broken bonds, the constant stress—has taken its toll. She wonders, briefly, if Jade feels the same. If the bruises on her back ache just as much inside as out.

"Okay," Harper says softly, her voice threading through the quiet. "I love you, sister."

The words hang in the air, unanswered. Jade doesn't move, doesn't turn. She just stands there, her grip on the sink unyielding, as though holding on is the only thing keeping her upright.

As Harper turns to leave, the weight of it clings to her, heavy and unrelenting, sitting in her chest like a stone she can't dislodge. Her steps falter at the doorway, and she glances back, hoping for some sign that Jade is still there, still reachable.

But all she sees is a figure carved from steel, standing alone in the kitchen. Jade bows her head as she slowly pushes her thick locs over her shoulder, hiding the bruises, hiding her secret. The motion is small but deliberate, and it speaks louder than any words ever could.

Harper swallows hard, the ache in her chest spreading through her like a slow burn. She knows the pain of carrying too much, of holding it all inside, and now it's written all over Jade. The bruises, the tension, the defiance —it's all there, a mirror to Harper's own struggles.

For the first time, she feels the distance Jade is putting between them—a gulf that wasn't there before but now feels impossibly wide. And the worst part? Harper isn't sure how to cross it.

LUCAS LEANS against the doorway to their room, arms crossed, staring into the hallway like it holds the answers he needs. Harper's been too quiet since dinner—her version of quiet, anyway. It grates on him, gnawing at the edges of his already frayed control.

His wolf stirs, restless and pacing within, a low growl echoing at the back of his mind. Ethan's name beats like a war drum in his chest, a constant reminder of unfinished vengeance. Dragging a hand over his face, his palm scrapes against the rough stubble on his jaw. Harper's planning; he knows it. She's just as hellbent on tracking Ethan as he is, and it pisses him off that she hasn't told him a damn thing.

"Fine," pushing off the doorframe. "If she won't tell me, I'll find out myself."

The house is quiet, as he makes his way to Luna's office. Neon colors from her monitors spill into the hallway, cutting through the dim light like a beacon. He knocks once, not waiting for an invitation before stepping inside.

Luna doesn't look up, her fingers flying over the keyboard with sharp, deliberate keystrokes. One of her screens flickers as Lucas steps in, and she quickly clicks a window closed.

"Harper, if you're here to pester me about Ethan again, I swear—"

"Not Harper," Lucas cuts in, his voice low and gravelly.

Her head snaps up, sharp eyes narrowing. "Lucas. Of course. If you thought you just heard my eye roll, it's because you did."

He doesn't rise to the bait, his gaze flicking to the monitors lining her desk. "What are you working on, Luna?"

"Nothing you need to worry about," she says briskly, swiveling in her chair to block his view.

Not fast enough. A picture of Jase lingers on one of the open monitors, his face unmistakable amid a string of scrolling data. Lucas's wolf bristles, suspicion threading through him. "What's this?"

Luna leans back, arms crossing as her expression cools. "It's exactly what it looks like—a file on Jase. Someone has to keep an eye on him."

Lucas's jaw tightens, his wolf pressing at the edges of his control. "You're digging into him behind Charlotte's back?"

"Not everything's about Charlotte," Luna snaps, her tone sharp enough to cut. "I have my reasons. Drop it, now."

Stepping further into the room, Lucas folds his arms across his chest. "Fine. What did you tell her?"

"Tell who?" Luna's smirk is casual, almost mocking, as she swivels her chair slightly.

"Don't play games with me, Luna," Lucas growls, his jaw tightening. "What do you know?"

Luna studies him, her bravado flickering before she

exhales, pressing her lips into a thin line. "Northern Nevada. A motel off Highway 50. That's it."

Lucas curses under his breath, fists clenching at his sides. "And you thought it was smart to tell her that? She's already itching to go after him."

"Like you're not?" Luna arches a brow. "At least I'm keeping tabs on her, which is more than I can say for you."

The tension stretches taut, Lucas's wolf pacing within. Luna exhales sharply, leaning back in her chair. "Listen, big guy. I get it—you both want revenge. But charging in without a plan will only get you killed."

His eyes flash gold, his voice a dangerous growl. "Don't lecture me. Just tell me if you've got anything else."

She shrugs, spinning back toward her monitors, the rhythmic click of her keyboard breaking the silence. "Not yet. But I'll let you know—because you're clearly the calm and rational one in this scenario."

Luna pauses, her fingers hovering over the keys. Without looking back, she calls, her voice deceptively light, "And Lucas, if you ever step into my lair again without my permission, I'll release my beasts so fast you won't have to worry about revenge. I'll laugh—ha, ha, ha—over your dead body."

Her words linger like smoke in the air before she adds, almost cheerfully, "Have the day you deserve."

Lucas pauses at the door, his wolf rumbling low in his chest. He stalks out without looking back, unsure if he just got his ass handed to him—or if Luna is simply that good at keeping him on edge.

WAIT. I'M THE ASSHOLE?

The smell of coffee and bacon wafts through the air, but Harper barely registers it. Her eyes feel gritty from a night of tossing and turning, her mind looping the same restless thoughts. She glances at Lucas, seated next to her, his posture rigid and his jaw tight. The tension between them is almost palpable, thick enough to cut with a knife.

She stabs at her scrambled eggs, trying to focus on anything but the silence stretching between them. Around her, the usual hum of breakfast conversation carries on, a sharp contrast to the turbulence swirling inside her.

Ivy steps into the room with Henry, her voice soft but clear. "Morning."

Her gaze flickers around the table. Ryan catches the movement and stands, his grin easy and warm as he gestures toward his chair. "Here, Ivy. Take my seat. I was just about to grab more coffee anyway."

Her cheeks flush, and she dips her head, her voice barely above a whisper. "Thank you."

Henry offers her a reassuring smile as she slips into the

chair, her movements careful and reserved. Ryan tousles Henry's curly blonde hair with a chuckle before grabbing his mug and heading for the coffee pot.

The chatter picks up again, and for a moment, Harper lets the noise fill the empty spaces in her head. Then Luna strides in, her pink mug in hand, and makes a beeline for the coffee pot.

"Rough night, Harper?" Luna asks without looking over, her tone dripping with faux concern.

Harper tenses, her fork freezing mid-air. "Why do you ask?"

"You look like shit," Luna says, her smirk practically audible as she fills her mug. "Figured all that late-night snooping for info might've kept you up past your bedtime. And don't worry—I have nothing new to report this morning."

Lucas sets his mug down with a thud, the sound sharp against the chatter around them. But Harper speaks first, her voice clipped. "You've got such a big heart, Luna. Truly, it's inspiring."

Luna leans casually against the counter, taking a slow sip of her coffee. Her smirk deepens when Lucas finally speaks, his tone edged with irritation. "You have something to say, Luna, or are you just here to stir the pot?"

"Oh, I'm just here to help," Luna quips, pushing off the counter and sauntering toward the table. "You both looked so... lost yesterday. Figured I'd do my part to keep the ship from sinking."

Harper's fork clatters against her plate, her eyes narrowing. "What the hell is that supposed to mean?"

Luna raises her mug in a mock toast. "Nothing. Just that Harper came by first, full of questions and theories. Then you showed up with your own agenda. Neither of you thought to check if the other had already been there. Honestly, it was adorable."

Harper's jaw tightens, her glare snapping to Lucas. "You went to her?"

Lucas's golden eyes narrow as they lock on Luna. "Funny, she didn't mention you were there first."

Kai shifts in his seat, his head swiveling between Harper and Lucas like he's watching a tennis match. "Well, this just got interesting," a grin tugging at the corner of his mouth.

Jaxson elbows him hard, but even he can't hide the flicker of amusement on his face.

"Relax, both of you," Luna says, taking a deliberate sip from her pink mug. "You got what you wanted, didn't you? A breadcrumb here, a breadcrumb there. It's not my fault you didn't communicate." She gives a innocent shrug. "I'm just the messenger."

Lucas pushes his chair back with a sharp scrape, his voice low and dangerous. "Careful, Luna.

"Oh, don't you growl at me. You're both pissed because I'm right," Luna snaps, meeting Lucas's glare head-on. "And for the record, I didn't tell either of you anything you couldn't have figured out yourselves—if you knew how to communicate. Kind of a key ingredient for a true mating, don't you think?"

Ivy flinches at the sound of Lucas's chair falling to the floor, shrinking back in her chair, her wide eyes darting nervously toward Henry.

Kai stands smoothly, positioning himself between Lucas and Luna with an exaggerated grin. "No, no, brother," he says, voice calm but firm. "Don't even think about going after my not-girlfriend."

Ryan is on his feet a second later, his relaxed demeanor gone as he steps forward. "Kai's got a point,

Lucas. Take a breath. No one needs to shift over breakfast."

The room feels like it's teetering on the edge of chaos when Charlotte strides in, her voice slicing through the tension like a whip. "For fuck's sake, can't I leave you all alone for one meal without it turning into a goddamn circus?"

Everyone freezes.

Charlotte surveys the scene with a mix of exasperation and authority. "Sit down. Now." Her glare sweeps from Lucas to Kai to Ryan. "And you," she snaps at Luna, who is grinning behind her mug, "stop poking the... bear before I have to deal with more than bruised egos."

Luna raises her mug in mock surrender. "Yes, Alpha. Anything for you."

Charlotte snatches a piece of bacon off the nearest plate and bites into it as she turns to leave. "Idiots," she grumbles under her breath, walking out of the room.

"Yeah, I'm suddenly not hungry," Lucas says, his stomps echoing through the archway as he leaves.

Harper sits with her head down for a few more seconds, the room uncomfortably silent. Finally, she speaks, her voice quiet but firm. "Luna, you're my sister, and I love you, but you could've handled that differently. Maybe cut us some slack. He's still trying to find himself again, and I'm just... along for the ride."

She leaves her words at the table, pushing back her chair to follow Lucas. As she steps into the hallway, Luna's tiny voice reaches her ears. "Dammit. I didn't want to be the asshole."

SHOULD I STAY OR SHOULD WE GO?

"Lucas, wait." Harper's voice cuts through the echo of his heavy steps as she hurries to catch up.

He doesn't slow down, his shoulders rigid with anger. "What, Harper? Want to rub it in some more?"

"What the hell is that supposed to mean?" she snaps, her frustration boiling over as she grabs his arm, forcing him to turn and face her.

His golden eyes blaze with fury. "You were planning to go after him. Alone. Weren't you?"

Harper's mouth opens, but no words come out. She straightens, her jaw tightening. "And what if I was? You're not exactly innocent here, Lucas. You had the same damn idea."

He takes a step closer, his voice a dangerous growl. "I didn't plan to leave you out of it because I think you're weak, Harper. I planned to leave you out of it because I need this kill."

Her wolf bristles, and Harper doesn't back down. "And you think I don't? You think I don't deserve to take him down after what he's done to my pack, to me? You're not the only one carrying scars."

His fists clench at his sides, his wolf pacing just beneath the surface. "This isn't about scars. It's about justice."

"Bullshit," she fires back. "It's about revenge, and you're acting like you're the only one who has a right to it."

They stare each other down, the tension crackling between them like a live wire. Harper's wolf howls, pushing her toward action, but she reins it in, her breathing shallow.

"You're reckless," Lucas says finally, his voice low but cutting. "You'd charge in blind and get yourself killed."

"And you wouldn't?" Harper counters, stepping closer until they're practically nose to nose. "Don't act like you've got some grand plan, Lucas. You're just as reckless as me."

His lips curl into a snarl, but he doesn't deny it. "At least I'd stand a better chance on my own than dragging you along."

She lets out a bitter laugh, the sound cutting through the tension. "Don't forget who got you out of that mine, Lucas. I'm the reason you're standing here to even have this argument. You're not leaving without me."

"Funny, because the same goes for you," he snaps, though she catches the faint flicker of hesitation in his eyes. Her words had chipped away at his resolve, just enough to notice.

They stand there, neither willing to back down, until Harper finally breaks the silence, her voice icy. "Fine. We're both too stubborn to stay out of this. But don't think for a second I'm letting you take him from me."

Lucas exhales sharply, his gaze still blazing. "And don't think I'll let you do the same."

Without another word, he turns and stalks off, his boots echoing against the hardwood floor.

Harper watches him go, frustration simmering just below the surface. "I have to go to work," she calls down the hallway after him. "I'll see you later."

"Yeah. See you later," comes his clipped reply, disappearing around the corner.

Her wolf paces restlessly within her, claws scraping at her resolve. The tension thrums through her like a live wire, and she knows this isn't over—not even close.

A COUPLE OF HOURS LATER, Harper tosses a dirty towel into the red rag bin, the lid clanging as it closes. "Great job, everyone," she calls out, her voice cutting through the post-lunch bustle of the kitchen. "That was a busy service, but we handled it like pros."

The maitre d's voice sounds behind her. "Chef, someone's here to see you."

"A guest?" Harper's hands are already unbuttoning her chef's coat, her fingers moving automatically as she grabs the clean one she always wears for front-of-house interactions.

"No, he didn't eat here. He just walked in." Harper notices the faint blush, coloring the young human's cheeks. "Do you know any ugly people, Chef? Because this guy is gorgeous."

Harper snorts, a laugh escaping before she can stop it. "Yes, I definitely know some very ugly people."

Her amusement fades as she steps into the opulent dining room. Crushed deep purple velvet booths line the walls, and crystal chandeliers cast a warm glow. Jase is seated in one of the high-top booths, his long frame stretched out with infuriating ease. His fingers drum idly against the menu in front of him, his trademark charming smile firmly in place.

"Hey, Harper," he greets, in his tone casual, as if his presence there was completely natural.

"What are you doing here, Jase?" Harper crosses her arms, caught off guard by the unexpected visit.

"What's good here?" he asks, ignoring her question as his eyes skim the menu.

She scoffs, her tone sharp. "I'm sure Vanessa already told you we're closed. Lunch is over. So, I'll ask again—what are you doing here?"

He looks up, finally setting the menu down with deliberate care. "Would you believe me if I said I was in the area and thought I'd stop by to check in? We never get much one-on-one time."

Harper raises a brow, unimpressed. "No, I wouldn't. Try again."

He chuckles softly, leaning forward. "Fair enough. Honestly, I wanted to ask you something—about Ethan."

Her stomach twists at the mention of the name, her wolf stirring uneasily. "What about him?"

"Your last interaction with him," Jase says, his tone still light, though his gaze sharpens. "Did you see anything unusual? Anything that might explain his next move?"

"Define 'unusual,'" Harper replies, keeping her voice even.

"Like powder," he says, lowering his voice slightly, the word laced with significance. "Did you see any of it? Did Ethan mention working with someone else?"

Harper hesitates, her wolf pacing in the back of her mind. "Why are you asking?"

Jase leans back, his fingers resuming their drumming.

"Just trying to piece things together. Ethan doesn't operate alone. He never has. If someone's pulling his strings, I'd like to know who."

Her gaze hardens, though concern flickers beneath her calm surface. "With Miles in prison, who else could be pulling his strings? As far as we know, he's still the Beta of the Cascade pack." She shifts on her feet, debating whether to reveal what Ethan told her in the mine. "He looked terrible. It seems like the Cascade pack bond is tearing them apart. The enforcers were definitely weakened."

Jase's fingers stop, his eyes narrowing slightly. "Anything else I should know about?"

"No," Harper says, her tone turning firmer.

He studies her for a moment longer, then offers a faint smile, standing and smoothing out his jacket. "Well, it was worth a try. Thanks for indulging me, Harper."

Before she can respond, he adds casually, "By the way, your new pack members. How are they adjusting?"

"What's it to you?"

"Nothing, really," Jase replies, his tone light. "Just curious. A female and a kid—that's not exactly your usual addition."

"They're fine," Harper says, her voice clipped.

"Good to know," he replies, his gaze lingering a moment longer. "How old is the kid? Pretty young, right?"

Harper straightens, crossing her arms tighter. "He's fine," she repeats.

"And the mom?" Jase presses, his tone still infuriatingly casual. "She seems... well, scared. Is she okay?"

Harper's patience thins, her wolf bristling at the veiled question. "What are you really asking, Jase?"

He shrugs, offering an easy smile as he scoots out from

behind the booth. "Just making sure everything's as it should be." His voice remains light, but his words carry a weight that lingers. "Sometimes, the smallest cracks are the ones that bring the whole thing down. And I'd hate to see that happen to the Red Rocks."

Harper's eyes narrow, suspicion flashing in her gaze. "What the hell's that supposed to mean?"

Jase pauses, glancing over his shoulder with that same calm smile. "Only that a pack as strong as yours shouldn't let small things fester. It's just an observation, Harper."

Her jaw tightens. "You don't get to waltz in here and act like you're doing us a favor. If you're trying to say something, spit it out."

He raises his hands in mock surrender, "No hidden message, I promise. Just looking out for the pack—same as you."

As he walks away, his footsteps echoing in the lavish dining room, Harper's mind churns. The timing of his questions, the deliberate way he phrased them—none of it sits right. Her wolf stirs uneasily, echoing her doubts. Whatever Jase was after, she couldn't shake the feeling that it wasn't purely for the greater good.

LATER THAT AFTERNOON, the tension between Harper and Lucas remains thick, like an unspoken inferno hovering between them. Harper slams the trunk of her car shut, the packed duffle bag inside mocking her with its finality. She doesn't know where this adventure will take them, but one thing is clear—once Ethan is gone, maybe she and Lucas can begin piecing their life back together. That is, if her Lucas is still in there somewhere.

"One. Do. Tree!"

Harper looks up, spotting Henry standing in the corner of the hallway leading to the open garage door.

"Henry? What are you doing all the way out here?" she asks, keeping her tone light. She knows Ivy had set strict boundaries for him to stay near the game room—hell, even Harper has gotten lost in this house a few times.

"Hi, Hoppa," Henry chirps, his little face lighting up. "Mommy said I can go anywhere as long as Una knows where I am. Una said I have to be the finder!"

"Okay," Harper says, crouching to his level with a soft smile. "How about I help you find Una?" She holds out her hand, and Henry eagerly grabs it.

"Yeah! You help me!"

Hand in hand, they make their way past the kitchen, where Isabell's voice carries over the rhythmic clatter of knives and pans.

"Una! I going to find you!" Henry's excited voice echoes off the foyer's stark white walls. Harper's pack bond instinctively pulls her toward Luna, even if they're still on uneven ground after the morning's spat.

"I think we should look in here, Henry." Harper gestures toward the game room, where Luna's silhouette is faintly visible behind the ceiling-to-floor curtain.

Henry dives into his search with gusto, peeking under the couch, behind the fireplace, and even lifting a corner of the pool table cover. Harper's amusement fades as she notices his tiny nose tipping into the air. His sense of smell shouldn't be that sharp yet. Shifter senses don't usually develop until puberty—just like their first shift. But Henry is breaking all the rules.

"Ha!" Henry exclaims, yanking back the curtain to reveal Luna standing with her hands in the air in surrender.

"You got me, kiddo," Luna says with a chuckle, her voice softer than Harper expects.

"Henry." Ivy's voice draws their attention as she steps into the room. "Time to relax before dinner."

Henry's little shoulders slump, but he obediently pads back toward his mother. She gives Harper a quiet nod before leading him away, leaving her and Luna alone.

"Well, fuck," Luna sinks onto the oversized sectional with a heavy sigh. "I'm sorry, sister. My attitude got the better of me this morning." She tucks herself into the corner of the couch, her usual sharpness dulled with regret.

"I know, Luna. Really, it's not your fault," Harper says as she sits down a few cushions away. "Lucas and I... we should be talking, but..." She trails off, her throat tightening. "He's not healed yet."

Luna leans forward, her elbows resting on her knees. "He'll heal, Harper. It just takes time. You brought him back from hell, and that's not something either of you can just bounce back from. Do you want me to dig deeper into the Bond of Light? If there's anything in the archives about its healing power, I'll find it."

"Yes, please," Harper says, her voice quieter now. "Our bond is there, but it feels... off. Hollow, almost. I can't explain it." She shifts uncomfortably. "I know he feels it too, but he thinks it'll be fixed once he kills Ethan." Her voice drops, her fingers twisting together. "But I already know that won't fix anything. It'll only solidify the darkness in him. That kill—it'll leave a mark, Luna. A dark, permanent mark on his heart. I just... I know it."

Luna's brow furrows, concern tingling through their bond. "Okay, sister. I'll see what I can find."

Harper hesitates, her hands tightening into fists as her

voice drops to a near whisper. "There's something else. Something I haven't told anyone. Not even Lucas."

Luna straightens, her expression sharpening. "What is it?"

"When I had Ethan in the mine," Harper begins, her voice trembling slightly, "he told me... Miles is his mate."

The words hang heavy in the air, suffocating the small space between them. Luna's eyes widen, shock flickering into disbelief. "What the actual fuck?"

"Yeah," Harper says, forcing out a humorless laugh. "I couldn't believe it either. It explains so much about his obsession with Miles and his hatred for me. But Lucas doesn't know. I don't think he can handle it—not yet."

Luna exhales slowly, processing. "That's... a twist I didn't see coming, but it makes sense."

Harper gives her a faint smile. "Knowing this, I'm a bit afraid this kill will leave a dark mark on my heart too."

"You've killed before, Harper. What's different about this?"

Harper exhales, her voice barely above a whisper. "Ethan's a monster, Luna. He's hurt so many people—my pack, Lucas, me. But now that I know about Miles... I can't stop thinking about what that bond must've done to him."

Luna leans back, her voice steady. "Sympathy doesn't make you weak, Harper. It makes you human—or wolf, I guess. But if you let it stop you from doing what's right, it'll eat you alive."

Harper stares at the floor, her voice soft. "That's just it. What if killing him isn't right? What if it just makes everything worse—for me, for Lucas, for everyone?"

Luna reaches out, gripping Harper's hand. "That's why you have the pack, Harper. If it starts to weigh you down, we'll carry it with you. Whatever happens, you're not doing this alone."

Harper squeezes Luna's hand, a faint smile tugging at her lips. "Thanks, Luna. I needed to hear that."

Luna's smirk returns, softer this time. "Don't mention it. Now, let's figure out how to stop you from losing your mind over this."

SECRETS AND DINNER TIME

The scent of roasted chicken and warm bread drifts down the hallway, tugging at Lucas, but the thought of sitting around that table gnaws at him more than hunger ever could. He leans against the wall, his arms crossed tightly over his chest, debating whether to disappear into the night or face whatever chaos waits inside.

Laughter ripples through the house, warm and carefree, followed by Kai's booming voice. "Spin it, or lose it!"

Lucas exhales a long breath, his shoulders sagging. Avoidance doesn't fix anything. With deliberate steps, he pushes off the wall and enters the dining room.

The scene inside is as chaotic as he expected. The lazy Susan at the center of the massive round table spins like it's the sun in its own bizarre solar system, dishes and bowls orbiting in wild circles.

Harper's laugh rings out above the hum of conversation, clear and unguarded. She sits with her head tipped back, her shoulders loose, her whole being glowing with a warmth that makes Lucas's chest tighten.

His stomach knots as he slides into an empty chair, his

gaze brushing hers for a fleeting second before darting away. The aftermath of their argument coils between them, an unspoken hurricane waiting to strike again.

Kai tosses a roll high into the air, catching it with dramatic flair. "And the crowd goes wild!"

"Wild with irritation, maybe," Luna quips, snatching a salad bowl from the spinning lazy Susan before it gets away. "Seriously, Kai, do you ever turn it off?"

Lucas barely registers the banter. The noise blurs into a swirl of energy he doesn't want to step into. His wolf stirs uneasily beneath his skin, its restlessness prickling like static along his spine.

The front door creaks open, breaking the rhythm of the room. Heavy boots thud across the marble floor, each step deliberate, slow, and full of intent. Silence ripples outward like a shockwave, conversation screeching to a halt as all eyes turn toward the doorway.

Charlotte's sharp tone slices through the air. "Who the hell let him in?"

Jase steps into view, his broad frame filling the space with an air of practiced arrogance. His gaze sweeps over the table, brushing over Luna before landing on Charlotte with a smirk that sets Lucas's teeth on edge.

"I did." Maddy ducks under Jase's arm, her expression completely unbothered. "He was out there lurking like some douchebag, just staring at everything."

Jade cackles, spraying a few drops of beer across the table.

Before Charlotte can respond, Isabell strides out of the kitchen, brandishing a towel like a weapon. "Muchos pueden comer aquí," she snaps, her tone dry as she rolls her eyes. She points a floured finger at Jase. "Siéntate. Ahora. No me hagas repetirlo."

Jase arches a brow, but he doesn't argue. He slides into an empty chair at the far end of the table, unhurried and entirely too comfortable. For a beat, no one speaks, the lazy Susan grinding to a halt under the weight of tension.

Lucas feels it first—a faint ripple in the bond enough to pull his focus to Harper. Her shoulders stiffen, her earlier laughter evaporating into a guarded stillness.

Harper doesn't look at Jase, but her silence feels deliberate, protective, as if she's bracing for something she can't name.

Kai's jaw flexes, his eyes locked on Jase with the intensity of a predator sizing up a rival. "Nice of you to grace us with your presence," he says, his voice deceptively light.

Jase shrugs, snagging a roll, "Just thought I'd check in. See how everyone's holding up."

Charlotte doesn't miss a beat, her irritation sharp and clear. "No, Jase. You never just 'check in.' You always want something or have a mess to dump on us."

"Is that what we're calling it now?" Kai's grin is razor-sharp, his words dripping with challenge as his gaze locks on Jase.

Before the tension spirals further, Luna cuts in with her signature flair. "Damn, Jase. I knew you were a pain in the ass, but this? You walk in, and suddenly it's a live-action soap opera. I could cut the tension with this spoon—it's so jelloey in here."

Jase, unfazed. "I wasn't planning to stay. Isabell yelled at me. She's terrifying."

Luna snorts, twirling her fork like a baton. "Yeah, she terrifies us too. That rolling pin of hers is nightmare fuel."

Kai shifts in his seat, his body still taut, but the sharpness in his expression dulls slightly. "Maybe she's onto something," he mutters.

Luna doesn't miss a beat. "Relax, Captain Brood. Your title's safe. No one's gunning for your throne tonight."

A ripple of laughter breaks the tension, soft and uncertain but enough to lift the room's weight. Harper's lips twitch, the ghost of a smile she quickly hides behind her glass.

Lucas leans back in his chair, his focus never straying from Jase. The lazy Susan spins again, the room settling into a fragile rhythm, but Lucas can't shake the simmering heat of the moment. Jase doesn't just enter a room—he upends it. And Harper knows this havoc is far from over.

"Spill it, Jase. Why are you really here?" Charlotte's voice cuts through the low hum of conversation, sharp and direct. She points her fork at him, her tone leaving no room for games.

"Easy, Charlotte. I'm not here to ruin your dinner." He glances at the table.

"Jase," Charlotte warns, her patience thin.

He leans forward, setting his beer down with a soft clink. The humor in his eyes dims, replaced by something more serious. "I've been able to confirm that the Cascade Pack is regaining its footing. Their bond isn't broken anymore—it's mending."

"How is the possible?" Harper asks

Jade's voice is matter of fact. "Ethan's back."

Jase nods, his expression softening. "Yeah. It all lines up. He's back with his pack. They must be accepting him as their Alpha. It's the only way a pack bond can fill the cracks."

Harper's heart sinks. She glances at Lucas, whose jaw tightens as his gaze remains locked on Jase. The darkness in his eyes feels almost palpable, like a shadow stretching across the table.

"Shit," Harper had hoped to take Ethan alone, to make him pay without involving anyone else. But now? If Ethan is back with his pack, there'd be children. Mothers. The thought twists her stomach.

Charlotte exhales slowly, placing her fork down with deliberate care. Her Alpha power rises like a quiet storm, commanding attention. "You two aren't going anywhere near the Cascade Pack. Do you hear me?" Her gaze flicks between Harper and Lucas, hard and unyielding.

"Charlotte—" Harper starts, but Charlotte cuts her off.

"No. This isn't a negotiation. That pack has been through enough."

Lucas finally speaks, his voice low and steady, but laced with danger. "He's a threat. We can't just ignore that."

"And we won't," Charlotte replies, her tone clipped. "But we handle this on our terms, not his. If he's hiding behind his pack, then he's using them as a shield. I won't give him the fight he's trying to provoke."

Jase leans back, his gaze flicking between them. "She's right, you know." His usual bravado softens, his tone measured. "I get it. Believe me, I do. But walking into another pack's territory to drag Ethan out? That's not just reckless. With their bond strengthening, they're more dangerous than ever. And if you rip that bond apart again, you could kill the entire pack."

Harper leans forward, her frustration bubbling to the surface. "So what? We just sit here and wait for him to come for us? Because trust me, Jase, he *will* come for us."

"No," Jase says firmly. "You prepare. You outthink him. Maybe he takes his seat as Alpha and decides to leave you alone."

Harper shakes her head, her jaw tightening. "He won't."

She takes a deep breath, glancing around the table. "There's something I haven't told you."

"What are you talking about, Harp?" Jade asks, leaning in, her curiosity piqued.

All eyes shift to Harper, the weight of their attention pressing on her.

"When we were in the mine," Harper begins, her voice quieter now, "Ethan lost control." She swallows hard, then forces the words out. "I asked him why. I needed to know why he follows Miles so blindly. He told me..." She hesitates, the memory flashing in her mind. "He told me Miles is his mate."

The silence is thunderous.

"Well, shit on a cracker if that doesn't make all the sense in the world," Luna breaks the tension with her usual irreverence.

Charlotte's eyebrows lift, her expression caught somewhere between surprise and understanding. "I didn't see that coming either, but I agree with Luna. It explains a lot."

Lucas scoffs, his fingers gripping the edge of the table. "Doesn't matter. He won't stop until someone stops him."

Charlotte exhales slowly, her tone calm but firm. "Then we'll be ready if he comes back to Red Rock territory," she says, her gaze steady. She locks eyes with Lucas, her authority radiating through the room. "But you will *not* go after him, Lucas. That's an order."

The silence that follows is suffocating. Harper glances at Lucas, her chest tightening. She can feel the fury rolling off him, thick and suffocating, matching the frustration simmering in her own blood.

Jase clears his throat, cutting through the tension. "Look, I get it. You're pissed. I didn't come here to stir the pot—I came to help. I care about this pack, believe it or not." He flashes a grin, his cocky charm sliding back into place. "Even if you all make it damn near impossible sometimes."

Harper exhales, leaning back in her chair. "Fine. But if Ethan so much as looks in our direction—"

Charlotte's phone buzzes sharply, cutting her off mid-sentence. She holds up a finger, her tone brisk.

"Go."

A brief pause, then she nods. "Yeah, I'll be there in a few minutes." Rising from her chair, she addresses the room, picking up where she left off. "Then we'll deal with it, *together.*"

After dinner, Jase says his goodbyes—for now—but Lucas doesn't linger inside. The weight in his chest feels heavier tonight. He makes his way toward the back patio, pausing when he spots Harper sitting in the shadows by the hot tub. The light rippling across the water casting soft, dancing patterns on her skin. She's still, her posture rigid, as if the weight she's carrying matches his own.

He doesn't move, just watches her. The way she stares at the water, lost in thought, twists something deep in his chest. She doesn't deserve to feel this burden, this darkness. This is his cross to bear.

She should be the light, and here I am, dragging her into my shadows.

Her phone buzzes, the glow cutting through the dark as she reads the screen. Lucas strains to catch the faint sound of her sigh, the slight slump of her shoulders as she types a reply.

Her voice breaks the quiet before he can say anything. "Lucas," she says without turning, her tone softer than usual, though it carries an edge of exhaustion. "Why are you just standing there?"

"I just needed to watch you for a minute," he admits, his voice low and gravelly, surprising even himself.

He moves closer, closing the distance between them. The night air carries her scent—fresh and grounding—wrapping around him like a lifeline. His presence reaches her first, his warmth pressing against her back before his hands do. Her stillness anchors him, but his wolf urges him to claim, to take what's his before the darkness swallows him whole.

"Stalker," her lips quirking just enough to tug at the corner of his heart.

"Drug addict," he counters, his tone dark. "And you're my drug. I need to feel you right now."

His hand slides down the front of her loose-fitting harem pants, the fabric soft under his fingers. The anticipation thrums in his blood, the tension in his chest momentarily forgotten as his fingers ghost over her folds, teasing, testing. Her breath hitches, and the sound makes something feral stir inside him.

When she leans back into him, her body trembling, he tightens his hold, his free hand steadying her against his chest. He moves deliberately, each touch precise, like this moment is the only thing tethering him to the world.

"I just got a text from Jade," she whispers, her voice catching as his fingers press just enough to make her shudder. "We need to meet in the game room in ten minutes."

"I don't need that much time," he breaths against her ear, his voice dipping lower, thick with need.

His fingers slide into her, and the tightness inside him begins to unravel with every subtle movement. He doesn't rush, savoring the way her body responds, the way her breath hitches and her grip on his arm tightens. Her warmth surrounds him, her trust grounding him in a way nothing else can.

"No sounds, Harper. None." The command is barely a whisper, but it holds all the intensity roaring inside him. Her lips part, but she bites down, silencing herself as her body bows against him.

Her knees buckle, and he wraps his arm around her waist, keeping her upright as his fingers continue their steady rhythm. Her quiet gasps, the tension quivering through her, fuel something primal in him. She's close—he can feel it, the way her body trembles, the way her breath catches.

"Lucas..." Her voice is barely audible, more a plea than a name, and it pulls at the darkness threatening to consume him.

He presses a kiss to her shoulder, his teeth grazing her skin with just enough pressure to send her over the edge. She shatters against him, her body trembling as waves crash through her, her quiet whimper the only sound breaking the stillness of the night.

For a moment, he holds her, their breathing the only noise between them. The world tilts back into focus, and with it, the ever-present weight of reality, but for this brief moment, the darkness inside him feels just a little quieter.

Finally, he chuckles, low and satisfied. "Still plenty of time to make it to the game room."

Her laugh is shaky, but it warms him. She turns to meet his gaze, her cheeks flushed, her eyes soft but bright with exasperation. "You're impossible."

"And you love it," he says, his voice quieter now, but the darkness lingers beneath it. He knows it. He feels it. And he can't shake the fear that she might one day feel it too.

A few minutes later, when Harper and Lucas step into the game room, the buzz of casual activity fills the space, masking the tension simmering beneath the surface. This big, sprawling house feels too small sometimes, but right now, it's holding up. Everyone has found their routines while waiting for Charlotte.

Luna sits cross-legged on the floor, her focus locked on another ridiculous paint-by-numbers masterpiece. Kai is perched behind her on the couch, grinning as he plucks colors from the palette like he's orchestrating chaos. "Go with this purple. It screams 'dignified dick.'"

"Perfect," Luna replies without missing a beat, her brush tapping against the canvas with the precision of someone who's found her rhythm in the absurd.

Lucas's gaze flicks to Harper, catching the faint smirk playing on her lips as she glances toward the infamous "dickshroom" painting in the foyer. It's a masterpiece of torment for Charlotte, and he doesn't doubt Luna's new creation will end up right next to it. Harper would usually laugh out loud at the thought, but not tonight. The heaviness of the day still clings to her, and to him.

His wolf shifts restlessly beneath his skin, the ever-present itch of anger threatening to claw its way out. Not here. Not now. He shoves the thought down, his jaw tightening as he scans the room.

"Listen up." Charlotte's voice slices through the low hum of activity, sharp and commanding. She strides into the room, making her way to her usual spot in front of the floor-to-ceiling windows. The glittering Las Vegas skyline stretches behind her, casting her in sharp relief, a silhouette of authority against the vibrant city lights.

Lucas's gaze lingers on the view, the city glowing like a beacon in the darkness. It's a stark contrast to the shadows that have taken root inside him, the kind that Vegas's neon glow could never reach. He hasn't had the chance to claim this city as his territory officially, but something about it pulls at him—a strange, quiet weight that settles whenever he looks out at it. For a fleeting moment, the chaos in his mind stills, but it never lasts.

Harper straightens beside him. She's always ready, eager for whatever Charlotte is about to say. He envies that part of her—the ability to find purpose in the fight. For him, it's not purpose anymore. It's just... rage.

"Ignore that order I gave at dinner," Charlotte begins, her tone measured but firm. "That was for Jase's benefit."

Lucas's head snaps up, her words cutting through his fog. "You're serious?"

"Williams, calm down," Charlotte says, giving him a pointed look. "I don't need you going all wolfie on me."

He bites back the growl rising in his throat, forcing himself to unclench his fists. The darkness inside him stirs, a low rumble that mirrors the tension in his body. It's always there now, just beneath the surface, waiting for an excuse to take over.

"What are you thinking, Alpha?" Harper asks, her excitement barely contained.

Charlotte stops pacing, her gaze sweeping over the room. "Luna, dig up everything you can about Ethan going home. I want to know if his pack is really healing from his return or if Jase is blowing smoke up our asses."

Luna doesn't even look up. She shoves her paint aside, her laptop appearing in her lap like magic. Her fingers fly across the keyboard, her focus unshakable.

"You don't believe Jase?" Liam asks, his voice steady as he stands in his usual sentinel stance, always ready to shield Charlotte from threats that don't exist.

Charlotte shakes her head. "I don't trust anyone outside this room. Jase may mean well, but he's not pack. If we're going after Ethan, I need to know exactly what we're walking into."

Lucas's fists tighten again, the barely suppressed anger roaring back to life. *We shouldn't even be talking about this. I should already be out there, hunting him.*

"And if it's true?" Harper's voice falters, a rare hesitation creeping into her words. "If his pack is stronger because of him?"

Charlotte's gaze hardens, her tone cutting through the charged air. "Then we do what we must. I'm not spending the rest of my life looking over my shoulder, wondering when he'll strike next."

She steps closer, her presence grounding, though her words carry the weight of finality. Now standing beside Lucas, her voice drops just enough to feel like a personal command. "Besides, no one hurts one of my wolves and gets away. The kill is yours, Williams."

"Alpha!" Harper's voice slices through the moment, sharp with anger.

"Shut up, Harper. This is not up for debate." Charlotte's tone brooks no argument as she saunters back to her pacing spot, cutting off any retort before it can form.

The words hit Lucas like a blow, heavy and undeniable.

He doesn't look at Harper; he doesn't have to. He knows the fury brewing in her, the resistance that matches his own in strength but comes from a place of light. His, though? His is different. It's darker.

Charlotte's declaration echoes in his mind. *The kill is yours.* It's not just about Ethan anymore. It's about the void Ethan left behind, the shadow Lucas has carried since the day he was taken. The light he once had is gone, replaced by something jagged, something heavy. *There's no light to go back to. Just this.*

Charlotte's voice softens as she shifts her focus. "Humboldt's, I need you to stay behind. Protect Maddy, Isabell, Ivy, and the boy. We can't leave them vulnerable."

Ryan doesn't hesitate. "Of course. We'll hold the line." His gaze flicks briefly to Ivy, and something shifts in the air. It's small, fleeting, but Lucas catches it—a quiet moment charged with unspoken meaning.

Ivy, seated by the window, straightens ever so slightly, as if she feels the weight of Ryan's attention. It's subtle but enough for Lucas to file it away. Another puzzle piece in a room full of unfinished edges.

"Thank you," Charlotte says, her voice resolute again.

"Is there a plan for taking Ethan out?" Lucas's voice is low, rough.

Charlotte's gaze locks onto his, unwavering. "There will be. But not tonight. Luna's digging, and we'll gather everything we can before making a move. No one acts until I give the word. Is that clear?"

The room grumbles its agreement, but Lucas doesn't move. The weight of Charlotte's command presses against him, but it's not enough to quell the fire raging in his chest. Ethan doesn't deserve patience. He deserves punishment.

Lucas doesn't give a damn that Ethan was only trying to protect his mate. *So am I.*

The thought twists in his mind, sharper than he expects. Ethan's loyalty to Miles, warped as it is, gnaws at him. *He would destroy anything for his mate, and I'd destroy myself before I let anything happen to Harper.*

The weight of that realization tightens in his chest. Ethan's choices left destruction in their wake, but Lucas feels the darkness clawing at him, threatening to pull him down the same path—and maybe further.

As the group begins to disperse, Lucas feels Harper's eyes on him. She doesn't say anything, but the concern is written all over her face. He doesn't meet her gaze. *If she knew what was really inside me, she wouldn't look at me like that. Not anymore.*

THE UNSHAKABLE CAN BE SHAKEN

S tanding in what was supposed to be his new part-
time den, Lucas feels the weight of the luxury
around him. The sleek lines, the indulgent decor—
it all feels foreign, like it belongs to someone else.

This was supposed to be different, he thinks, his gaze
tracing the neon lights stretching into the horizon. The idea
of living part-time in this city had felt like a promise—freedom, belonging, a life with his mate. But now, it feels like
that dream is slipping through away, crumbling under the
weight of everything that's happened.

Behind him, Harper sits cross-legged on the edge of the
bed, her quiet presence grounding him even as tension radiates from her in waves. She doesn't say anything, but he
knows her too well to think she's at ease. She's waiting—
waiting for him to speak, to give her something, anything, to
break the silence.

Charlotte's words press down on him, relentless. *The kill
is yours.*

The sentence still echoing in his mind. Killing Ethan

wasn't supposed to be complicated. It was supposed to be simple—justice for what he'd done, for what he'd taken. But now? Now there's a pack, shattered and unstable, waiting in the aftermath. If Lucas kills Ethan, he'll inherit it.

Fuck you, Miles. His thoughts spiral, jagged and raw. *I protected you all these years. I tried to help you, tried to make you better. And this? This is what you leave me? Fuck you.*

The bitterness claws at him, but it's Harper who pulls him back. He turns abruptly to face her, needing to be sure his thoughts stayed where they belonged—inside his head.

"Harper," his voice breaking against his will. "What do I do?"

He meant to sound strong, steady, but the words betray him, thick with the weight of doubt and anger that churns like a storm inside him.

"Baby," Harper says softly, her voice steady even as her eyes glisten with worry. "This is an impossible decision."

Lucas drops his gaze, his hand curling into a fist at his side. *Impossible. That's exactly what it feels like.* He swallows hard, the taste of bitterness lingering. "It's not just about Ethan anymore," his voice low. "It's about the pack. About Miles."

She shifts, leaning forward, her elbows resting on her knees as she watches him carefully. "Miles did this," she says, her tone sharper now. "Not you."

Lucas flinches, the words cutting through him like a knife. "I let him do it," he snaps, his anger flaring. "I stood by for years, thinking I could fix him. Thinking I could make him better—make him decent. But I couldn't. I failed, Harper. And now this... this mess... it's mine to clean up."

Her voice softens, but it doesn't lose its edge. "You didn't fail, Lucas. Miles made his own choices. You didn't put that darkness in him. He let it consume him. That's on him, not you."

His chest tightens, the words crashing into the wall of guilt he's built around himself. "You don't get it," he says, his voice rough. "I protected him, Harper. I covered for him. I thought—fuck, I thought if I just kept trying, he'd change. But all he wanted was power. That's all he ever cared about."

"And now?" she asks gently.

Lucas exhales shakily, running a hand through his hair. "Now he's gone, but everything he touched is still rotting. And if I kill Ethan..." He trails off, the weight of the unspoken words settling in the room.

Harper's gaze sharpens, her wolf stirring behind her eyes. "If you kill Ethan, you'll inherit the Cascade Pack."

His jaw tightens, his eyes dark as he meets hers. "Yeah. And what the hell am I supposed to do with that? I don't want it. I don't want any of this."

"You don't have to decide right now," she says softly. "But you need to stop blaming yourself for what Miles did. You tried to help him. That doesn't make you responsible for the mess he left behind."

Lucas turns back to the window, his reflection faint in the glass, distorted by the glow of the city. *She's wrong.* He can't say it aloud, but the thought claws at him. *I was supposed to stop him. I should have stopped him.*

Harper rises, crossing the room to stand behind him. Her hand rests lightly on his shoulder, her touch grounding. "We'll figure this out. Together."

For a moment, the strife inside him stills, but it doesn't last. It never does.

Harper rubs her eyes as she makes her way downstairs, her body heavy with exhaustion. *Coffee. Coffee, help me, please coffee.*

Thank God she knows these stairs by heart because her gaze is glued to her phone. The restless night had taken its toll—every moment filled with tension, half-spoken words, and the weight of Lucas's turmoil pressing down on her. She feels like she's running on fumes.

Her thumb hovers over the screen. The decision had come to her in the early hours, long after she'd given up on sleep and stared at the ceiling in frustration. *Get Spencer involved.*

They all grew up together. If anyone could shed some light on this for Lucas, it was Spencer. Their bond wasn't just history—it was a kind of understanding few could match.

Lucas wouldn't like it. She knows that. But she's not about to sit by and watch him spiral into a darkness she can't pull him out of. Not when there's even a chance Spencer could help.

Spencer. He needs you.

> Ok. Text. Call. In-Person?

Is that your way of gauging?

> Yup.

Ok. Well call then.

> Oh. So it's bad. I'll call in a few minutes.

Hang on. Is a call worse than in person?

> Yeah. Here's the levels. Text is, Hey Bud, how ya doin? In person clearly could wait a couple of days for the travel. And the call is right now.

Well, shit. I can see that logic.

The early morning light filters through the windows, casting long shadows across the compass inlaid in the marble floor. Harper has decided, she has a love-hate relationship with this part of the floor. There are days that the walked over it has brought comfort in knowing she will always find her way home and other days... *shut the fuck up compass.*

Harper slows, her ears picking up the low hum of voices drifting from the kitchen. *Hang on.* Rounding the corner, she stops short, her eyes landing on Ivy and Isabell. Their heads are bent close over the oversized island deep in conversation, their voices too quiet to catch.

Conversing in Spanish, their words flowing between them with an ease Harper didn't expect. Ivy's voice is soft but animated, her hands moving to emphasize her point. Isabell nods, her expression calm and measured, offering a quiet response that sounds like advice—or maybe reassurance.

Harper leans against the doorway, watching for a moment before clearing her throat. "Secret meeting?"

Ivy startles, her cheeks flushing as she glances at Harper. "Oh, no, sorry. We were just—" She falters, her gaze darting to Isabell.

Isabell waves a hand dismissively, a small smile tugging at her lips. "Café?" she asks, gesturing toward the coffee pot on the counter.

"Uh, yeah, sure." Harper steps into the room, pouring herself a cup. The air feels warmer here, cozier, but there's a tension she can't quite name. "Didn't know you spoke Spanish, Ivy."

She shrugs, a faint smile playing on her lips. "It's my first language. I don't use it much anymore, but... with Isabell, it feels natural."

Harper sips her coffee, her gaze flicking to Isabell, who is now chopping vegetables with an effortless precision that catches her attention. The knife moves so fast it's almost a blur, each piece perfectly uniform. Harper blinks. "I'm the chef but you are the magician."

Isabell chuckles softly, her voice low and musical. "Comida es importante," she says simply, her eyes crinkling with amusement as she adds the freshly chopped vegetables to a skillet on the stove.

"Food is important," Ivy translates, though Harper got the gist. There's something about the way Isabell moves, the way she carries herself—it's almost... instinctual. Everything she does seems deliberate, like she's in tune with a rhythm no one else can hear.

"How long have you been a friendly, Isabell?" Harper asks, leaning casually against the counter. She tries to sound nonchalant, but her curiosity simmers beneath the surface.

Isabell's lips quirk into a knowing smile. "Oh, so long, señora. Hard to remember years." Her hands move with practiced ease, chopping vegetables with precision. "Males be down soon. Eat like it's their last meal every time."

Harper chuckles but doesn't let her off the hook. "Did you work with shifter packs in Mexico?"

Isabell's hands pause for the briefest moment before resuming their rhythm. "Oh, sí," she says lightly, her tone smooth. "I lived with jaguars for many years. Always secrets, always someone needs me."

There's a weight to her words, though she delivers them with an almost casual air. Harper narrows her eyes slightly, filing the comment away. "Yeah, well, we certainly need you. I can't even remember a time without you now. You've made our lives better, for sure."

"Stop, Miss Harper. You too kind." Isabell waves her off with a flick of her wrist, but her smile softens, warm and genuine.

Sitting quietly at the table, she watches their exchange with a small smile. "She speaks about all of you with love," Ivy says softly. "Love like family."

"That's because she *is* family." Harper throws an air kiss toward Isabell, her tone light but sincere. "Well, guess I'll leave you two to your breakfast prep. Thanks for the coffee."

As Harper walks out, she glances back over her shoulder. Ivy and Isabell have resumed their conversation, their voices low and fluid, like a stream winding through familiar terrain. Something about the scene tugs at her—not quite unsettling, but impossible to ignore.

Heading into the conversation, Harper had hoped to gain some insight into Ivy, but she's walking away with more questions about Isabell.

Ivy isn't a wolf—that much she knows. But... Isabell? Harper's lips twitch into a small smile as she shakes her head. *That woman is definitely an angel. She was probably kicked down here for being too bossy.*

Harper turns the corner, heading back to her room where her beautiful mate is undoubtedly still sleeping. The promise of the quiet morning and fresh coffee grounds her... until it doesn't. The hot liquid sloshes over the edge of her mug and splashes all down her front as she collides with what feels like a brick wall.

"Jaxson." Her tone is sharper than she intends, but she's already assessing the situation, wiping at the mess.

"Sorry, Harper. I didn't hear you." The usually calm, unflappable Jaxson stands before her, disheveled and breathing heavily. His hair's a mess, his usual neat appearance replaced by something frayed at the edges. This isn't like him.

Harper narrows her eyes. "What's going on, Jaxson? Clearly, you're not okay."

"Bad dream, I guess." His voice is strained, his breathing still labored.

Harper's wolf stirs uneasily, sensing the tension radiating off him. This isn't just a bad dream, not with the way his hands are trembling. Efficiency takes over as she grabs his wrist, steering him down the hallway. If there's one thing she knows, it's that sitting and talking it out is better than letting it stew.

"Come on." She leads him to one of the wingback chairs tucked into one of those pointless alcoves—the kind architects throw in to look fancy but only succeed in wasting space.

She gestures for him to sit, already calculating the fastest way to find a towel for her shirt and figure out what's rattled Jaxson.

He slumps into the chair, his head in his hands. "It felt so real, Harper. Like I couldn't... couldn't stop it."

She softens, the practicality giving way to something more patient. "Couldn't stop what?"

"The explosion. The mansion exploded, and I couldn't get in fast enough to save it. To save Isabell." The defeat in his voice is profound. She's never seen the unshakable shaken.

"It's okay, Jaxson," she says gently, her tone steady, grounding. "The house is here, and I just left Isabell in the kitchen. She's fine. Those dreams suck, but that's all they are —dreams."

Jaxson exhales shakily, his shoulders dropping slightly, but his gaze remains distant, his jaw tight. Harper watches him for a moment, unsure if her words have landed.

"I need to see her," he says finally, rising from the chair with a quiet determination. He turns toward the stairs without waiting for her reply, leaving Harper with the lingering weight of his unease.

The significance of seeing Jaxson rattled isn't lost on her. The stress of Ethan still being out there seems to be affecting them all in different ways. The lingering question of the powder gnaws at her. Is it being used on other shifters? Jase sniffing around for his mole only adds to the mounting pressure. How bad is this going to get?

"Babe?" Harper calls as she steps into their room, her voice faltering when her gaze sweeps over the scene. The bed is empty, the sheets disheveled, hanging more off than on. A pillow lies abandoned on the floor, and a broken glass glints faintly in the moonlight, water pooling around it.

Harper sprints toward the sound of running water, her heart pounding. She skids to a stop in the doorway, her breath catching at the sight before her. Blood. Everywhere. Her once-pristine white tile now streaked with crimson, the stark reality stealing the air from her lungs. "Lucas. Baby, what is going on?"

Her voice shakes, but it barely registers over the roaring in her ears. She lunges toward the shower, her bare feet slipping slightly on the wet floor. "Lucas!"

He's there, sitting under the pounding stream, his naked body curled into himself, the water cascading over his trembling form. His shoulders shake with silent sobs, his face buried in his arms. He's crying. Broken. A shell of the man she once knew—the man Ethan stole from her.

"Baby. It's me. It's Harper. I got you, babe." Her voice is soft, steady, though panic claws at her insides. She reaches for him, her fingers brushing against his slick skin, but he flinches, curling tighter, recoiling like a wounded animal.

"I'm no longer who you fell in love with, Harper," he chokes out, his voice raw, each word scraping against her soul. "I can't be him anymore."

The words pierce through her, but before she can respond, the door slams open behind her. Charlotte and Liam burst in, their eyes darting between the blood-soaked scene and Lucas's trembling form.

Lucas's head snaps up, his entire body going rigid. His growl is deep, guttural, and primal. The sound reverberates through the small space, a warning as his wolf prowls dangerously close to the surface.

"No, Lucas," Harper pleads, shifting to block him from their view. "No. They're leaving. It's just me. Focus on me, baby. Not them."

Her tone is firm but soothing, a lifeline she throws out with everything she has. Charlotte and Liam exchange a brief glance before stepping back, their retreat slow and deliberate. The soft click of the door as it shuts echoes like a relief valve releasing the building tension.

"Thank you, Alpha," she whispers under her breath, her focus snapping back to Lucas.

"Ok, Lucas. It's just us now. Just talk to me." She inches closer, lowering herself to his level, her voice steady but aching with desperation. Her gaze drops to his forearms, to the fresh cuts that crisscross his skin, the crimson evidence of his pain already beginning to heal. The sight tears at her, a silent scream of anguish she swallows for his sake.

The shower water beats down relentlessly, mingling with the blood as it swirls down the drain. Harper presses her palm gently against his cheek, guiding his face toward her. "You're right, Lucas. You're not the same man I fell in love with."

His eyes flicker to hers, a storm of guilt and despair warring in their depths.

"And that's okay," she continues, her tone soft but unyielding. "What you went through, what you survived— of course you're not the same. I'd be more worried if you were."

He blinks, the tension in his shoulders easing ever so slightly. She brushes her fingers lightly through his damp hair, her voice steady but filled with raw emotion. "You don't need to be the man you were. You just need to keep walking toward the man you're meant to become."

Her words linger, delicate yet unyielding, a fragile truth offered with open hands. "Because at your core, you're still you. Still my mate. The darkness can take everything else, Lucas, but it can't have your core. Not while I'm still breathing. I'd rip apart the fabric of the universe if it meant stitching your soul back together."

Lucas's eyes fill with tears, his breath hitching as he leans into her touch. The walls he's built around himself finally begin to crack, letting her in. For the first time in what feels like an eternity, Harper sees it—a flicker of hope, a spark of the light she's always known still burns within him.

PLANS

The sound of laughter and heavy breaths carries through the open patio doors as the Humboldt pack strides into the backyard, the afterglow of their pack run still radiating off them. The afternoon breeze carries a faint warning of winter, the scent of desert sage mingling with the tang of chlorine from the pool. Harper trails behind the four larger-than-life men who have seamlessly become her second pack.

Her blonde hair hangs loose and damp from the run, beads of sweat still clinging to her temple. There's a lightness in her step that she hasn't felt in days. The tension in her chest loosened, by the rhythm of paws pounding against the desert floor. Pack runs always have a way of grounding her, bringing her and her wolf into harmony.

They've seen eye to eye on most things: good food, good fucks, and even better margaritas. The essentials of life, as far as her wolf is concerned. Harper smirks at the thought, brushing back her damp hair as she catches up to the others. These moments—this unity—are a reminder that no matter how chaotic things get, there's strength in the bond they've built.

Ryan slaps Jaxson on the back, a rare grin splitting his face. "You're slowing down, man. Lay off the second helpings."

Jaxson smirks, ruffling his damp curls. "Or maybe you've finally caught up."

Harper snorts, dropping onto one of the cushioned chairs by the oversized sectional. "You two sound like old married wolves."

"Jealous, Harp?" Jaxson shoots back, tossing her a towel.

She catches it mid-air, shaking her head. "Not even a little."

Luna sits criss-cross apple sauce on the sectional, her laptop perched on her knees. The massive TV mounted above the fireplace is already lit up, the image of a grainy security camera feed flickering on the screen. "Oh good, the pack's back. You're just in time for the main event."

Behind her, the soft splashes of the pool provide a subtle backdrop to the tension in the room. Maddy's laughter rings out as she tosses a bright green pool noodle to Henry, who gleefully paddles toward it, his curls sticking to his forehead. Ivy sits on the edge of the pool, her legs submerged, a watchful yet relaxed expression on her face as she keeps a gentle eye on the boy.

Luna glances back briefly, her fingers still flying across the keyboard. "Can we take a moment to appreciate the level of chill out there? It's like they missed the memo that we're about to hunt down the guy who's been a walking shitstorm for us."

"Please tell me you found something useful," Charlotte says as she steps onto the patio, Liam trailing just behind her. Her tone is clipped, all business, and she doesn't bother sitting. Even in the relaxed backyard setting, her Alpha presence cuts through the casual air like a blade.

"Wow, Alpha. Straight to business, huh? No 'Hey Luna, thanks for the hard work?' or 'You're amazing for doing the impossible?'" Luna leans forward, the glow of her screen casting a mischievous shadow across her face. "You could at least acknowledge the child zen happening in the background. Look at that—pure, unbothered bliss."

Charlotte doesn't flinch, her brow arching in silent expectation.

"Fine, fine," Luna huffs, rolling her eyes with theatrical flair as her fingers dance over the keyboard. "Don't all thank me at once." She leans back, shooting the screen an exaggerated glare. "I didn't find much, but I managed to hack into a couple of low-grade security cameras. Turns out the Cascade Pack isn't exactly tech-savvy."

She smirks, her tone dripping with sarcasm. "The best I could scrape together was someone's fancy-ass doorbell feed and a few random home cameras. Really cutting-edge stuff." Her hands gesture dramatically to the screen. "Shoutout to modern technology for giving me the absolute bare minimum. Truly, I feel so appreciated."

The pack gathers around as Luna projects the feed onto the TV. The footage is shaky, catching glimpses of figures walking past a front porch. Ethan's lean, familiar form flickers into view, his movements unmistakable.

"There he is," Harper leans forward, her wolf stirring just beneath her skin.

"And there's the pack," Luna says, pointing to another figure. "Look at them. They're moving like a unit. Strong-ish. Not perfect, but definitely better than broken."

"They're healing," Charlotte says, her tone heavy.

Harper's jaw tightens. "And getting stronger."

Luna taps a few keys, freezing the frame on Ethan. "This camera doesn't catch much—just their comings and goings. But look at him. He's not hiding. He's walking around there like he's untouchable."

"Because he thinks he is," Lucas growls, his voice low and dangerous.

Luna leans back, tossing a handful of popcorn into her mouth as if the tension isn't cutting the air. "I gotta say, the whole vibe of the pack screams, 'We're barely holding it together but trying real hard.' It's almost cute. Almost."

Ryan crosses his arms, his gaze fixed on the screen. "Cute doesn't matter if they're strong enough to fight."

Charlotte nods, pacing along the edge of the pool. "Luna, keep digging. This isn't enough. I want to know how many males they have left. We eliminated their enforcers in the mine so who's left?"

"I'm on it," Luna says, her fingers flying across the keyboard. "But you guys might want to consider a Plan B, just in case."

Charlotte stops mid-step, turning to face the group, her expression steeled with determination. "That's exactly what we're here to figure out. We also need to assess what's around the territory. If we can draw the fight away from the women and children, that's what we'll do. I want precision. No mistakes. Is there another pack nearby the Humboldt's know about?" Her gaze lands on Ryan, sharp and expectant.

Ryan shakes his head slightly. "Not that I know of, but I'll call Spencer and see what he knows." Without waiting for a response, he strides toward the sliding glass door, his phone already in hand.

Harper's eyes flick to Lucas. The simmering anger in his eyes is unmistakable, his fists clenching at his sides as if he's barely keeping himself in check. Her chest tightens at the sight, the raw energy radiating off him making her wolf restless.

"He's not untouchable," Harper says softly, stepping closer. Her voice is calm, but the fierce resolve beneath it feels like a blade unsheathed. Her wolf stirs, restless and ready, and for once, Harper doesn't fight it. She leans into the dark edge creeping through her, letting it fuel the quiet fire in her chest. "We'll let the dark guide us on this one, Williams."

Lucas's gaze meets hers, and Harper sees it—the anger in his eyes softening, not because the rage is gone, but because he sees the reflection of his own shadows in her. Her words settle into the space between them, heavy and deliberate, a bond forged in something more primal than understanding. She's not afraid of his darkness. She's embracing her own.

His nod is slow, deliberate. It's not just agreement—it's a recognition, a silent acknowledgment that she's stepping into this with him, no matter how far they have to go. For Harper, it's not just about revenge anymore. It's about survival, about protecting what's hers. And if it means letting the dark consume her for this fight, so be it.

Luna pops another piece of popcorn into her mouth. "Oh, we'll find a way, all right. And when we do, I'll person- ally hack into their Spotify and replace their workout playlist with the Barney theme song."

Jaxson smirks, his earlier tension easing. "That's the kind of psychological warfare we need."

Charlotte's expression softens just enough for a faint smile to break through. "Focus, Luna."

"Oh, I'm focused," Luna replies, her tone dripping with feigned innocence. The mischievous twinkle in her eye, however, tells a different story as she shoots Jaxson a quick wink. "Multitasking is my superpower."

Jaxson raises an eyebrow, fighting the tug of a smirk. "That's one way to put it."

The air shifts suddenly, thick and electric, as if the world itself is holding its breath. Jaxson is on his feet in an instant, his movements fluid and sharp.

His gaze snaps upward. "Ravens," he says, his voice low and edged with something Harper can't quite place. "Not the eat-garbage-to-survive kind either."

Harper follows his line of sight, stepping into the yard as her wolf stirs uneasily. Above them, the unkindness circles directly over the backyard, a black swirl of sharp beaks and glinting eyes. The birds are too close, too deliberate in their movements. This isn't nature—it's something else entirely.

"Why are they here?" Luna's voice is a hushed whisper, as though speaking too loudly might bring them crashing down.

Harper narrows her eyes at the ravens, their formation almost too perfect, too synchronized. "They're not just typical birds. They are way too big," her wolf pacing beneath her skin. "They're watching us."

"Or waiting," Jaxson adds grimly.

The group stands frozen for a moment, the weight of the circling birds pressing down on them. Harper's fingers curl into fists, her wolf itching to shift, to do something. The ravens feel wrong in a way that makes her skin crawl, like they're being hunted without even realizing it.

Charlotte steps forward, her gaze fixed upward, sharp and unyielding. "Alright," she says finally, her voice cutting through the oppressive quiet like a blade. "Let's lock this in. No missteps. Luna, keep digging. Find out if this is Ethan's doing or something worse."

Luna nods, her eyes wide as she glances back at the birds.

Charlotte's tone hardens as she turns to the others. "The rest of you—be ready for anything. We're not just fighting Ethan. We're fighting everything he's built."

Jaxson lets out a low growl, his wolf clearly on edge. "If this is what he's built, we're in for more than a fight. This is a warning."

Harper glances at Lucas, her heart thudding in her chest. The ravens continue their slow, deliberate circles above them, the sky thick with their presence. She forces herself to breathe, to focus. If this is a warning, they'll meet it head-on.

The unkindness caws as if in agreement, their calls sharp, a sound that seems to echo in her bones.

Surrounded by a symphony of howls, laughter, and low murmurs, Lucas feels the weight of it all—not like the steady comfort of a weighted blanket, but like a cinder block pressing against his chest, crushing with every breath.

Each new step towards Ethan feels both inevitable and impossible. The past drags at his heels, heavy and relentless, while the future claws at his chest, demanding a reckoning.

Lucas's gaze shifts to Harper. She's standing near the edge of the patio, the wind teasing strands of her blonde hair as she chats with Luna. Her laugh carries on the breeze, but his attention drifts to the faint scars crisscrossing her back, just visible through the loose neckline of her tank top.

Charlotte's voice cuts through his thoughts, firm and unyielding. "You've got something on your mind, Williams. Spill it."

Lucas exhales, stepping forward, his resolve hardening with every beat of his heart. "There's something I need to do before we leave."

The pack's voices die down, all eyes turning toward him. Charlotte tilts her head, studying him with that sharp, assessing gaze that makes it impossible to hide.

"I'm ready. I'm strong but having the Red Rock bond inside me as well, it might just be a bit more protection from the powder, if it comes into play." his voice steady despite the tension twisting in his chest. "I don't want to just fight beside you. I will give my body for this pack."

Charlotte's brow arches. "Has Harper gone over the initiation?"

Lucas nods, his eyes flicking to Harper's for a brief moment. The encouragement steadies him. "A little."

Charlotte steps forward, her Alpha presence radiating like a dam about to break. "Red Rocks."

Lucas squares his shoulders. "Tell me what I need to do."

Charlotte's gaze sweeps the pack stopping at Luna. "Will you be able to control them?"

"I'll go angel, Alpha." Luna's tone not exuding confidence.

Lucas has known there is more to Luna than meets the

eye and suddenly he isn't feeling as confident as he was just two seconds ago.

"Form the circle." Charlotte commands.

Lucas lets his wolf rise, the familiar burn of the shift grounding him. When it's over, he stands in the center of the circle, his dark wolf steady but alert, his eyes scanning the pack.

His scars ache faintly, reminders of the battles that brought him here, but tonight they're eclipsed by something deeper—a sense of belonging he hasn't felt in years.

Charlotte shifts first, her powerful black wolf stepping forward to make the first mark. Her bite is swift, precise, tearing into his shoulder with the controlled force of an Alpha. It's deliberate, measured—like everything she does.

One by one, the others follow. Liam's massive wolf looms over Lucas, his sheer size a reminder of the pack's strength. His strike is a brutal rake across Lucas's side, a mark that burns as much with respect as pain.

Jade's fierce wolf circles him with predatory intent, her golden eyes gleaming before her claws lash out, marking his flank with a flash of calculated ferocity.

Harper is next.

Her shift is fluid, seamless, her wolf a striking mix of grace and strength. She approaches him slowly, her amber eyes locking with his in a silent exchange. The bond between them hums with unspoken words, a shared understanding that cuts through the ritual's intensity. Her bite is firm but not cruel, her mark carrying the weight of their connection, a promise carved into his skin.

Lucas feels a flicker of something beyond the pain—a grounding force, a tether that steadies him in the storm of his own thoughts. Harper's wolf lingers for a moment, her nose brushing his as if to reassure him before she steps back, her gaze lingering just a beat longer than the others.

And then there's Luna.

When she shifts, the air changes, charged with an energy that prickles along Lucas's skin. Her sleek white fur shimmers faintly in the moonlight, her red eyes glowing like embers in the dark. She moves with deliberate grace, her steps almost too measured, too careful, as though every inch of her is controlled chaos.

As she approaches, Lucas's wolf stirs uneasily, caught between awe and uncertainty. The energy she radiates isn't like the others. It's primal, untamed, something he feels deep in his bones but can't fully grasp.

Her claws pierce his skin, quick and clean, leaving a mark that's deeper than the surface. The pain is sharp, but it's the intention behind it that rattles him. Unlike the others, her touch isn't about strength or dominance—it's restrained, almost thoughtful, as though she's holding back something far greater.

And then it's over. She steps back, her red eyes locking onto his for a fleeting second. There's no malice in her gaze, only something Lucas can't name. It lingers, leaving him more unsettled than he cares to admit.

As the pack shifts back to human form, Harper moves to his side, her hand finding his. The fresh scars burn against his skin, but her presence steadies him, her touch grounding him in a way nothing else could.

"Welcome to the Red Rock Pack," Charlotte says, her voice firm, but there's a softness in her eyes—a rare glimpse of approval.

Lucas glances around the circle, his gaze landing on Harper. Her hand tightens in his, her eyes full of quiet pride.

For the first time in a long while, he feels like he's exactly where he's meant to be.

The darkness inside him isn't gone, but it feels... shared. And that's enough.

The room is dark, the faint glow of the Vegas skyline slipping through the edges of the curtains. The steady rhythm of Harper's breathing fills the space, a quiet symphony of life that Lucas clings to. She's sprawled across his chest, her curves fitting against him like she was always meant to be there. One hand rests on his left pec, her fingers tracing absent patterns over the fresh bite mark, her mark.

"You're going to wear that thing out," his voice low and rough.

Harper hums, the sound soft and soothing. "It's mine. I'm just admiring my work." Her fingers press lightly, a reminder of the ceremony earlier that night. "Besides, you wear it well."

Lucas huffs a laugh, but it doesn't quite reach his eyes. His gaze drifts to the ceiling, the weight of everything pressing down on him like the heavy beams of the old cabin he used to call home. "It's better than what I came from," the words slipping out before he can stop them.

Harper's fingers still, her head tilting to look up at him. "What do you mean?"

His chest tightens under her gaze, and for a moment, he considers brushing it off. But this is Harper—his mate. If he can't share the shadows with her, who can he share them with? "Back home," he says, his voice quieter now. "My cabin... it's nothing like this. Dark wood everywhere, creaking floors that make the place sound haunted, and a kitchen so small you can't turn around without bumping into someone. Everything about it feels... temporary."

Her hand moves again, trailing soothing circles over his chest. "But it's home," she says softly.

"No," he corrects, the bitterness creeping into his tone. "I mean, I suppose, but it never felt like mine. Not like this place feels like yours."

Harper shifts, propping herself up on her elbow to meet his gaze. Her blonde hair falls around her pink face, a wild halo framing her face. "Lucas, do you think this place matters to me? The fancy walls, the big rooms, the view of the Strip?" She pauses, her lips curling into a teasing smile. "Well—they do," she admits, her tone light, drawing his attention to the room with a wave of her hand. "But this isn't home. You are."

The words hit him like a punch to the gut, raw and real. He doesn't know what to say, so he stays silent, his hand moving to rest against the curve of her waist. The warmth of her skin grounds him, her touch reminding him that, for all his doubts, she chose him.

"You're the strongest man I know," Harper continues, her fingers brushing against his jaw. "But it's okay to feel like this. To question. To carry pieces of where you came from. It doesn't make you less—it makes you real."

Lucas swallows hard, his throat tight. "What if I can't give you what you need? What if—"

She cuts him off with a kiss, soft but insistent. When she pulls back, her eyes are fierce and unyielding. "You already do. Every day."

The silence stretches between them, but it's not uncomfortable. It's heavy with meaning, with promises neither of them needs to say out loud. Harper rests her head against his chest again, her fingers resuming their lazy tracing over her mark.

Lucas exhales, the tension in his body easing as her weight anchors him. The cabin, the scars, the doubts— they're still there. But for now, with Harper in his arms, they feel smaller. Manageable.

She's right. She always is. Wherever she is—that's home.

WHY ARE THINGS NEVER WHAT THEY SEEM

The scent of coffee and maple syrup draws Harper toward the kitchen, mingling with the clatter of plates and the hum of the morning chatter.

She steps into the chaos, her brow furrowing slightly at the sight of everyone crammed into the kitchen instead of spreading out in the spacious dining room like usual. The tight quarters only amplify the noise, making the room buzz with energy.

"Okay," she says, leaning against the doorframe. "We've got a dining room big enough to seat a small army, so why are we all squished in here?"

Jade doesn't miss a beat, raising her coffee mug. "Because the kitchen has the good vibes, Harper. Everyone knows the dining room is for people who have sticks up their asses and call dinner 'supper.'"

Luna snorts from her perch on the counter, nearly spilling her coffee. "She's not wrong."

Harper shakes her head, a smirk tugging at her lips as she slides in next to Lucas. He's already halfway through a plate stacked with pancakes, his quiet presence grounding in the midst of the chaos.

Kai, seated at the end of the island, gestures dramatically to the spread of food in front of him. "Can we also talk about how Isabell has clearly outdone herself? Again. I mean, look at this—pancakes, waffles, bacon for days. It's like she's trying to fatten us up."

Isabell storms past him with a tray of fresh fruit, her rolling pin tucked under one arm like a weapon. "You no get fat, idiota. You shifters. Eat. Or don't."

Kai grins, completely unfazed. "So what you're saying is I can eat all the bacon I want without worrying about cholesterol?"

Isabell exclaims something in rapid Spanish that Harper doesn't catch, but the tone alone makes her snort. "I'm pretty sure she just said something about your arteries crying for help," Harper says, nudging Lucas with her elbow.

Isabell slams the fruit tray down on the counter with just enough force to make everyone pause. "I make you drop dead, idiota. Eat."

"See?" Jade says, smirking as she takes a sip of her coffee. "This is why we stay in the kitchen. Entertainment and snacks. Can't beat it."

The room erupts into laughter, the sound rolling over Harper like a warm wave. She glances at Lucas, who's quietly watching the banter unfold, his lips twitching with the ghost of a smile. She nudges him again. "You good?"

He nods, his hand brushing hers under the table. "Yeah. It's... nice."

Harper doesn't press. She knows this kind of loud, easy camaraderie is still new to him, but she also knows he's starting to find his place in it. Slowly.

Maddy, seated across from them, pokes at a waffle with her fork, her gaze bouncing between the others. Harper catches her eye and grins. "Better eat that waffle, Maddy. Kai's looking hungry, and I wouldn't put it past him to steal it."

Maddy's lips twitch into a shy smile. "He can try," she says softly, her voice laced with quiet defiance. "But he'll lose a hand."

"Damn, Maddy!" Luna cheers, raising her coffee mug in salute. "That's the energy we need more of. You're officially one of us now."

Kai clutches his chest dramatically. "Betrayed by the baby of the group. I never thought it would end like this."

"Not the baby," Jade quips. "The quiet assassin. You've been warned."

Isabell returns with a fresh stack of plates, her scowl only half-hearted. "Idiots. All of you." But there's a softness in her tone that doesn't go unnoticed.

The laughter settles, the air shifting as Charlotte strides into the room, her presence commanding as always.

Liam follows close behind, his usual stoic calm in place.

"Alright," Charlotte says, her tone all business. "Let's eat and get moving. The Red Rocks are leaving right after breakfast."

The weight of her words presses down on the room, but it doesn't dampen the warmth entirely. Harper takes a deep breath, savoring the fleeting moment of togetherness. This is what they're fighting for—the bonds, the laughter, the ridiculousness of it all.

Luna, of course, is the first to break the tension. "A toast," she announces, lifting her coffee cup high. "To bacon, sass, and surviving another day without Isabell murdering us."

Kai raises a fork loaded with pancakes. "Hear, hear!"

Harper clinks her mug against Lucas's, a soft smile playing on her lips as the room fills with laughter once more.

A FEW HOURS into the drive, and the Red Rocks are heading to Oregon to finally finish this bullshit once and for all.

Harper stares out the window, trying to ignore the way her wolf claws at her insides, restless and demanding action. It's like a slow-burning itch she can't scratch, and no amount of deep breathing or internal pep talks is going to fix it.

Her hand rests on Lucas's knee, though she's not entirely sure why. Maybe it's to stop her wolf from tearing out of her skin, or maybe it's to remind Lucas not to lose his cool either. *Let's be honest... it's probably a little of both.* The energy in the truck is so tense, she half expects sparks to start flying from the seats.

Then there's the truck itself. Harper can't keep quiet anymore. She blurts out, "Charlotte, when the hell did you go and get a Lincoln Navigator? Like, was this a 'treat your-self' moment or a 'we need to look badass on the road to murder' kind of deal?"

Charlotte doesn't even flinch. Eyes on the road, from the passenger seat. Harper can see her profile that she's the picture of calm efficiency. "Yesterday," she replies, her tone clipped, like that answers everything.

"Yesterday?" Harper echoes, her eyebrows climbing into her hairline. "You just woke up and thought, 'You know what this team of feral wolves needs? A luxury SUV.'"

Charlotte doesn't bite. She never does. "It's armored,"

she says, as though that explains everything. "Reinforced suspension, bulletproof windows, the works."

Luna's laugh bubbles up from the backseat, breaking the tension for a moment. "We're mother-ducking wolves, Char. We don't need bulletproof."

Charlotte's lips twitch, but she doesn't take the bait.

Before she can respond, Liam's voice cuts in from the driver's seat, low and steady, but carrying an unmistakable growl beneath the surface.

"We don't trust those assholes. I don't know this guy like you ladies do, but he's off his rocker. Even shifters can escalate to the level of pulling in human weapons."

Harper shifts in her seat, a chill running down her spine. *Fuck. He's right.* Her hand, resting lightly on Lucas's knee, jerks involuntarily, her fingers tightening before she catches herself.

Liam's calm tone might fool someone who didn't know better, but Harper isn't one of them. The tension radiating off him is palpable, his wolf bristling beneath the surface, protective and ready to spring into action. The low vibration of his growl doesn't just carry a warning—it's a promise. A promise of what he's willing to do if this all goes sideways.

Harper sneaks a glance at Lucas, whose eyes remain locked on the road ahead, his body tense and unmoving. Her wolf shifts uneasily, feeding off the simmering energy crackling between the three of them.

"Liam's got a point," Lucas says finally, his voice calm but edged with steel. "We can't assume Ethan will play by the rules, even shifter rules. If he's desperate enough to bring weapons into this, we're all in deep shit."

The weight of his words settles over the cab, thick and suffocating. For a moment, no one speaks, the hum of the engine the only sound.

"Sometimes we have to fight fire with fire," Charlotte says, turning slightly in her seat to look at Liam. Her tone is measured, but there's a glint in her eyes that Harper recognizes. It's the same fierce determination she's seen a thousand times before. "Our claws won't stop bullets though."

The words settle over the cab like a heavy blanket. Harper watches Charlotte closely, catching the way her jaw tightens, the way her shoulders square. Charlotte might be practical to a fault, but Harper knows this isn't just about strategy.

This is about survival. This is about protecting their pack at any cost.

"What do you think we'll walk into, Alpha?" Luna's voice pipes up from the backseat, small but steady.

Charlotte exhales, her eyes flicking to the side mirror as if she can see the answers somewhere in the blur of the road behind them. "I don't know, Luna. That's the problem. They've always come after us. Now we're walking into their territory. That puts us at a disadvantage."

Her voice softens slightly, but the edge remains. "They have the upper hand. We have to keep that in mind. Our goal is as little bloodshed as possible. Keep the young ones out of it. And the females, too—unless you have no other choice. There has to be someone strong left to take over if..."

Her voice trails off, the unspoken words hanging heavy in the air. Harper shifts uncomfortably, glancing at Charlotte's profile. The steel in her voice doesn't fully mask the fear Harper knows she won't admit—not out loud.

This isn't just about protecting the pack or winning a fight. Harper knows Charlotte has lived this before—making the impossible choice to kill an Alpha, carrying the weight of that decision, and ridding the world of a cruel and

unjust leader. But that choice didn't come without consequences.

It wasn't just the bloodshed; it was the burden of stepping into the role of Alpha for the Sidney Pack, a title Charlotte never wanted.

Shifter politics is a precarious, brutal game, and she'd
navigated it with grit and determination, clawing her way
out of that position by finding someone strong enough to
take her place—someone who could stabilize a pack
teetering on the edge of chaos without spilling more blood.

Now, Harper sees that same weight in Charlotte's expression, the same fear—not of the fight, but of what comes
after. The fear that Lucas won't—or can't—make the choice.
That the burden will fall on her to end Ethan and deal with
the fallout, the politics, and the consequences that will
ripple far beyond their pack.

Harper clears her throat, trying to break the heavy
silence. "So, what's the plan, then? Walk in, shake hands,
and hope for the best?"

Charlotte glances over her shoulder, her expression
unreadable. "We don't get caught off guard. That's the plan."

Luna snickers softly from the backseat, the sound brittle.
Harper doesn't miss the way even Lucas shifts beside her,
his hand brushing against hers for a brief moment, a silent
tether in the growing tension.

The Navigator hums, the bustling chaos of Las Vegas
fading into a blur of tan-colored buildings and speeding
cars. Inside, the atmosphere is thick, the weight of what lies
ahead pressing down on all of them.

Harper shifts in her seat, unease coiling tighter in her
chest. Her wolf paces restlessly, claws scraping at the edges
of her control. The air feels electric, charged with the
certainty of the pandemonium waiting for them.

She glances at the others—Liam gripping the wheel with white-knuckled focus, Charlotte scanning the road like she expects it to attack, and Lucas, his jaw tight, his gaze locked ahead. Each of them is consumed by their own thoughts, but the silence speaks volumes.

Harper turns her gaze to the window, watching as the city dissolves into the vast emptiness of the desert. The open stretch of interstate feels like a void, swallowing them whole.

For a fleeting moment, she wonders if this is what walking into a trap feels like—knowing it's coming but being unable to stop it.

And yet, despite the fear twisting in her gut, she knows one thing for certain: whether Lucas makes the kill or Charlotte does, this ends with Ethan.

The sharp chime of Charlotte's phone shatters her thoughts. Charlotte grabs it, her face tightening as she reads the message. "Turn around," she barks, her voice cutting through the hum of the Navigator.

Liam spins to look at Charlotte, his brow furrowing. "What? Why? What's going on?"

"I don't know yet," Charlotte snaps, her fingers flying across the screen. "But we need to get back. Now."

Harper's stomach twists, her wolf snapping to attention. The unease she'd been trying to ignore morphs into something heavier, sharper. "What's happening?"

"Alpha?" Jade growls from behind Harper.

Charlotte doesn't answer, her gaze glued to the phone. The silence stretches unbearably, thick with unspoken dread, until she finally growls, "The mansion might be under attack."

Liam curses under his breath and jerks the wheel, the Navigator lurching hard as he pulls off at the next exit.

Harper grabs the door handle to steady herself, her heart hammering against her ribs.

"Who?" Lucas's voice is calm, clipped, but Harper can hear the barely-contained edge beneath it. His wolf is ready to explode.

Charlotte shakes her head, her lips pressed into a thin line. "It's not who. It's what."

The chill crawling up Harper's spine turns into an icy grip as the realization clicks. Her voice is barely above a whisper, yet filled with dread. "Ravens?"

Charlotte's silence is answer enough.

She presses the phone to her ear, "What the fuck, Ryan?"

Harper doesn't need speaker mode to hear Ryan's voice —it carries clearly thanks to her shifter hearing.

"I don't know, Charlotte. It's not good. There are at least two-hundred birds up there. Just circling." His voice is strained, a mix of frustration and something Harper doesn't hear often from Ryan—fear.

Charlotte growls low in her throat. "Okay, we just turned around. We'll be there as soon as we can. Listen carefully— get all the ladies into the panic room. You remember what I showed you?"

Harper's eyes snap to Charlotte, confusion twisting her features. She glances over her shoulder at Jade and mouths, *panic room?*

Jade's brow furrows, and she shrugs, but her expression darkens. If Jade doesn't know, it means this is something new—something Charlotte hadn't told even her closest packmates about.

Harper files that away for later, her wolf pressing closer to the surface, itching to do something, anything, to fix this.

Charlotte's voice cuts through the thick tension. "Ryan, you keep them safe. Don't open that door for anyone but us.

And for the love of everything, don't try to fight those birds. This isn't a regular unkindness."

"Got it," Ryan says, though his voice wavers slightly. Harper closes her eyes, picturing him standing in the mansion, trying to keep everyone calm while staring down two-hundred shifter ravens.

Charlotte hangs up, her jaw set, her fingers gripping the phone so tightly Harper half expects it to shatter.

"What's the panic room?" Harper asks, breaking the silence.

Charlotte doesn't answer immediately. Instead, she meets Harper's gaze over her shoulder, her expression guarded but tinged with something Harper can't quite place —maybe regret.

"It's a last resort. The realtor showed it to me during one of the walk-throughs."

Harper raises an eyebrow. "The realtor? And you didn't think to mention this to the rest of us?"

Charlotte exhales sharply, her fingers tightening around the headrest in front of her. "Honestly, I never thought we'd need it, so no, I didn't bring it up. If you'd asked me three months ago if I'd have a child, an elder, and a couple of battered women in my house, I would've laughed in your face."

The words hang in the air, heavy and raw.

Harper feels a pang in her chest as she takes in the weight of everything Charlotte has been carrying. The mansion might be big enough to house them, but the burdens it held were crushing.

"I told Ryan about it..." Charlotte continues, her voice trailing off for a moment before she steels herself. "Because I don't know if Ethan has more of that powder. If he does, and we're caught off guard again, we'd be in trouble. Not just in trouble—done. No recovery. No return."

Harper feels a chill crawl down her spine at Charlotte's words.

The mention of the powder brings flashes of the chaos it caused last time—how it weakened one of the strongest of them. *Lucas.*

The memory stirs something primal inside her, and she clenches her fists, her wolf snarling softly in agreement, ready to protect at all costs.

Her gaze shifts to Lucas, sitting beside her, his body tight with tension, every muscle coiled and ready. His eyes remain fixed on the road ahead, his focus unshakable, but Harper doesn't miss the subtle twitch of his jaw or the way his hands grip the edge of his seat.

The sight steadies her, even as her wolf pushes closer to the surface, aching to do something. She places a hand on his arm, a quiet gesture that says, *I see you. I'm with you.*

Luna, perched in the backseat, breaks the tension with a quiet but pointed question. "So what's in this magic panic room? Is it just a fancy closet, or are we talking an actual stronghold here?"

Charlotte's lips twitch, though the humor doesn't reach her eyes. "It's reinforced steel with a separate ventilation system and enough space to hold everyone safely for a few days, maybe longer if necessary. It's not perfect, but it's better than nothing."

Harper raises an eyebrow, her fingers unconsciously drumming against her thigh. "Days? Wow. That's a big place then. Where'd you fit that? Under the wine cellar?"

Charlotte turns slightly, meeting Harper's gaze with an expression that's half-amused, half-dead serious. "Actually, yes. It's underground. Accessible through a hatch in the cellar."

Harper blinks, caught between surprise and a grudging sense of respect. "Well, damn, Charlotte. I didn't know we were living in a villain's lair."

Luna lets out a nervous laugh, but the tension in the air doesn't fully dissipate.

"Call it what you want," Charlotte says, her voice firm. "But it's there for a reason. I just hoped to hell we'd never have to use it."

Harper glances out the window, the weight of Charlotte's words lingers, heavy and unshakable, as the faint unease in her chest sharpens into something more.

For a moment, the car falls into silence again, the hum of the engine the only sound. But Harper's wolf stirs restlessly, and she knows everyone in the Navigator feels the same creeping dread—an unspoken understanding that whatever lies ahead might be more than they're ready for.

"Let's just hope Ryan remembers where the hatch is," Harper mutters under her breath, breaking the silence with a touch of dry humor.

Charlotte's lips curve into the faintest hint of a smile, but her eyes remain sharp. "He will. Ryan doesn't forget details. Especially where that mama and cub are concerned. Now let's focus on getting back before it's too late."

"Oh, so you saw it too?" Luna asks from the backseat, her tone light but curious.

"Blind men in London saw it," Liam quips, trying to cut through the tension. His grin is faint, but the attempt at humor earns a soft chuckle from Luna.

Harper glances out the window, her mind drifting for a moment. She hadn't missed the way Ryan's energy shifted around Ivy and Henry, the way his focus zeroed in on them like they were already his to protect. It's not something Ryan talks about, but in a pack full of shifters, unspoken feelings tend to scream louder than words.

"Alright," Charlotte cuts in, her voice pulling them back to the task at hand. "No more distractions. We've got bigger things to worry about."

The mood sobers instantly, the weight of their new mission settling over the cab once more. The interstate stretches endlessly ahead, the hum of the tires against the asphalt the only sound as minutes tick by.

Charlotte's phone rings again, the shrill sound cutting through the tense silence in the Navigator. She snatches it up, answering with a sharp, "Ryan?"

The yelling on the other end is immediate, loud enough for everyone to hear even without shifter hearing. "The birds—they're breaking the windows! They're everywhere! I've got all but Isabell in the panic room, but they're attacking us—"

"Where's Isabell?" Charlotte demands, her voice cutting through Ryan's panic.

"She's not here!" Ryan shouts. "She went to the store earlier! I thought she'd be back by now, but—shit!" A loud crash echoes through the phone, followed by a stream of curses. "They're getting in!"

Charlotte barks orders at Liam without hesitation. "Liam, faster!"

The Navigator screeches into the driveway moments later, gravel spraying as it comes to a halt. Harper barely waits for the engine to stop before throwing open the door, her wolf surging to the surface. The mansion is in chaos, the sounds of breaking glass and frantic shouts echoing from inside.

The Red Rocks spill out of the car and rush toward the

house, Lucas at Harper's side as they charge through the front door. Ravens dive and claw at them, their beady eyes gleaming with an intelligence that frightens Harper. Feathers and glass litter the floor, the destruction worse than Harper imagined.

Ryan stands at the base of the stairs, swiping at a raven as it lunges for his face. Its talons slice across his forearm, and he snarls, shaking it off. "Get these things off me!" he yells, his voice hoarse.

The front door slams shut behind them, the weight of the attack pressing in from all sides. Wings beat like a thunderstorm, a relentless onslaught of claws and beaks. Shadows dive at their faces, ripping at their clothes, yanking at their hair.

A shriek tears through the air as one of the ravens locks onto Charlotte's shoulder, its beak plunging into her flesh. She staggers back, shaking violently to dislodge it. "Red Rocks, shift, now!" she roars over the chaos.

The command hits like a trigger. Bones snap, bodies twist, the room filling with the sickening crunch of transformation. Claws rip through skin, clothes shred, and fur erupts in waves.

The Red Rocks explode into motion—now wolves, now fury, now war.

Harper rakes her claws through a raven mid-dive, sending it spiraling into the wall. Her wolf howls, rage driving her forward. Teeth snap. Feathers scatter. The fight has truly begun.

Jase bursts through the door moments later, his usual swagger replaced with urgency. "What the hell is going on here?" he shouts, batting away a raven as it dives at him.

Before anyone can answer, the air shifts.

The chaos halts.

Every raven freezes mid-flight, wings suspended as though time itself has stopped. Blood drips from claws and fangs, but the fight is over in an instant—unnaturally, impossibly.

The Red Rocks and Humboldts stare in stunned silence, their heaving breaths the only sound in the room. Harper's wolf growls low, unsettled. Her fur bristles, instincts screaming that this isn't right. But her human side pushes back, forcing her to release the shift.

She shudders as her bones begin to break and realign, claws retracting, fur sinking beneath skin. The cool air hits first, sending a shiver down her spine as she rises on two legs once more. "What the hell..." her voice raw.

Beside her, Jaxson follows, his massive frame trembling as he shifts, his hands flexing where claws once gleamed. His gaze sweeps the room, scanning for a threat that no longer moves.

Ryan is next, staggering back as his limbs stretch and twist, his chest heaving with exertion. He rolls his shoulders, wincing at the claw marks left by the ravens, now stark red against his skin. "That was some fucked-up shit."

Jade exhales sharply as she shifts, her posture still rigid, ready to fight.

One by one, the rest of the pack follows, the snap and pop of shifting bodies filling the silence. Lucas shakes out his hands, flexing his fingers as if testing the strength in them.

Kai, the last to shift, swipes a hand down his face, dragging in a ragged breath, "That was not normal."

The room remains still, every frozen raven a haunting reminder of the power at play.

The answer comes when Jaxson turns toward the doorway. His eyes widen in horror as he spots her. "No... No, no!"

All eyes follow his gaze to Isabell, standing in the doorway. Her hands are raised, her fingers trembling as she chants softly. Her lips move in a language Harper doesn't recognize, the words laced with power. A faint glow surrounds her, pulsing in rhythm with her words.

"Isabell!" Charlotte calls out, her voice sharp and demanding. "What are you doing?"

Isabell doesn't respond. Her focus is unbroken, her voice rising as the chant builds.

Jaxson takes a step forward, his expression twisting with alarm. "No! Stop her!"

But it's too late.

Isabell's chants grow louder, the words shifting into something older, more primal—an ancient language that seems to hum with power. The air around her crackles, a faint glow surrounding her as if the energy itself is responding to her call.

Harper stares, frozen in place, her wolf retreating in stunned silence. She's heard rumors, whispered stories passed down about witches still existing, hidden among humans and shifters alike. But those were just that— rumors.

And now, standing before her, is living proof.

The realization hits her like a freight train. She's been living with one. Eating with one. Trusting one. *This explains so much.*

"What the... hell..." Harper's voice is barely a breath over the rising intensity of Isabell's chant. The ancient, guttural words vibrate through the air, thick with power, sending a shiver down her spine as the hair on her neck stands on end.

Above them, the ravens begin to move. It's subtle at first —small jerks in their suspended forms, like marionettes with tangled strings. Then, one by one, they start to retreat, their movements sharp and erratic, as if something unseen is pulling them back.

"They're not flying away," Lucas mutters, his voice low and uneasy. "They're being pushed."

Harper swallows hard, her gaze snapping between Isabell and the jagged, unnatural flight of the ravens. It's not freedom. It's force.

Suddenly, the air begins to swirl, a low hum rising in intensity as Isabell's chants grow louder and more forceful. Her voice carries an ancient, unrelenting power that seems to come from everywhere and nowhere at once. Harper claps her hands over her ears, the sound cutting through her like the sharp edge of a blade.

The wind picks up, swirling chaotically around them, whipping Harper's hair into her face. Her wolf bristles, unsettled and unsure, as the storm intensifies. Yet, despite the chaos, Harper notices something strange—the household items, the furniture, even the scattered feathers on the floor, remain completely still, untouched by the unnatural gusts.

"What the hell is happening?" Harper's voice swallowed by the *low, resonant hum* building in the room. Her eyes dart to Isabell, whose small frame stands firm and unyielding at the center of the storm.

Isabell's hands rise higher, her fingers splayed as if pulling power from the very air around her. The *sharp crackle* of unseen energy fills the room, punctuated by the rhythmic cadence of her chants. The words vibrate through the air, resonating deep in Harper's chest, like the *low thrum of distant thunder*.

The ravens screech, their cries a piercing cacophony as their jagged movements turn frantic. They're forced back, retreating toward the shattered windows as if dragged by an invisible tide.

The glow around Isabell intensifies, a soft, golden light that ripples outward, accompanied by a faint buzzing, like the crackle of lightning just before it strikes. Harper gasps as the bite marks and bruises on her arms begin to fade, the sting and ache replaced by a soothing warmth that spreads through her limbs.

She glances around, catching flashes of relief on the faces of the others. Their wounds—the scratches and bruises left by the ravens—are disappearing right before her eyes, leaving smooth, unbroken skin in their wake.

"She's healing us," his voice low and filled with awe. He presses a hand to his side, where a particularly nasty gash had been moments ago, now nothing more than a memory.

The ravens let out a final series of shrill cries, the sound reverberating off the walls as they're pushed out through the shattered windows. Their wings beat in wild, uneven flutters, and one by one, they vanish into the night. The house falls silent, save for the faint whisper of the wind through the broken panes.

The air stills as Isabell's chanting stops abruptly. The golden light flickers, then fades, leaving the room eerily silent. Harper stares at Isabell, her chest heaving as she tries to process what just happened.

Isabell lowers her hands slowly, the energy in the room still buzzing like a live wire. She rolls her neck, the movement deliberate, almost casual, as if the chaos she just unleashed was nothing at all. Brushing a stray hair from her face, she turns to the group, her expression unreadable.

"What... was that?" Harper asks, her voice barely a whisper.

"Fue yo cumpliendo mi promesa de proteger a esta manada," she says quietly, her voice firm, unyielding.

The silence stretches, thick and deafening, until Jaxson finally finds his voice, cutting through the shock. "She says... she kept her promise to protect her pack."

No one moves. The tension in the room clings to them, tangible and alive. Harper's eyes flick back to Isabell, who now stands impossibly calm, as if she didn't just wield magic that defied everything they thought they knew about her.

Jase, still frozen near the doorway, stares at Isabell, his eyes wide. "She's not human..." he mumbles, the words more to himself than anyone else.

Charlotte exhales slowly, the sound unnaturally loud in the stillness. She points at Isabell, her voice tight. "We'll unpack this later." Her gaze lingers on Isabell for a moment longer before sweeping across the room. "Is everyone okay? Roll call."

Kai pats his chest with exaggerated motions, his lips quirking up into a grin that doesn't quite reach his eyes. "I'm good."

"Good," Jade chimes in, her tone clipped, her shoulders stiff but steady.

Charlotte's sharp gaze snaps to Liam, her hand reaching for his shirt where blood has seeped through. She grabs the fabric, her voice hard. "You're good?"

"Yes, Red, I'm good," Liam replies, his voice steady but softening as he grabs her face, gently forcing her eyes to meet his. "I shouldn't be. I was bleeding pretty good. And we didn't have to do the light show."

"I know." Her voice wavers for a split second before the steel returns. She steps back, straightening. "Finish roll call."

One by one, the Red Rocks and their allies call out their

status. Even Jase manages to chime in, though it requires him to close his mouth for a moment.

A minute later, Ryan strides in, Maddy, Ivy, and Henry in tow. Relief flickers across Charlotte's face for just a moment before she schools her expression back into something unreadable.

The weight of it presses down on Harper's chest—the uncertainty, the raw power they've just witnessed, the questions that no one dares to voice. Lucas's hand slides into hers, grounding her. She squeezes back, her grip firm, matching his unspoken reassurance. His breaths are still uneven, but he doesn't let go.

For a fleeting moment, the quiet feels like a reprieve.

Crash. The door bursts open, slamming against the wall with enough force to rattle the frames hanging nearby. Harper's wolf snaps to attention, the sudden noise a jolt to her already frayed nerves.

The frames shake precariously, one tilting Luna's infamous "dickshroom masterpiece" to a slant. Harper's eyes catch on it for a split second—the crude mushrooms, rendered with Luna's exaggerated artistic flair, somehow managing to feel wildly inappropriate and oddly comforting in the chaos.

A guttural growl escapes Lucas, low and feral, snapping Harper's focus back. Ethan strides in, flanked by a group of shifters, their eyes sharp and glinting with malice. The tension in the room thickens, the air growing heavy with the unmistakable promise of violence.

"Well, isn't this cozy," Ethan sneers, his voice dripping with disdain. His hand lifts, revealing a small pouch that Harper instantly recognizes.

"Get down!" she yells, but before anyone can react, Ethan throws the powder into the air.

Time slows as the fine, glittering dust hangs in mid-air, its trajectory halted. The air crackles with energy, sharp and alive, and Harper's heart pounds as she turns toward the source of the power.

Isabell stands in the doorway, once again, hands raised, her eyes glowing with an otherworldly light. Her chants low and furious, the words rhythmic, vibrating through the room. The powder swirls, twisting unnaturally, before reversing direction entirely.

Ethan's smug grin vanishes as the powder flies back toward him and his men, coating them in an iridescent cloud. They cough and stumble, their movements jerky and uncoordinated.

"What the—" Ethan's words are cut off by a snarl that rips through the room.

Lucas shifts mid-charge, his massive grey wolf barreling into Ethan with bone-crushing force. The sound of flesh tearing, echoes as Lucas's jaws find Ethan's throat, ending him in a swift, brutal motion.

The room falls eerily silent, broken only by the wet *thud* of Ethan's body hitting the floor. Blood pools beneath him, dark and final, a grim punctuation to the chaos.

The Cascade pack members who had flanked Ethan moments before now stand frozen, their expressions caught somewhere between shock and fear.

One of them stumbles back, his hands raised in surrender. "We... we didn't know," he stammers, his voice trembling. "We just followed orders."

Another, younger shifter hesitates, his gaze darting between Ethan's lifeless body and Lucas, who stands motionless in the center of the room. Slowly, the young man drops to his knees, bowing his head. "Alpha," he whispers, the word barely audible but heavy with meaning.

Lucas stiffens, his wolf snarling in response. The word echoes in his mind, sharp and unwelcome, clawing at the edges of his resolve.

Charlotte steps forward, her sharp gaze snapping to the remaining shifters. Her voice is cold, commanding. "You have a choice," the words cutting through the tension like a blade. "Leave now and stay out of our way, or you'll follow your Alpha to the grave."

Harper watches as Charlotte positions herself beside Lucas, the limp body of Ethan at their feet. It's a power move, deliberate and undeniable. Lucas's giant wolf form looms beside her, a silent reminder of the force they've just unleashed. The Cascade shifters exchange uncertain glances, their loyalty crumbling in the face of the new, unspoken threat.

The remaining pack members hesitate for only a moment before one of them tugs at the others, urging them to retreat. "We're gone. We don't want any trouble." Their steps are hurried and unsteady as they back out of the house, disappearing into the night.

But the one on his knees remains, his head bowed, his posture unwavering. "I ask for sanctuary," he says, his voice steady despite the chaos around him.

"Oh, fuck me," Charlotte shakes her head. "Like we have time for this shit."

Jase's gaze flicks to Charlotte, then back to Isabell. His voice, steadier now, cuts through the tension. "She's not human," he repeats, like he's finally grasping the weight of the revelation. "I can't hold Miles now. His charge was shifting in front of a human. She's not human! This changes everything."

Charlotte's sharp laugh is devoid of humor. "Are you fucking kidding me, Jase?" she snaps, her tone razor-edged. "Those assholes can break into my house, attack my pack, and all you care about is some technicality? You're telling me you have to let the dickwad who started all of this go because she's not human? Fuck off, Jase. Get the hell out of my house."

Jase flinches but holds his ground for a beat too long, then shakes his head. "You think this ends with Miles? It doesn't. You're not ready for what's coming."

Charlotte steps forward, her eyes blazing with fury. "Get out. Now."

For a moment, Jase looks like he might argue, but the fire in Charlotte's gaze leaves no room for debate. He nods stiffly, still stunned, and backs toward the door. With one last glance at Isabell, he mutters something under his breath and disappears through the rot-iron doors.

As the silence settles over the foyer, Luna pipes up from her corner, her voice cutting through the tension like a blade. "Okay, so, note to self: don't piss off Isabell. Ever. I mean, she just weaponized glitter."

Harper snorts despite herself, the humor breaking through the weight of the moment. "Pretty sure that's not glitter, Luna."

"Glitter, chaos dust, whatever," Luna shrugs, leaning against the wall with a smirk. "I'm just saying, if I ever get on her bad side, I'll start packing my bags immediately."

Lucas exhales a short, sharp laugh, shaking his head as he leans against the counter for support.

Harper glances at him, her chest tightening as she takes in the raw exhaustion etched into his features. For the first time in weeks, though, there's something else there too—clarity.

Charlotte's her sharp gaze sweeps over the group. The weight of her presence fills the space, and even the new guy —the wiry one who hasn't yet said a word—flinches under her scrutiny.

"Alright," Charlotte says, her voice cutting through the thick tension. "Everyone, clean up and meet in the game room in twenty minutes. Isabell," she points at the short Latina woman that Harper now has so many questions for, raises an unimpressed brow, "take the new guy to one of the smaller rooms. Get him towels, let him catch his breath— but not too much."

Charlotte's focus shifts to the traitor, her expression turning steely. "You," she says, her voice dipping into a low growl that sends a shiver down Harper's spine, "don't try anything stupid. If you do, I will kill you. Slowly." The guy's throat bobs as he nods quickly, his submissive stance almost exaggerated in its eagerness.

"And don't get comfortable," Charlotte continues, her words deliberate. "You've got twenty minutes to be ready for an interrogation. Understand?"

The man stammers out a quiet, "Yes, ma'am," as Isabell rolls her eyes and jerks her head for him to follow her.

Charlotte claps her hands, snapping Harper's attention back to the room. "Move. Now."

TRUTHS ARE SO REVEALING

Harper pulls a clean hoodie from the shelf, tugging it over her head with a sharp yank at the hem. She grabs a headband next, sliding it into place to push her short blonde hair off her face. The motion is deliberate, grounding, as she watches Lucas move around the walk-in closet like he's carrying the weight of something unspoken.

"What were their houses like?" she asks, breaking the silence. Her voice is casual, but the question lingers. "The Cascade Pack, I mean. Were they big? Fancy? Small?"

Lucas freezes for a moment, his hand brushing over a folded stack of shirts. "Why do you want to know?" he asks, his tone wary. His eyes dart to hers, guarded and tense.

Harper shrugs, standing in the doorway as she adjusts the cuffs of her sleeves. "Just curious," she says lightly. "I mean, you lived there, right? Spent enough time to notice the details."

"I wouldn't call it living," Lucas grabs a shirt and tosses it onto the fancy pink bench. "It wasn't permanent. Just a place to sleep while I did what needed doing."

"So, it wasn't home?" Harper presses, her voice softer now.

Lucas exhales sharply, shaking his head. "No. Not even close. It was... functional. Basic. Walls and a roof. Nothing more."

Harper nods slowly, taking in his words as she slides her hands into her hoodie's pocket. "The dude confirmed it, though," she says, her tone gentle but direct. "Ethan had taken the pack, or he wouldn't have said what he said after you killed him."

Lucas stiffens, his hand clenching into a fist at his side. "I didn't want this," he bites out, his voice low, rough with restrained emotion. "It was instinct. To kill him. My wolf took over." His jaw tightens, and his gaze drops to the floor. "I couldn't stop him, even if I wanted to."

"I know." Harper's voice softens, a thread of humor weaving through her words as she steps closer, her smile warm and teasing. "I'm just surprised Isabell didn't voodoo the shit out of you for shifting in her house."

The corner of Lucas's mouth twitches, a ghost of a smile flickering across his face. "She probably thought about it."

Harper chuckles, the sound light but grounding, and her hand brushes his arm. "But seriously, Lucas... you're the one who can make them better. You know what they've been through. You could heal them."

His jaw tightens, staring at the wall like it holds the answers he doesn't want to say out loud. "What if I don't want to?"

His voice drops to a whisper as he reaches for her, pulling her close like she's the only thing tethering him to reality.

"We planned a life. Not just in one pack but two. And now..." He drops his forehead to meet hers, his voice breaking. "Now if I follow shifter laws, I have to go in and lead a pack that only knows a patriarchy I've never believed in."

"Then we figure it out together," Harper says, her voice steady and sure. She tilts her head up, meeting his eyes fully. Her truth is written in every line of her face, in the unwavering strength of her gaze. "We've already had so much time stolen from us, Lucas. Maybe it's time we set our own path. Maybe this is it."

Lucas looks into her eyes, searching for a flicker of doubt, for any hesitation that could anchor him to the safety of his fears. But all he sees is conviction, as solid and unyielding as the earth beneath them.

"You'd have to leave your sisters. Your job. Everything you've built here in Vegas," he says, his voice barely a whisper as his hands cradle her face, desperate for some resistance to this insane idea.

Harper's lips curve into a smirk, her voice calm, unwavering. "So." She throws in an exaggerated hair flip, and it's so over the top it pulls a shaky laugh from him, softening the tension in his shoulders. "It's not the first time I've recreated myself."

Lucas breathes a laugh, shaking his head. "How do you make everything sound so easy?"

"It's not," Harper replies, her tone softening.

Her hand slides up to rest over his, her touch grounding.

"Nothing about this is easy, baby." She lifts her gaze to his, her eyes fierce yet tender. "But that's life, isn't it? It breaks you. It takes things you think you can't live without. But somehow, you find the pieces that really matter. Some you leave behind, and the rest? You rebuild with what's left."

Lucas swallows hard, his chest tightening at the truth in her words. "And what if there's not enough left to rebuild?"

Her grip on his hand tightens, her voice steady but rich

with emotion. "There always is," she whispers. "Because the pieces that matter? The ones that make you who you are?" Her soft hands slide to his cheeks, cradling his face and forcing him to meet her gaze. "They don't get left behind. And together, we'll make them enough."

After hugging tight for longer than they should've, they are the last to show up in game room.

"I should've known it would be you two that's late to the party," Charlotte says, pacing as usual.

The game room feels stifling, the tension thick enough to choke on. Lucas leans against the wall on the opposite end from the doorway, his arms crossed as he scans the room.

Both packs are crammed into the space, their quiet intensity filling every corner.

Luna and Kai have claimed the sectional, their relaxed postures at odds with the sharpness in their eyes.

Jade and Ryan lean against the wall near the pool table, their conversation muted but charged. Scattered throughout, the rest of the packs hold positions that seem casual but are anything but.

The hum of the ceiling fan does nothing to cut through the heavy air.

Lucas straightens as Jaxson fills the doorway, his presence commanding even in silence. Brock follows close behind, his steps hesitant but steady.

Charlotte's gaze shifts to Jaxson. "Are the other guests tucked away in their rooms?"

Jaxson gives a curt nod, his expression unreadable. "All accounted for."

Isabell breezes in moments later, a tray balanced expertly in her hands. The mismatched mugs and steaming plates of nachos threaten to tip, but she moves with practiced ease.

"If we're interrogating someone, might as well have snacks," Luna says, her tone breezy, though the glint in her eyes suggests she's enjoying the tension far too much.

She leans back into the sectional, casually kicking her feet up onto Kai's outstretched thighs. "Nothing says 'welcome to Vegas' like nachos and a good old-fashioned grilling, right?"

A ripple of exasperation passes through the room, the weight of her words cutting through the thick atmosphere.

Isabell sets the tray down on the table, her no-nonsense gaze sweeping over the room. "Well? Eat. Stay strong," she says, her tone brisk but with an undercurrent of warmth. She flicks Lucas a pointed look before turning back toward the kitchen.

Charlotte's voice cuts through the room before Isabell can fully leave. "Don't go far," she warns, pointing toward her. "We have unfinished business to discuss."

Isabell pauses, turning back with a small, knowing smile. "Sí, Señora. I be in the kitchen when you ready." Her tone is calm, almost too calm, as if daring anyone to push her further. Without another word, she disappears through the door.

For a brief moment, Lucas catches the faintest twitch of amusement at the corner of Charlotte's jaw, but it's gone just as quickly as it appeared. Her attention snaps back to Brock, the weight of the room's collective unease shifting back to him.

The younger man's broad shoulders are hunched, his steps hesitant as he steps fully into the room. His dark brown eyes flicker over the gathered crowd, taking in every face, every corner, before finally landing on Lucas.

For a moment, their eyes lock, and Lucas sees it—uncertainty, mixed with something else. Recognition? Respect? It's gone too quickly for him to decide as Brock's gaze drops to the floor.

"Sit," Charlotte commands, gesturing toward the single chair placed conspicuously in the center of the room. Her tone brooks no argument.

Lucas studies Brock as he hesitates, hands flexing briefly before gripping the chair's armrests. The kid's trying hard not to let the room rattle him, but the slight tremor in his fingers gives him away. He sits on the edge of the chair, his body coiled tight, ready to spring.

There's something faintly familiar in the set of his jaw, the flicker of his eyes as they sweep the room, and Lucas can't quite place why it gnaws at him.

"Who are your parents?" Lucas asks, his voice cutting through the quiet like a blade.

Brock's head jerks up, surprise flashing across his face. "Why does that matter?" he asks, his tone steady but low.

"Answer the question," Lucas says, stepping forward. His voice isn't loud, but it carries the weight of something more —commanding, Alpha-like.

The room seems to shift with it, the air charged. Lucas feels a tingle roll down his spine, sharp and unfamiliar. His eyes flick to Charlotte, who gives him a subtle nod, her expression unreadable but knowing.

Brock's shoulders stiffen under the weight of Lucas's words, his gaze dropping reflexively to the floor. "My parents were Marlene and Jason Devlin," he says finally, his voice quieter now, almost reverent.

Lucas's stomach tightens at the names. Marlene and Jason—two Cascade Pack members who had quietly opposed Miles's rise to power. Lucas remembers their steady resilience and unwavering determination to shield their family, even as Ethan's control tightened around the pack like a noose.

"You're their son," Lucas hums, almost to himself.

Brock nods, his fingers tightening on his knees. "They... they didn't make it," he adds, his voice breaking slightly. "Ethan saw to that."

The room falls silent, the gravity of his words sinking into the space like a lead weight.

Charlotte clears her throat, snapping the tension. "What do you know about any plans that Miles or Ethan had?" she asks, her voice brisk and cutting.

Brock hesitates, his gaze darting to Lucas before settling on Charlotte. "I know enough to know it's enough," he says cautiously. "I'm not here to fight you. I want help."

"Help?" Harper leans forward, her arms crossed. "Why should we believe you?"

Brock lifts his head, meeting her gaze with surprising steadiness. "Because I want the Cascade Pack to be better," he says simply. "We've heard about the Red Rocks—not in the best light. But the way I saw it, if Miles hated you, it was because you were good." His eyes flicker with quiet intensity. "Evil never likes what it can't control."

Lucas studies Brock, his chest tightening at the quiet conviction in the younger man's voice. For the first time in what feels like forever, he wonders if maybe, just maybe, this broken pack can be rebuilt.

"Tell me about the ravens," Lucas says, his tone steady as he steps closer, the air in the room growing heavier with his presence.

Brock swallows hard, his fingers flexing on the armrests. "They're not just birds," his voice low, hesitant. "They're shifters... I think. I don't know much about them. No one does. But they've worked with Miles before."

Lucas's expression darkens, his jaw tightening. "Worked with him how?"

Brock shifts uneasily, his gaze darting between the gathered pack members. "Spying, mostly. Sometimes more. They're good at what they do—flying in and out unnoticed, seeing everything. If they're attacking, though..." His voice trails off, and he glances up at Lucas, the unease in his eyes unmistakable. "It means Ethan made a new deal."

Harper leans forward, her arms crossed tightly. "You mean coming here, you didn't know about the ravens?"

"No. No, ma'am. I don't think any of us knew," his voice firm but calm. "Me and the other boys, I mean."

"What did you think you were coming here to do, then?" Charlotte demands, her frustration rippling through the room like a wave.

Luna leans back on the sectional, her lips curving into a smirk. "Probably not to sit in the hot seat and get grilled by a badass Alpha," she quips, earning a few snickers from the pack.

The humor momentarily cuts through the tension, eliciting a few reluctant chuckles around the room. But Char-lotte's sharp glare sweeps over them like a blade, silencing the laughter immediately. "Enough," she snaps, her tone brooking no argument.

Brock hesitates, his shoulders stiffening under the weight of their stares. "The mission was to kill you," he admits, his voice quiet but steady. Lucas narrows his eyes, watching closely for any sign of deceit. His gut, however, tells him the young man is speaking the truth.

"But I was hoping..." Brock's voice wavers, his head dipping slightly as if the words weigh too much. "I was hoping there'd be a way to get one of you to listen to my pleas. To see reason. And maybe—" His voice fractures, and he swallows hard, forcing the words through. "Maybe one of you would kill him."

Jade exhales sharply, shaking her head as disbelief twists her features. "There is so much to unpack here."

"Yeah, there is," Charlotte agrees, her focus unwavering as she studies Brock. She tilts her head, assessing him like a puzzle with missing pieces. "So, are there others like you? Others who want a pack of peace?"

"Yes." The word bursts out of Brock without hesitation. He lifts his head, his gaze locking with hers, steady and unflinching. "There are. We need a strong leader to help clear out the ones who won't change."

Eyes lock on Lucas, the intensity clawing under his skin. Shoulders stiffen as unease coils tight in his chest. The wolf stirs, bristling at the weight of unspoken expectation pressing between them.

That silent plea burns louder than words, a challenge and a call to step into the role earned at such a cost. Dark-ness lingers there, a black spot etched onto his heart.

The wolf growls—not in resistance, but with the

simmering promise of what it could mean to lead, to protect. Holding the gaze takes everything, the question hanging heavy in the air: *is he ready?*

Charlotte doesn't miss the moment. Her eyes flick between them, sharp but silent. "Jaxson, take him back to his room," her tone clipped, firm. Her attention snaps back to Brock, her voice cutting through the air. "Don't leave that room until someone comes for you."

Brock nods, slow and deliberate, but there's a hitch in his movement, his hesitation clear. "Can I let my brother know I'm not dead?" His voice dips, raw with desperation.

Charlotte's lips press into a line before she answers, her tone softening just enough to offer a sliver of mercy. "Yes. But Jaxson will be with you the entire time. If he feels anything is out of sorts..." letting the silence draw the rest of the threat. Her meaning is crystalline. "He will end you."

The blood drains from Brock's face, his jaw tightening as he nods. "Understood."

Lucas tracks every movement as Jaxson steps forward, a silent shadow of strength. His sheer presence dwarfs Brock, who shrinks slightly under his looming frame. Jaxson offers Charlotte a curt nod before turning to guide Brock toward the hallway.

The quiet that follows feels heavier than any words. Lucas exhales slowly, the room still thrumming with the residue of unspoken truths and jagged tension.

"Holy fuck, Charlotte. Ravens?" Liam's voice cuts through the silence, snapping Lucas out of his thoughts. "The ravens I know would never be involved in something like this."

Charlotte meets his gaze, her expression unreadable. "From what I've always known, raven unkindnesses are rare. I don't know where these guys came from." Her attention shifts to Ryan. "Have the Humboldt's had any interactions with them?"

"Not that I know of," Ryan says, his tone cautious but firm.

Charlotte nods once before turning to Luna. "Do some digging. See if you can find any ties—Miles, Ethan, family connections, financial debts. Anything."

Luna raises an eyebrow, her arms crossing in defiance. "Oh, no. I'm not going anywhere until you deal with Isabell. I'm not missing that circus."

"Fine," Charlotte bites out, irritation flickering in her tone.

As if summoned by the mention of her name, Isabell appears from the shadows, her small frame exuding confidence. "I here."

Charlotte's gaze narrows, her voice sharp. "Okay. How long ago did she ask you to start watching us?"

The question slices through the air, pulling everyone's attention. Glances dart between faces, silent questions rippling through the group like a rising tide. No one speaks, but the unspoken thought is clear: *What the hell is Charlotte talking about?*

"Since lost so many pack, year ago." Isabell says, her confidence growing with each word, her voice steady and unapologetic.

The room shifts again, tension thickening as shoulders stiffen and breaths catch. Lucas's gaze settles on Charlotte, catching the flicker of emotions playing across her face—grief, anger, and something else. Her hands curl into fists at her sides, the weight of Isabell's words landing like stones.

"She get me here," Isabell states plainly. "Help me watch over you. She love you, Miss Charlotte." Her words soften as she switches back to her favored language. "Ella te quiere como a una hija."

Jaxson translates, his tone low but steady. "She loves you like her daughter."

A hushed "Oh shit" escapes Harper, barely more than a whisper. "Does Lyla know? Does she know you're a witch?"

Lucas glances around the room, confusion etched into every face except Harper's, Jade's, and Luna's. The air feels electric with unanswered questions. But then Isabell's smile unfurls, and it's warm, like sunlight breaking through clouds, easing the tension knotting Lucas's chest.

"Of course, cariño. We are the oldest of friends," Isabell replies, her tone carrying a gentle fondness.

Lucas can feel the love she holds for Lyla in every syllable. It's genuine, almost tangible, and it takes the edge off the unease building inside him.

Charlotte's voice cuts through the moment, her tone sharp with curiosity. "Why didn't we meet you before? We lived with the Black Canyon's for along time."

"I was away for years," Isabell explains simply, her calm demeanor betraying nothing.

"So, she sent you to watch over us. Protect us if needed, I suppose," Charlotte says, her voice softer now, the edge tempered by curiosity.

"Sí, Señora," Isabell replies with a slight nod. "She know you strong, but she hears rumors. She know why you no allow males into your pack, but not having numbers made you weak. She afraid for Red Rocks." A sly smile spreads across her face as she glances at Harper. "Plus, I cook better than Miss Harper." She throws Harper a wink, the teasing note cutting through the tension.

"Okay, so does someone want to explain what storybook we just walked into?" Kai says, now perched on the edge of the couch, his expression a mix of disbelief and amusement, looks bouncing between Harper, Charlotte, and Isabell.

"Shh, big man," Luna whispers, patting his back as though he were a child needing comfort. "This is about Charlotte's mentor. Only the greatest She-Alpha of all time."

"This does pose a problem, though," Lucas interjects, his tone heavy with concern. "Jase is going to release Miles because of this. He'll go straight back to the Cascade Pack."

"Yes, he will," Harper agrees, her gaze meeting Lucas's with unwavering intensity. "But they'll need a strong Alpha to make sure the pack doesn't spiral back into darkness." She steps closer, her voice firm yet gentle. "Lucas, you can do it. You can help those people."

Lucas doesn't know how to untangle the emotions crashing through him—doubt, fear, and something danger-ously close to hope. But he knows one thing: she's right. He has the strength the pack will need. The dark within him, the part that has weathered pain and carried the weight of survival, will keep them strong, unyielding when it matters most. And Harper's light will remind them what they're fighting for. To be better. To show mercy. Together... maybe they can give the Cascade's what they've never had—a pack worth believing in.

"Yeah. I know, Harp." Lucas's voice carries more resigna-tion than he intended, but it's there. The truth. The accep-tance. The weight of what's to come settling squarely on his shoulders.

Charlotte clears her throat, bringing the focus back to Isabell. "You're staying, then? With us?"

Isabell's smile is warm, her calm presence softening the edges of the room. "Sí, Señora. I stay. Lyla sent me to protect you, I will. Until you no need me."

"Well, it sounds like I'm losing two good wolves," Charlotte says, her voice steady but edged with something softer —relief and a touch of pride woven into her tone. "But if tonight's taught me anything, it's that we need all the help we can get."

"Plus, her cooking is better than mine," Harper adds, rolling her eyes with mock annoyance.

"That's debatable," Isabell quips, throwing Harper another wink.

Luna breaks the moment, flopping dramatically onto the couch, her arms thrown wide as she stares up at the ceiling. "Ugh, fine. Isabell stays, Lucas and Harper go play Alpha's in the Cascades, and I'm just left here, a lonely middle child of this dysfunctional family. Who will comfort me when I'm sad? Who will—"

"Me, my love," Kai interrupts, "I will always take care of my 'not girlfriend'"

"Rude," Luna says, clutching the pillow dramatically to her chest. "I'll miss you both terribly, of course, but I'll survive. Somehow. Probably by bothering Jade until she tries to kick my ass."

"I can always kick your ass." Jade sighs, shaking her head. "Don't test me."

Luna smirks, unrepentant. "What's life without a little fun?"

Lucas lets out a low chuckle, the tension in his chest easing just slightly. "You'll be fine, Luna. You'll annoy everyone into keeping you around."

Luna grins wide, throwing an exaggerated wink his way. "Damn right I will."

The humor lingers for a moment before fading, the reality of the decisions made settling over the room like a quiet lullaby.

Lucas looks at Harper, the weight of their shared future heavy, but not unbearable. Not with her beside him.

"Let's get this done," he says quietly, the resolve in his voice solidifying. Harper nods, her fingers brushing his in a silent promise.

As the room falls silent, Lucas allows himself one final glance at the faces around him—this family that's not perfect but theirs. And for the first time in a long while, he feels the stirrings of something he thought he'd lost... purpose.

SHHHH,

A few hours later, Harper finds herself sitting alone in the kitchen she redesigned when they bought the house. It has her flare.

Her fingers trace the edge of the island, a small smile tugging at her lips as she takes it all in—the polished marble, the black gothic style cupboards, the carefully chosen light fixtures that cast a warm glow over the space. She hasn't been in this house long, but it feels like home in a way she never expected.

As she looks around, her heart clenches. She knows she and Lucas are making the right decision. There's an entire pack that needs him—needs them both. But the weight of leaving this house, this pack, presses heavy against her chest.

"Can I interrupt your thoughts?" Charlotte's voice breaks the quiet, warm but tinged with something deeper.

Harper inhales, letting the familiar sound of Charlotte's voice ease the ache in her chest. "Always," she says, gesturing for Charlotte to sit with her.

Charlotte moves to the stool across from Harper, leaning

forward slightly. "This leaves the Red Rocks with low numbers again," Harper says, her voice soft but tinged with worry.

"I know, Harp," Charlotte replies, her tone steady but gentle. "But with you and Lucas at the Cascade's, we don't have an entire pack to worry about. It's just Miles now."

"And any allies he has in his pockets," Harper reminds her, her gaze searching Charlotte's face for any sign of hesitation.

Charlotte nods, a small smile tugging at her lips. "Yeah, but we've got more allies now than we've ever had before. You and Lucas made sure of that."

Harper hesitates, her fingers drumming lightly against the counter. "Are you sure about this? You've been my rock, Charlotte. I don't want to leave you."

Charlotte's gaze softens, a rare vulnerability shining through. "Harp, you've been more than a sister to me. You've been my anchor. But you don't need to worry about me. You and Lucas—you're doing what's right. And honestly? I'm proud of you."

The words catch Harper off guard, a lump forming in her throat as she swallows hard. "You're going to make me cry," she whispers, her laugh shaky but sincere.

Charlotte smirks. "Good. Someone needs to remind you that you're part human once in a while."

Harper smiles through the sting of tears,. "I guess you have a witch on your side now too. I mean woah, who would've saw that coming?" Harper heads toward the pantry.

"Lyla, obviously." Charlotte's tone is laced with amusement. "I sent her a text."

Harper scoffs. "Yeah? And how'd that go?"

"Exactly how you'd expect." Charlotte smirks. "She sent me three laughing emojis."

"Well, that woman has always been one step ahead of us. I wonder if we will ever save *her* life?" Harper crawls back up the bar stool with a box of Chicken In A Biscuit crackers. *They are her favorite.*

Tearing into the ridiculous plastic bag inside the little blue box, Harper grunts, "Do you think Isabell really goes shopping or can she just wiggle her nose and this shit pops out of thin air?"

They share a laugh, the sound easing some of the tension between them.

As Charlotte stands to leave, she pauses in the doorway, glancing back. "You're going to do great things, Harper. Don't doubt it for a second."

Harper watches her go, the words lingering in the air like a quiet promise. She exhales slowly, the weight on her shoulders easing just a fraction.

Popping another cheese-covered bite into her mouth, savoring the sharp, salty flavor, the quiet of the kitchen wraps around her like a blanket, offering a rare moment of peace. She leans back in her chair, sighing softly—until her phone buzzes against the counter, breaking the silence.

Reaching for it, she swipes the screen to find a message from Lucas.

> What are you doing, troublemaker?

She smirks, already feeling the corners of her mouth curl into something less innocent.

> Eating. Alone.
>
> For once.

The dots appear almost immediately.

> Alone, huh? That doesn't sound right. You should be upstairs. With me.

She chuckles softly, glancing toward the darkened windows as if the night might be listening.

> I'm busy enjoying my cheese-covered bites of heaven. And peace. Both of which will disappear if I come up there.

> They'll taste better when you're up here.

She rolls her eyes, warmth pooling low in her belly as her fingers dance over the keyboard.

> Elevation makes food lose it flavor.

Her heart skips as the dots pop up and vanish, only to return a moment later.

> Harper, you taste perfect at any elevation.

Her breath catches. Damn him for knowing exactly what to say to make her pulse race. But she's not giving in that easily.

> Big words. But I'm not moving. My cheese and I are a package deal.

She pops another bite into her mouth, smirking at her own stubbornness—until her phone buzzes again.

> You're playing with fire, baby. Last chance

Her lips part to retort, but another message follows before she can type.

> Or maybe I'll come down there and show you what happens when you tease me.

Her stomach flips. She straightens in her seat, suddenly very aware of the quiet house around her. He wouldn't, would he?

> You wouldn't dare.

Her heart pounds as the seconds stretch too long without a reply. Then, just as she's about to fire off another text, a shadow moves in the doorway. Her head snaps up, and there he is.

Lucas leans against the frame, arms crossed, a slow, wicked smile curving his lips. Nothing but a pair of jeans clings to his body, the top button undone, teasing at the promise beneath. His abs—sharp and carved like sin itself—catch the soft glow of the kitchen light, looking downright lickable.

Before she can form a response, he moves—silent, barefoot, and deliberate—crossing the room in an instant. Suddenly, she's acutely aware of how her oversized t-shirt and sweats make her look like a purple hot air balloon.

"Lucas—" she starts, but he doesn't stop. His hands grip her hips, pulling her off the chair and spinning her toward the counter. The round edge presses against her thighs as he lifts her effortlessly onto it.

"You think I'd let you sit down here alone," lips brushing her ear, "when I could have you up there, in our bed?"

Her breath hitches as his hand slide down the front of her sweats, his touch firm and deliberate. His fingers brush against her, teasing, before his middle finger runs right through her center, stealing the air from her lungs.

She stiffens for a moment, the old whispers of insecurity clawing at the edges of her mind. But then Lucas's gaze locks with hers—dark, unyielding, and full of something that makes the world tilt.

"Don't," he orders, his voice a low rumble that sends shivers racing down her spine. "You're mine, Harper. Every inch of you. You are an Alpha Female now. And you are perfect."

And just like that, doubt melts away—replaced by the heat of his touch and the steady intensity in his eyes. His fingers slide into her, stealing her breath as a gasp escapes.

Heat floods her cheeks, but there's no time to dwell on it because he's kissing her—hard and deep—short-circuiting every coherent thought.

"Lucas, someone could—" she starts, her voice breathless, but he cuts her off with a sharp nip at her neck.

"They won't," he growls, his hands gripping her thighs as he steps in, his body caging her against the counter. "But even if they do... let them. Let them see. Let them know I'm yours." His breath is hot against her skin, his voice rough with devotion. "I may be Alpha now, but I will always bow to you."

Her heart races, a wild mix of nerves and desire as his lips trail down her neck, his hands gripping her hips to keep her steady.

He slowly withdraws his fingers, leaving her aching from the loss. Holding her gaze, he brings his fingers to his mouth, licking them slowly, deliberately. "You taste like honey baby," he teases, his mouth brushing the corner of hers before capturing her lips fully, swallowing her reply.

And just like that, the world narrows to the heat of his

touch. His hands grip her hips firmly, pulling her closer to the edge of the counter until her knees part to make room for him. The cool marble presses against the backs of her thighs, but it's nothing compared to the fire building between them.

His kiss is relentless—hungry, demanding—and she can't think, can't breathe, as he claims her mouth like it's the only thing keeping him alive. Her hands clutch his shoulders, desperate for balance, but it's impossible to stay steady when his touch is unraveling her piece by piece.

His hands trail up under her shirt, calloused fingers brushing over the softness of her stomach, then higher. He groans into her mouth as his palms cup her breasts, thumbs grazing over her hardened nipples through the thin fabric of her bra.

"Lucas," she breathes, her voice shaky, but he doesn't stop. He presses a knee between her legs, spreading her wider, and she feels him—hard and unyielding against her core.

"God, Harper," he rasps, pulling back just enough to look at her. His pupils are blown wide, and his chest rises and falls with each labored breath. "You have no idea what you do to me."

She opens her mouth to respond, but the words die in her throat as his hands slide back down, hooking into the waistband of her sweats. He tugs them down in one swift motion, leaving her exposed to the cool air—and him.

Her cheeks flush, a rush of heat crawling up her neck as his eyes roam over her. She moves to close her legs, suddenly very aware of being in the kitchen, but he's there, his hands on her thighs, keeping her open.

"Don't hide from me," his voice low and rough. "You're beautiful, Harper. Every inch of you."

Before she can argue, his fingers slide back to the apex of her thighs, parting her gently. His touch is firm yet deliberate, his middle finger glides through her damp surrender. She gasps, her head tipping back against the cabinet as her hips buck toward him.

"Fuck, woman," he groans, his free hand gripping her hip to hold her still. "You're so wet for me. Do you have any idea how crazy that makes me?"

She doesn't respond—can't respond—as he circles her clit with a feather-light touch, teasing her until she's trembling. Her fingers dig into his shoulders, her nails biting through his shirt as he builds her higher, faster.

"Lucas," she gasps, her voice breaking as a wave of pleasure crashes over her. Her head tips back, her lips parting for a moan—but his hand is suddenly over her mouth, silencing her.

"Shh," he growls, his eyes locked on hers, wild and unrelenting. "You don't want to wake the whole house, do you?"

Her heart races, the fear of getting caught mixing with the heat of his touch, making her head spin. She nods faintly, her breath hot against his palm as he pulls his fingers from her center, only to drop to his knees before her.

Her hands fly to his shoulders as his mouth replaces his fingers, his tongue finding her with devastating precision. The need to cry out claws at her throat, but his earlier warning echoes in her mind.

She bites down on her lip, trembling as his tongue works her over, his grip on her thighs keeping her wide open for him.

"Lucas," she whispers through clenched teeth, her voice barely audible. Her thighs quake, her entire body coiled tight as he pushes her higher, faster.

"That's it, my perfect mate," he praises against her, the

vibration sending shockwaves through her core. "Stay quiet, Harper. Let me take you there."

The tension inside her snaps, her release crashing through her in silent, shuddering waves. She clings to him, her fingers digging into his hair as he draws every last ounce of pleasure from her.

Before she can recover, he's standing, his hands gripping her thighs to pull her flush against him. His lips are slick, his smile wicked as he pulls down the zipper on his jeans. Slow, teasing her even more.

"You're incredible," he says, his voice thick with lust. "But I'm not done with you yet."

She starts to protest, her voice barely above a whisper. "Lucas, seriously, what if Isabell—"

"I don't care." he cuts her off, his tone firm but teasing. He positions himself at her entrance, his eyes locking with hers.

Her breath catches as he pushes into her, slow and deliberate, stretching her until she feels utterly consumed. His hand slides to the back of her neck, pulling her forehead to his.

"But, stay quiet." His voice a rough whisper, the command sending a shiver down her spine.

The quiet of the kitchen feels deafening, broken only by the soft sounds of their bodies moving together. His thrusts are slow at first, deliberate, dragging out every second like he's savoring her. Each movement sends a ripple of pleasure through her, tightening the coil inside her with unbearable precision.

Her fingers grip the edge of the counter, her knuckles white as she struggles to stay silent. Every muffled moan, every whispered breath she holds back feels like a spark, feeding the fire burning between them.

Lucas's hands are everywhere—on her hips, sliding up her back, tangling in her hair as he tilts her head back to capture her lips. His kiss is raw, desperate, and she's powerless to do anything but fall into him, her body arching to meet his.

"You're so fucking perfect," he murmurs against her lips, his voice rough and breathless. His hands grip her thighs tighter, pulling her closer, deeper, until there's no space left between them.

Her heart pounds, every nerve in her body alive with sensation. She bites her lip to stifle a moan, the fear of someone walking in heightening every touch, every thrust, until she's trembling in his arms.

The creak of floorboards upstairs sends her breath hitching, her fingers digging into his shoulders as her body tenses. "Lucas—" she starts, her voice a breathless whisper, but he cuts her off with a soft growl.

"They won't come down," his lips brushing her ear. "And even if they do..." He thrusts deeper, stealing her breath. "Let them see. Let them know who you belong to."

The flush on her cheeks deepens, her pulse racing as the thrill of being caught heightens every nerve in her body. The sound of muffled footsteps upstairs grows fainter, but the fear lingers, twisting deliciously with the fire he's building inside her.

Her teeth sinking into her bottom lip to hold back the moan threatening to escape. His hands slide down her back, gripping her hips as he sets a brutal pace, driving her higher and higher until she's trembling.

His name becomes her prayer, a breathless whisper, her nails raking down his back as she battles the moans threatening to escape.

"Shh," he soothes, his mouth finding hers in a desperate kiss. "I've got you, baby. Just let go."

The coil inside her tightens, her entire body trembling as he takes her apart piece by piece. The fear of being caught, the heat of his touch, the rasp of his voice—it all blends into a heady cocktail that has her shattering in his arms.

Her release crashes through her, and she clings to him, burying her face in his neck to muffle the soft cry that escapes. He groans against her skin, his movements growing rougher, more desperate as he chases his own end.

The faint creak of a door upstairs sends another jolt of adrenaline through her, her thighs trembling as Lucas buries himself deeper. She can't help herself—she bites down on his neck, the familiar taste of copper hitting her tongue. The sharpness of it pushes Lucas over the edge, a growl of her name rumbling from his chest as his release tears through him.

For a moment, they stay there, their breaths mingling in the heavy silence of the kitchen. His arms wrap around her, anchoring her to him as he presses a lingering kiss to her temple.

"You're going to get us caught one of these days," she whispers, her voice shaky but filled with a hint of laughter.

He pulls back just enough to smirk, fingers grazing the fresh brand she left on his neck. The bleeding has already stopped, but the sting lingers—and he wants to savor it before it fades.

"You like it, and you know it." His voice is a low drawl, rough with satisfaction. "You always try to deny the thrill gets to you, but your body, mate?" His smirk deepens as his thumb brushes her swollen lips. "It betrays you every time."

Her cheeks flush, but she can't help the grin tugging at

her lips. The moment lingers, her pulse still racing as she tilts her head toward the ceiling. The sound of muffled footsteps echoes faintly, and she shakes her head.

"Well, we're lucky they didn't come down," her voice softer now.

Lucas leans in, brushing a kiss against her jaw. "Maybe. Or maybe I wanted them to come down just so they'd know you're mine."

She laughs softly, her fingers brushing his hair as she shakes her head. "You're insatiable."

"And you love it," he replies, his grin widening as he presses another kiss to her lips.

She does. God help her, she does.

I DIDN'T SEE THAT COMING

The hum of conversation fills the dining room, a soothing mix of clinking silverware and soft chatter.

Harper sits back in her chair, letting the familiar noise wash over her. Glancing around the table, her chest tightens at the thought of leaving this behind.

The warmth, the laughter—it's been their anchor after everything they've been through. Her wolf shifts uneasily in her mind, letting out a low whine of discomfort.

Lucas's hand brushes hers under the table, grounding her. His touch, steady and sure, quiets the ache in her chest. "You okay?" he whispers, the question meant only for her.

She nods, the corners of her lips curving into a faint smile. "Yeah. Just... it feels weird."

His thumb strokes slow circles over her knuckles. "It'll be okay. We'll come back," his tone firm, like a promise.

Across the table, Ivy carefully cuts Henry's pancakes into neat squares. The boy's chatter is soft but happy, his small blue fork stabbing at the pieces as his mother fusses over him. Harper's wolf huffs in approval at the sight, instinctively drawn to the tenderness of the moment.

Charlotte clears her throat from the head of the table, her gaze settling on Ivy. "Are you sure you're comfortable staying here with the Red Rocks?"

Pausing, her knife hovering mid-slice. "I think... yes," she says, glancing at Ryan. "You've all been wonderful, and Henry loves it here."

Ryan meets her gaze, his smile warm, steady. "You'll be safe here."

Harper's wolf stirs at the subtle blush that spreads across Ivy's cheeks. The protective energy radiating from Ryan is impossible to ignore, and Harper can't help but smirk, though she stays silent—for now.

Jade strides in, her movements purposeful as her sharp eyes sweep the room. She zeroes in on Ryan almost immediately.

"Ryan, can you guys stay a little longer? A week or so?"

Ryan raises an eyebrow, leaning back in his chair. "Probably. Why?"

Jade exhales, "I've got a high-end client who needs special protection, and I'll be gone for about a week. With Miles getting out, I don't want the ladies without extra claws."

Ryan nods, already pulling out his phone. "I'll call Spencer, but it should be fine."

Jade nods her thanks, then turns to Maddy, who's been unusually quiet, pushing her eggs around her plate. "Maddy, as soon as I'm back, we'll pick up on your training. You're making great progress."

Maddy's face lights up, her shyness momentarily replaced by pride. "Thanks, Jade. I'll keep practicing while you're gone."

Harper leans back in her chair, her lips twitching into a smirk. "The ladies will be fine. I mean, they've got a mother-fucking witch living with them now."

As if on cue, Isabell appears in the doorway. Her small frame is impossibly confident, her gaze sweeping the room with an arch of her brow.

"Damn yes, they will," Isabell says, her tone sharp with satisfaction.

The room goes silent for a beat, tension and awe coiling in the air, before Kai breaks it with a laugh. "Still not over how you do that, Isabell."

Isabell grins, a playful sparkle in her eyes. "Y nunca lo harás," she replies smoothly.

Kai turns toward Jaxson, his expression curious, a glint of mischief sparking in his eyes. "Speaking of which... Jaxson, why the hell did you yell like that when you saw her casting her *voodoo*?"

"No voodoo. Spell." Isabell's voice cuts through the room, quiet but firm, as she retreats into the kitchen. Her back is straight, but the sharpness in her tone lingers in the air like a warning.

Kai winces, rubbing the back of his neck. "Sorry, Isabell. Spell." He glances her way, but her focus is already on picking up plates, moving with purpose as if the conversation is no longer worth her attention.

Kai shifts his gaze back to Jaxson, his curiosity unrelenting. "So? What was that about? You looked like you'd seen a ghost."

The tension in the room sharpens, Harper's wolf bristling at the shift in energy. Jaxson stiffens in his seat, his jaw clenching.

"I knew what she could do," he says, his tone flat, carefully measured.

Kai leans forward, his brows drawing together. "How? Did she tell you?"

Jaxson's hand tightens into a fist on the table, his voice dropping into a low, dangerous growl. "It's none of your fucking business."

Harper's heart skips a beat as her wolf growls softly in the back of her mind, sensing the barely contained agitation radiating from Jaxson. The air thickens, charged with tension, as if one wrong move could shatter the fragile hold keeping him together. Without a word, Jaxson rises and leaves the room.

"That was... interesting," Lucas hisses.

Kai, ever the one to lighten the mood, leans back in his chair, nudging Luna with his foot. "So, are you going to tell everyone we're not boyfriend and girlfriend, or should I?"

Luna smirks. "Yup. It's true. We are *NOT* boyfriend and girlfriend. Sex toys for each other works just fine for me."

Charlotte rolls her eyes before shifting her gaze to Lucas, her tone light but probing. "So, how did the conversation go with Spencer? I'm guessing he wasn't thrilled to hear you're an Alpha now—and that he's losing not one, but two wolves."

She looks down at her plate, her voice dipping. "I'm happy for you, but this fucking sucks."

Lucas leans back, crossing his arms. "He's ok. I think I heard him swear in five different languages, and he barely speaks English."

Harper arches a brow. "Did you actually say the words 'I'm an Alpha now'?"

Lucas chuckles. "Not in so many words. But he figured it out when I told him we're taking Brock and leaving after breakfast."

Charlotte smiles faintly, shaking her head. "Call

anytime. The Alpha bond can be... tricky. You'll get confused why you're angry, then realize it's because Luna's pissed at Kai." Throwing the two of them her famous death stare.

Lucas rises, extending a hand toward her. "Thank you, Charlotte. For everything. As long as I'm Alpha, the Cascade Pack will be your ally."

"Fuuuuuck, I never thought I would hear those words in a sentence." Charlotte stands, pulling him into a tight hug. "You will make a fierce Alpha, Lucas Williams. Take care of my girl," her voice carrying the weight of a promise. "Or I'll kill you myself."

Harper rises, drawing everyone's attention. "Alright, guys, Lucas and I need to get going. We've got a lot to figure out." She glances at Ivy and Henry. "You'll be okay here. The Red Rocks have got your back. And Isabell." She smirks at the witch. "You've got this, right?"

Isabell winks. "Si."

Charlotte grabs Harper, pulling her into a hug that's firm and unrelenting. "Be careful out there. I love you, Harp."

"I love you BIG, Char," Harper whispers, her voice trembling. "You'll always be my favorite Alpha."

"I heard that," Lucas hisses from nearby, his tone teasing. The room erupts into soft laughter, the sound breaking some of the heaviness hanging in the air.

But Harper doesn't pull back. She doesn't care that tears are slipping down her cheeks, soaking into Charlotte's hoodie. She giggles through the tears, clutching her sister tighter. "I'm not ready to let go," she admits softly, her voice muffled against Charlotte's shoulder.

Charlotte's hand strokes Harper's back, her voice steady and comforting. "You don't have to, Harp. I'm always here. You got that? I am always here."

Harper nods, her wolf giving a low whine in agreement. Charlotte isn't just her Alpha—she's her north, the steady point she's relied on when everything else felt like chaos. Letting go feels like losing a piece of herself.

Finally, Harper forces herself to step back, wiping her eyes with the sleeve of her shirt. Charlotte cups her face, her thumb brushing a stray tear away.

"You're going to be okay," Charlotte says, her tone full of quiet strength. "And if you're not, you call me. Got it?"

Harper nods, her chest tightening, but her voice steadies. "Got it."

Charlotte smiles, pressing her forehead to Harper's in a way that feels more human than wolf. "Text when you get there."

COMING SOON

REDEMPTION OF THE DESERT WOLF

Some battles are fought with teeth and claws.

Others are fought in the dark—alone.

Jade Deveraux has always lived by three rules: routine, control, and never let anyone see her break. But when a new powder hits the streets and a shadowy trafficking ring resurfaces, those rules stop saving her—and start crushing her. Jade slips into the underground fights looking for answers... and a place to bleed out everything she refuses to feel.

When she vanishes, the pack scrambles—and the only one who can track her?

The man she hates more than the monsters hunting her.

Ryder Sheridan never claimed to be a hero. He's a storm wrapped in a smirk, a wolf built for trouble, and Jade's oldest wound. Their past is a landmine—one misstep and everything between them detonates. But the enemy closing in wants Jade alive for reasons far darker than vengeance, and Ryder will burn Vegas to ash before he lets them take her.

As alliances twist, frenemies emerge from the shadows,

and a new threat rises from the ruins of the old, Jade and Ryder are forced together by danger... and ripped apart by truth.

Trust won't come easy.

Forgiveness may never come at all.

And the past they've both buried might be the deadliest weapon pointed at them.

In the desert, nothing stays hidden—and love won't save them unless they survive the war coming for them both.

ALSO BY JD WOLFE

Reign of the Desert Wolf ~ Book 1 in the Red Rock Series